The Spy at the Embassy

SPECIAL EDITION

Also by E. R. Paskey

The Guardians

Bad Faith

Portal Woes

Treason's Edge

Freedom's Children

Ink Realm Duology

Lady Ink

Finder Series

Head Case

Magna

Old Wounds

Overload

Blowback

Standalone Novels

The Other Side of the Horizon

Galaxy's Way

In Plain Sight

E.R. PASKEY

SPECIAL EDITION

E Minor
Press

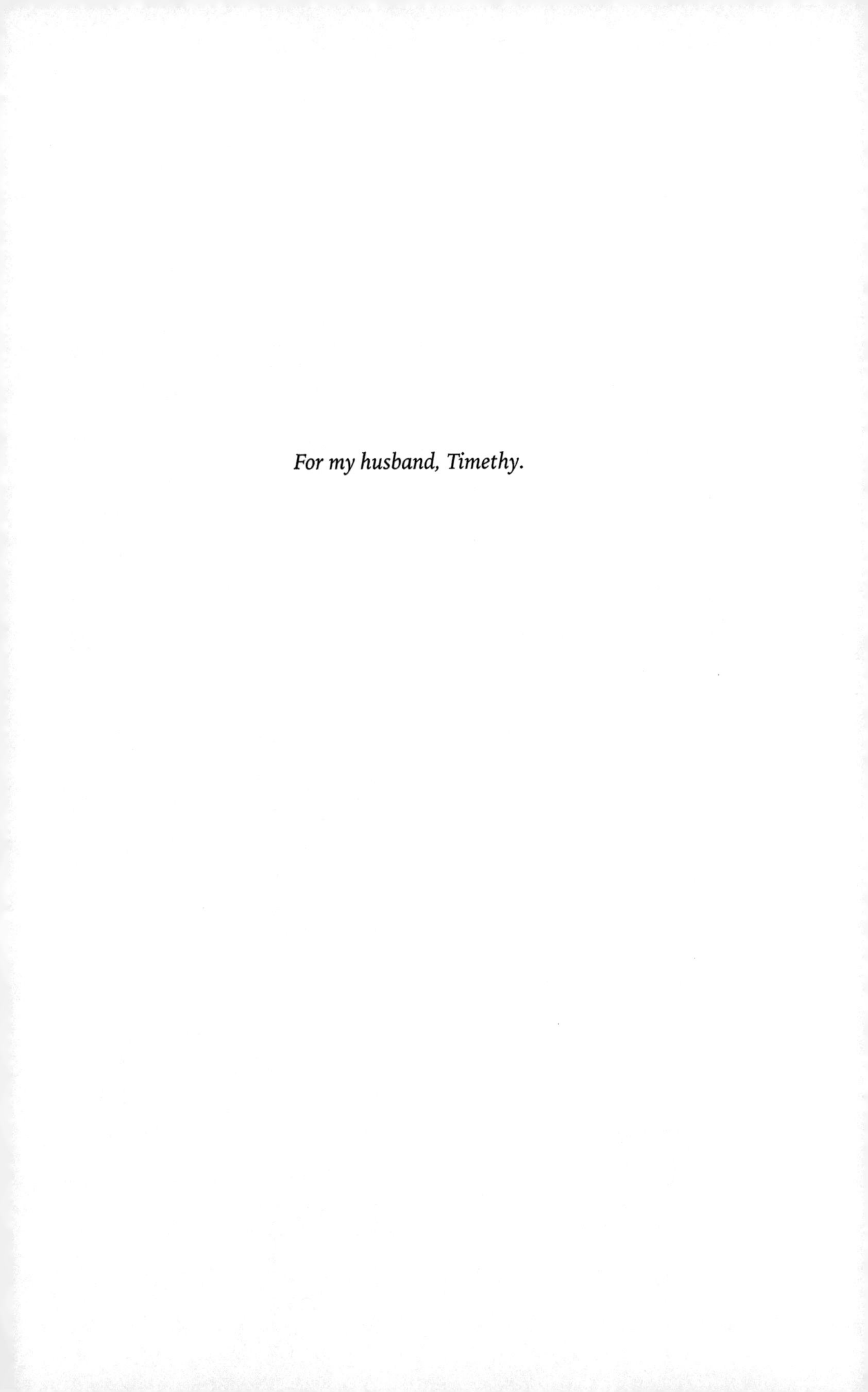

For my husband, Timethy.

Introduction

Welcome to *The Spy at the Embassy Special Edition*! I am beyond thrilled to be able to put this into your hands.

This Special Edition includes both *The Spy at the Embassy* novel and the novella that inspired it, *Danger at the Embassy*.

I wrote *Danger at the Embassy* after taking a workshop on writing romance spy stories. I've always loved espionage stories, and who doesn't love a good romance? Combining the two sounded like a ton of fun.

When I sent the novella off to my first reader, she told me that she loved it, but that there was a novel fighting to get out. (Which, honestly, didn't surprise me. Novels are my favorite thing to write.) And in hindsight, I could see where I'd snipped and altered story threads along the way to make the story fit within the prescribed word count and to wrap the ending into something satisfying for a novella.

Well, it didn't take much convincing to for me to decide to go back and write that novel. Hence, *The Spy at the Embassy* was born.

While the two stories do share a number of similarities in the beginning chapters, they branch out and end in two completely different ways. It was, frankly, amazing to go back and compare them.

I hope you enjoy reading both stories. (You can figure out which one is your favorite!)

Thanks for reading. Storytelling is my passion and it makes me happy to know that you wonderful readers enjoy these stories as much as I do.

~ E.R. Paskey

October 2023

The Spy at the Embassy

E. R. PASKEY

Chapter One

When Reine Delgado was a child, she'd thought the parties her parents occasionally hosted at the Denquay Embassy in Brazil were the epitome of what it meant to be an adult. Beautiful ladies in glittering evening gowns, handsome men in black tuxedos, and delicious little finger foods that floated through the air on trays held by all-but invisible waiters and waitresses.

She'd pouted when her parents left her for the night, and curled up in her bed, impatiently counting the days and months and years until she was old enough to attend those parties too.

Now that she was an adult, Reine knew better. Oh, the evening gowns were still glittering—in fact, getting dressed up was probably still her favorite part of attending a party—and the sharp-looking tuxedos hadn't changed much. The food was still good. (She adored shrimp puffs and little fruit creations best.)

But the people? She'd learned that in reality the women weren't as beautiful and the men weren't as handsome as they'd been when seen through a dreamy child's eyes.

Especially not now that Reine understood the motivations of most of the people attending these parties…herself included.

Tonight, the ballroom in the atrium that took up half of the top two floors of the Denquay Embassy in Washington, D.C. was resplendent. Made from bulletproof glass, the atrium provided a wonderful view of D.C.'s skyline, the Washington Monument just visible in the distance. A giant crystal chandelier hung from the center of the domed ceiling, providing most of the ballroom's light, though decorative lamps with sconces lined the walls and provided even more illumination.

Reine took a champagne flute off of a passing waiter's tray with a smile of thanks. She made it a point to thank the waitstaff when she could. People at parties like these only noticed waitstaff if something was wrong.

Plus, in her line of work, being kind to waitstaff sometimes came in handy.

Reine pretended to sip her champagne, surveying the room with keen interest. Even through the thin fabric of her deep purple elbow-length gloves, the glass stem felt cold. The steady influx of guests had slowed; she guessed most of the people Ambassador Ambrose had invited to celebrate his wife's birthday were here already.

She turned slowly, and the folds of her purple gown—the same shade as her gloves—swished against her legs with a delightful slide that made her feel like a princess, even now. The fabric shimmered with a subtle sheen in the light from the chandelier overhead. She loved this dress, with its halter neckline and tight bust. The fabric of the skirt draped in such a way that it looked like it hugged her hips, but it was loose enough that she'd be able to run if she had to.

Or if she had to scale the side of a building. (That had happened once, a year and a half ago. She still couldn't believe she'd managed to pull it off.)

On one side of the massive ballroom, a small white stage held an eight-person orchestra in formal black gowns and suits. They played various classical pieces from Mozart to Beethoven, interspersed with modern and classical pieces that were the pride of Denquay. The music was just loud enough to provide good background noise, but not so loud that it overshadowed conversation.

A spray of tables curved along another side of the ballroom, giving partygoers a chance to sit down and converse while they enjoyed the view of America's capital city outside. Most of those tables were empty; everyone here was much too interested in mingling to take a chance on sitting down and missing out on some choice piece of information or chance of a making good deal on something. Sitting down might come later, when the party finally wound down in the early pre-dawn hours.

The world of international relations might look glamorous on the surface, but over the years Reine had learned there were some wicked undercurrents. Her parents had been caught in one of those undercurrents. The aftermath hadn't been pretty.

Now that she was an adult, Reine had found a way to help keep other people from getting caught in those undercurrents.

It wasn't easy. And she'd learned that you couldn't save everybody. Still, she liked to think what she did helped.

At the very least, it meant she slept better at night.

Reine drifted across the ballroom's smooth, polished maple surface, pretending to sip her champagne while she surveyed the glittering crowd of guests. She caught whiffs of at least a dozen different perfumes and colognes along the way, though she knew for a fact that this Embassy building had a top-of-the-line air scrubber system.

Her internal sense of time told her that it was well after 8pm. Any minute, the Ambassador and his wife would make their grand entrance and the party would begin in earnest. When that happened, Reine would have a little time to kill before she set off to accomplish her mission.

She recognized many of the faces in attendance tonight. Some because she knew them personally, from her job traveling back and forth as needed from the Embassy here in D.C. to the Denquayan Consulates scattered in important cities across the United States. Others because she had been briefed on them—and she always studied those briefs thoroughly. There were American politicians and businesspeople here, along with an array of visiting Denquayan politicians and businesspeople, and those from other countries doing business with both Denquay and the United States.

Reine even spotted a couple of Denquayan celebrities in attendance—stars of one of her country's most popular television shows who had traveled from their home country for tonight's event.

In the background, the music suddenly shushed. A thrill of satisfaction curled through Reine. *There they are.*

She turned to face the ballroom entrance along with everyone else as the ornate double doors opened to admit Ambassador Ambrose and his wife, Karina. The middle-aged duo always looked elegant, but tonight they had outdone themselves. The cut of the Ambassador's black tuxedo and crisp white shirt camouflaged his middle-aged paunch, while his wife's slinky, off-the-shoulder mermaid blue gown highlighted her smooth, flawless shoulders.

Karina did a better job of staying in shape than her husband, that was a fact.

Reine had always suspected—and the rumors that swirled around the upper echelons of Denquayan politics echoed this—that the Ambassador had something of a wandering eye. Idly, she wondered how well that was going, giving that the Ambassador was stationed in the heart of American politics. There were plenty of opportunistic women here, she was sure.

The Ambassador held up a hand in welcome; his wife clung to his other arm, an elegant smile curling her pretty red lips. In the respectful silence that filled the ballroom, his cultured voice carried to everyone. "Welcome to the Denquayan Embassy. On behalf of myself and my wife, we would like to thank you for coming tonight to celebrate my Karina's day of birth. We will start the festivities with a dance—my Karina's favorite traditional waltz."

He turned his head to plant a kiss on his wife's dark brown hair, which was swept up into an elegant French twist and studded with glittering diamonds and peridots. She beamed up at him, and then the pair made their way out into the center of the ballroom.

Reine watched along with everyone else as the Ambassador and his wife settled into position. Perfectly on cue, the orchestra started up again. Beautiful strains of a violin and cello tangled together in an enchanting melody.

The song triggered a memory, making Reine's breath catch in her throat. Her mother had loved this song, and no matter how many times she had heard it in the years since, it always struck Reine the same way. She blinked and the memory—of her parents waltzing together and laughing in the large living room of their quarters in the Embassy compound—vanished liked mist.

She raised her champagne to her lips and drank—a real sip, this time. The fizzy liquid burned down her throat. *Focus*, she told herself. *What would Erica say if she knew that stupid song still affected you?*

Cold. Rational. Emotionless.

That was her goal right now. Emotion clouded judgment. The last thing she could afford right now was to make a mistake because of old emotion dredged up by a piece of music, of all things.

Her job might allow her to travel back and forth between the Embassy and various Consulates around the country, but only in prescribed measures. If she failed to complete her mission tonight, it could be weeks or even months before she had another shot—and by then it might be too late.

Lives depended on her. More lives than she cared to consider.

Reine took a deep breath. *Don't think about the pressure.*

She was up to the task.

She had to be.

Chapter Two

Officially, Reine was an attaché, which in her case meant that she was nothing more than a glorified secretary and messenger girl. A slightly cushy job, bestowed out of a lingering sense of guilt on a girl whose parents had given their lives in the service of their country.

Unofficially, she'd been recruited four years earlier by the Intelligence Division of Denquay's Department of Defense. They had used her job as a cover for many covert tasks, but tonight was a new wrinkle.

The Intelligence Division suspected that the First Secretary in the Embassy in D.C., a woman named Ariane Montoya, was involved with something illegal. They hadn't provided Reine with specifics. In this case, she didn't need to know.

Her job was to break into Ariane's computer, clone her hard drive, and get the evidence back to her handler, Erica.

It sounded simple, on the face of it, but the job was considerably more complicated than that. Denquay might be only a fraction of the United States' size, with a fraction of their national security budget, but they had good tech. *Really* good tech.

Reine had been secretly training for this for several months. She'd assured her handler she could, well, *handle* things. The party tonight was both her mission and a chance to dress up in fancy clothes. (She'd kept being excited about that part to herself.)

Now, standing here in the ballroom while couples flooded to join the Ambassador and his wife on the dance floor, she casually glanced around for anything out of the ordinary. Anything that might derail her mission.

She didn't expect anything, but of course, the only real rule of spying was to expect the unexpected. At some point tonight, something would probably go wrong. When it did, she'd deal with it just like she dealt with everything else.

Her problem now? She had entirely too much time on her hands until her window of opportunity opened.

A restless sense of energy filled her, curling and swirling through her nerves from her head, out to the tips of her fingers and all the way down to her toes. She did her best to banish it, to send a mental wave of calm through her body, like an imaginary wave of cool ice. Most of the time, this sort of exercise worked pretty well.

Tonight…tonight Reine was having a little trouble. She still felt on edge.

Maybe it was the fact that this was a big mission. Probably one of the biggest she'd been given, in her four years in the Intelligence Division. Everything else she'd ever done had involved a Consulate, and the Ambassador himself had only been there on one of those occasions. She'd never poked around the Embassy like this before.

Or perhaps, she mused, as she let her hips sway in time to the waltz's rhythmic beat, perhaps it was not so much her locale as the politics behind it. She'd been told once by one of her supervisors in the Intelligence Division not to worry about the politics. She was a delicate instrument—an instrument meant to perform an assigned task, not to think on her own.

Those instructions had been politely—but firmly—negated by

that man's supervisor. Marcus was sometimes a dinosaur, Reine had been told. There were areas of life in which he failed to realize that Denquayan culture had marched out of the Old Days and into a new world that required more resources and more finesse.

Politics—both internal and international—*absolutely* colored everything. Politics were the entire reason agents like Reine were necessary in the first place.

Well, that and greed, she thought with a wry smile, letting the glass rim of her champagne flute rest against her lips. Greed colored a great many things as well.

She froze imperceptibly as the hair on the back of her neck prickled. Someone was staring at her. Reine maintained her cool, pleasant expression, but inside all her senses went on full alert.

It was probably one of the older men here. Even though she was usually more of an invisible wallflower, she still couldn't escape. What was it about old people that they thought gave them the right to throw proper etiquette out the window and just openly stare? Or make comments that they'd never in a million years have made if they were two decades younger?

Slowly, Reine turned a little to the left, her hips still swaying to the music. Brown met hazel as her gaze collided with that of a man looking straight at her.

She took the measure of him in a quick once-over. He was perhaps early thirties, probably half a head taller than she was in her heels, with broad shoulders and an athletic build. Though dressed in an expensive black tuxedo and equally expensive Italian shoes, he had a look about him that screamed military. Or perhaps ex-military.

She wasn't entirely sure what nationality he was—European or American, probably, judging by his light skin and sandy brown hair. She *was* sure he was not a politician. His posture was too stiff, and he lacked that suave confidence that oozed out of every pore of every politician she'd ever encountered.

He also had entirely too much scruff for a politician. On him, however, the slightly unkempt facial hair was oddly attractive. Reine pegged him as either a bodyguard, or the brainless muscled arm candy of somebody else more important than he was. Attractive, but probably not much of a conversationalist.

No sense being rude, however. She inclined her head in a polite nod.

The man returned the nod with a smile that lit his entire face, lending a genuine warmth to his hazel eyes.

That smile hit Reine with the force of a small bus. A little shaken, she turned away, lowering her champagne flute as she took a steadying breath. Okay. Perhaps she needed to revise her initial impression of him.

That smile made him surprisingly attractive, in a subtle way that kind of crept up on a woman.

Still not a politician, she thought, resisting the urge to look over her shoulder, *but 'brainless' might have been too harsh.*

She felt a presence come up behind her a second before someone tapped lightly on her bare shoulder and said, "Excuse me."

Reine turned—and felt something flutter in the pit of her stomach as she found herself staring up at the handsome man.

"Hi," he said with another amazing smile that was just a little shy around the edges. "I'm Clay Dawson." His voice was a pleasant, husky rumble that was entirely too attractive.

He held out a hand to her. "May I have this dance?"

Chapter Three

His erstwhile partners had explained it twice, but Clay Dawson still wasn't entire sure what he was doing here at the Denquay Embassy tonight. He took a sip of chilled water from a fancy wine glass, gaze constantly assessing the ballroom, and let the buzz of conversation and the lovely strains of music wash over him.

In the grand scheme of things, attending the Denquayan Ambassador's wife's birthday party didn't seem very important. It was a birthday party, for crying out loud. Surely Blackthorn Security had higher priorities to attend to.

His partners, Naomi Jones and Rob Skelton, begged to differ. A birthday party on this level was *exactly* the sort of thing they needed to attend. As far as either of them was concerned, running a security firm required networking and getting fat contracts from people who knew people.

And here Clay had always thought that word of mouth advertising about them being reliable and good at what they did would be enough.

He kept that thought to himself, however. His opinions weren't very popular, lately. Going into business with his old buddy from the war in Afghanistan and a woman who'd worked in Naval Intelligence had seemed like a good idea at the time, but there were days that made him realize the three of them were lightyears apart in some of their ideologies and business practices.

Tonight was a case in point.

Hence the reason Clay still wasn't entirely sure why he was here. Rob wanted to show him off, wanted prospective employers to see that they could hire security people who were urbane, cultured —and could kick ass when the situation warranted it. Clay wasn't sure small talk at an international birthday party was the best way to get all that across, but what did he know?

He was just an ex-soldier who spoke five languages and could kill a man ten different ways with his bare hands alone.

Clay had to admit the venue was rather stunning, though. The ballroom in the Denquay Embassy was beautiful. He cast an appraising eye up at the domed glass ceiling that rose above them.

Not tactical at all, even if it *was* bulletproof glass, but definitely beautiful. Of course, they were in Washington, D.C. and not Afghanistan or Iraq, so it wasn't like they had to worry about somebody shooting a missile into the building, but his years in the Marines had left an impact.

Clay would probably never be able to walk into a room without immediately assessing the people in it and both its tactical advantages and disadvantages again.

Most of the time, he was okay with that.

He took another sip of his water. Rob teased him about it sometimes, but Clay preferred not to drink on the job. He didn't drink much period, anymore, but most definitely not when they were working.

Besides, he'd never much cared for champagne anyway. It had always struck him as one of those things people liked to say they enjoyed because it was fancy and expensive.

He glanced around the ballroom again. The food here would probably be good, though. Waiters hadn't started circulating with trays of hors d'oeuvres yet, but it was only a matter of time. That was one thing Clay had gained an appreciation for while stationed overseas—he'd tried a number of new foods and had really come to enjoy most of them.

His tie felt too tight around his throat, but he resisted the urge to loosen it. He also resisted the urge to tug at his cuffs. Naomi had pointed out once that when you thought about it, wearing a tuxedo wasn't really that different from wearing a dress uniform, but it felt a *lot* different in Clay's head.

Earlier that evening, Naomi had examined him critically when he'd showed up in the lobby of the hotel they were staying at while they were in D.C. She'd bemoaned his stubborn unwillingness to shave, but otherwise declared that his tuxedo and Italian shoes passed muster. On this stage, looks were just about as important as qualifications.

Deep down, Clay admitted he was a touch scared to find out what Naomi would do to him if he ruined Blackthorn Security's image tonight by looking sloppy. The third member of their trio looked cool and elegant herself, with her riot of dark curls and tasteful burnt orange evening gown, but Clay knew she wasn't above picking the locks on his hotel room door and waterboarding him in his sleep. There were days he wondered if her past in the military wasn't just a *touch* more extensive that what she told everybody.

A sudden hush flooded the ballroom, and Clay knew that Ambassador Ambrose and his wife had finally made their appearance. Dutifully, he turned to listen to the Ambassador's speech along with everyone else, but while all eyes watched the couple step out on the dance floor, he watched the crowd over the rim of his water glass.

Most of the people here were career politicians—regardless of their nationality. Then there was the usual group of businesspeople, celebrities, and other hangers-on. Here and there, he spotted members of various security details.

They'd been trained to do a good job of blending in, but like recognized like. Clay picked them out easily. It was something in the way these men and women stood—an alertness in their posture and attitude that couldn't completely be disguised.

It was the way the world worked now. Nobody on this level ever felt completely safe. Bodyguards and security details were as normal as meetings and long chats about the world's future over late lunches and dinners.

Some of the women in attendance tonight were beautiful. Some were married, though Clay had learned in the past that that didn't stop them from flirting outrageously at times.

His gaze caught on a young woman dressed in a deep purple gown that highlighted the olive tones of her skin. Thick, glossy dark brown hair was twisted up into a complicated knot on the top of her head, though a few tendrils framed her narrow face. She was watching the crowd too, a half-full flute of champagne in her gloved hand, her hips swaying in time to the music. What he could see of her expression was pleasant, but her eyes held an oddly thoughtful note.

It only took one glance for Clay to know that she exercised regularly. Her arms, which were bare from her shoulders to the top of her purple elbow-length gloves, were lithe and muscular. He wondered who she was.

He didn't remember seeing her face in any of the profiles Rob and Naomi had put together of potential employers at this soiree.

As though feeling his gaze on her, the woman turned slightly and their gazes met. Dangly silver earrings glinted in the light from the chandelier as she gave him a nod.

Clay felt a little shock go through him. Oh, yes, she was definitely beautiful. But there was something *more* about her—something breathtaking he couldn't even figure out how to put into words at the moment.

A little stunned, he smiled at her and nodded back.

After a second that seemed to last forever, she looked away and their connection broke. Clay felt a pang deep in his chest. He inhaled sharply and raised his free hand to scrub it through his hair, remembering at the last second that he couldn't do that right now. What was *that*?

He'd never experienced anything like that before. All she'd done was *look* at him and—

He swallowed. *Focus, Dawson. You're on the clock tonight. Don't get distracted by a pretty face.*

His feet, however, had a mind of their own.

Before Clay quite realized what he was doing, he found his feet carrying him toward the woman. Heart thudding in a way that it hadn't even the last time he'd taken point on a field patrol to sweep for IEDs, he reached out a hand and tapped her on the shoulder.

He introduced himself and asked her to dance before he could lose his nerve.

Clay was only mostly shocked when she accepted.

Chapter Four

Hiding the fact that there were butterflies doing a mad dance in her stomach, Reine allowed Clay Dawson to lead her out to the dance floor. Why not? She had time to kill and he might be a good distraction for a while.

On the way, they both set their half-empty glasses on a passing waiter's tray. Reine noticed with interest that Clay had been drinking water. That was unexpected. Either he didn't drink or he had a code of ethics that involved restrictions on alcohol.

That thought disappeared as Clay took her hand in his and settled his other hand at her waist. Even through the filmy fabric of her gown, his touch seemed to radiate heat. Hoping he couldn't hear the way her heartbeat had quickened, Reine placed her left hand on his shoulder, the loop securing her matching purple clutch to her wrist securely in place.

Clay waited a second, as though counting beats in his head, and then seamlessly swept her into the collection of couples swirling around the dance floor at the center of the ballroom.

Only years of experience kept Reine from raising her eyebrows in surprise. She tilted her head to one side, considering her dance partner. What was that old saying her grandfather, God rest his soul, used to say? Never give a sword to a man who couldn't dance?

Well, this man could dance. Reine had danced with better, but for someone who mostly likely had a military background, Clay was not bad at all. He was light on his feet and he didn't grip her too tightly.

This close to him, she noticed that he smelled good. His cologne, which he'd applied lightly, smelled fresh and clean. Through the almost sheer fabric of her gloves, she could tell that his fingers were strong and a little weathered. This was a man who worked with his hands.

Deep down, Reine approved. She could never openly admit it in her line of work, but she liked a man to have hands that were not as smooth—or smoother—than her own.

She looked up into Clay's face just as he looked down at her and lifted an eyebrow with a mischievous smile.

"So, I've told you my name, but you have yet to introduce yourself, Miss…?"

"Delgado. Reine Delgado."

"Miss Delgado." Clay cocked his head. "It *is* 'Miss', right?" He made a show of looking around them. "Don't have to worry about an angry husband coming after me, do I?"

This drew a laugh from Reine. "I don't think anyone has ever asked me if they had to worry about an angry husband before." Over the top of Clay's black-clad shoulder, she glimpsed the Ambassador and his wife waltzing together. Their posture was the easy familiarity of two people who lived their lives together, but there wasn't any obvious passion.

Maybe the rumors were true. Maybe the Ambassador did have a wandering eye and his wife tolerated it. Or perhaps they were simply private people, who kept their emotions and behavior tightly checked in public.

Eight years working in the diplomatic field, and Reine still had yet to figure that out.

She turned her attention back to her dance partner as he asked, "May I call you Reine?"

The sound of his voice saying her name sent a surprising jolt of pleasure through her. She regarded him steadily, a little surprised by his politeness. (Sometimes Americans were entirely too forward.)

Smiling, she inclined her head in a nod. "You may."

The waltz ended and changed to another, a lilting melody with a slightly slower pace that was more conducive to conversation. In the back of her mind, Reine marveled at how even tonight's music had been chosen deliberately with that in mind.

As they settled into a slow dance, Reine canted her head to one side, offering Clay a coy smile. "What brings you to the Embassy tonight, Clay Dawson?"

"Work, I'm afraid."

"Let me guess. Security?"

He pretended to look affronted, before grinning at her, a trifle ruefully. "Is it that obvious?"

Reine found herself smiling back at him, though she tried—and failed—to school her expression into something serious. Even through his tuxedo jacket, she could feel the hard muscles in his shoulder beneath her gloved fingers. "Well, you do have that…military…look about you."

"It's not the hair," he said. "Grew it out on purpose."

"No." Reine scrutinized his sandy brown hair, which curled just a bit around the edges, and her smile widened. "It's not the hair."

Clay spun her around in time to the music. The little girl inside Reine swooned at the way her skirt swirled out and then swished against her legs as he spun her back into position.

A little breathlessly, she said, "It's the way you stand. I've seen it before, in countless men and women who have served in various countries." She freed a hand to wave it in his general direction.

"There is an alertness about you, as though you are always watching everything around you."

"We *are* always watching everything around us," he said seriously, but then he grinned. It lit his entire face, making his hazel eyes sparkle. "Occupational hazard, I'm afraid. Drilled into us right from the start." The sparkle in his eyes abruptly dimmed, something somber flickering through his gaze. "Not sure it ever goes away."

"I'm inclined to agree with you." Reine's smile turned a little softer at the edges. "Have you ever been to South America?"

"No. Not yet. Spent most of my time in the Middle East. Marine Corps."

"Ah. May I ask where were you stationed?"

"Afghanistan, mostly. Did a few tours."

That was about what Reine had expected. She nodded, then tilted her head to one side again. "Do you miss it?"

Clay gave her a considering glance, as though debating the best way to answer this. Seeing her genuine curiosity, he shrugged. "I miss having a clear sense of purpose, maybe. This—" he jerked his chin to indicate their surroundings, "—isn't quite the same."

Reine thought of sand and rock and the smell of gunfire on the wind. "No," she said slowly. "I don't see how it could be."

"Don't get me wrong, I'm glad to have something to do." Clay twirled her around again in time to the music, and when he brought her in close again, he gave her a charming smile. "In this particular job, I get to meet lovely ladies like you."

She acknowledged the compliment with a smile of her own and a flutter of her eyelashes. This American was surprisingly easy to talk to. It would be time for her mission before she knew it.

Curiosity dug little pinprick claws into her again. She studied the bearded contours of Clay's face, noting a couple of faded scars along his hairline on his left side. "Why did you leave the military, if you loved it so much?"

She felt the muscles in his shoulder tense beneath her hand. He looked at her and then looked away, the expression in his hazel eyes going distant. A muscle twitched in his jaw, before he forced himself to relax.

"It was time." Clay turned his gaze back to her, his eyes full of shadows. "Lost a couple of good buddies to an IED. Damn near blew me up too." He shook his head. "When that last tour was up, I decided I'd had enough."

Reine held his gaze, nodding slowly. There was more to it than that, she was sure—there was always more to a story like that—but it would suffice for now. Honestly, it was more than she'd expected him to reveal.

Clay took a breath and the shadows cleared. He smiled, a touch self-deprecatingly. "Enough about me. Tell me about you, Miss Reine Delgado."

"Oh, well, there is not much to tell." Reine took her hand off of his shoulder long enough to wave it casually through the air. It was her turn to offer a self-deprecating smile. "I am basically a glorified diplomatic secretary and messenger girl."

"You're Denquayan, right?"

"Yes. Although I have spent a lot of time in Consulates in various cities here in the United States."

"So you travel around a lot?" Clay's eyes twinkled. "I can relate."

"I'm sure you can."

The music changed as the orchestra shifted to a slow, elegant ballad more suited for standing mostly still and swaying in place. (Not everyone who attended these parties knew how to waltz, and Karina Ambrose was well aware of that.)

Clay shifted his grip slightly, bringing Reine a little closer. Her heartbeat quickened again at this increase in proximity. She inhaled, feeling heat rise to her cheeks. Oh, he smelled amazing.

Something about the way he looked at her made her feel like she was the only woman in the room. She felt like he could *see* her—see straight past her defenses to the real her inside.

She drew in another, slightly shaky, breath. *This is dangerous.* She was a woman on a mission tonight; she didn't have time to get side-tracked by a charming American security contractor, no matter how…attracted…she was to him.

She was going to have to nip this in the bud.

Chapter Five

Clay couldn't remember the last time he'd felt so at ease around a woman he felt such a strong attraction to. It was beyond strange. Part of him felt like he'd reverted to his awkward teenager self again—all thumbs and left feet and hot and bothered under the collar—while at the same time another part of him marveled at how easy it was to talk to Reine.

For a lower middle-class boy from Northern Kentucky, an event like this one was so far out of his comfort zone it might as well have been in the stratosphere. He wasn't used to rubbing elbows with politicians, diplomats, and the extremely wealthy, even in a working capacity. Rob and Naomi kept assuring him he'd get used to it eventually, but most of the time Clay felt like an impostor walking around these parties in a tuxedo.

Right now, though…

Clay looked down at the woman in his arms. The lights from the chandelier gave Reine's dark hair a glossy sheen, and made the fabric of her purple dress shimmer. He wasn't sure if it was her hair or her perfume, but she smelled like cherries. The good kind of cherry scent, not the one that reminded him of nasty cold medicines he'd taken when he was growing up.

Like most of the women here, she was probably wearing heels, which put her head a few inches above his shoulder. Without them, Clay suspected the top of her head would probably be level with his shoulder. He couldn't help thinking that either way she was the perfect height for him.

He looked down at her as they swayed to a classical piece of music he didn't recognize. Unlike some of the other women here tonight, her makeup was tasteful and enhanced her features rather than just being caked on.

His eyes darted to her lips, before he forcibly dragged his gaze back up to her eyes. *Don't go there, Dawson,* he warned himself. She was out of his league and he knew it. (And even if she wasn't, he could practically hear the lecture Rob would give him about getting involved—or wanting to get involved—with somebody at an event they were working.)

To distract himself, he arched a playful sandy brown eyebrow. "I'm not keeping you from any other potential dance partners, am I?"

For an instant, Reine looked startled, and then she laughed. Clay instantly loved the sound of her laugh. It was like music—sweet, tinkling bells. A part of his mind started plotting how he could make her laugh again.

"No," she said, laughter still coloring her voice. She made an exaggerated show of looking around, mimicking his earlier motion. "No, I don't think anyone else is waiting."

"Good. Their loss." A flicker of satisfaction curled through Clay. He didn't want to share her attention with anyone else. Selfishly, he found himself wanting to spend as much time with her as he could at this fancy shindig.

Reine looked at him, and for a second, Clay thought he glimpsed surprise in her dark eyes, as though this sentiment wasn't one she encountered often. He pushed that aside; he'd probably imagined it. A woman as beautiful as she was, working in the diplomatic corps, probably had all kinds of opportunities to meet men.

He was just lucky to be in the right place at the right time tonight.

Chapter Six

"How long have you worked for the Ambassador?"

Clay's voice brought her back to herself. Reine lifted both bare shoulders in a careless little shrug. "Eight years, give or take. On the whole, I quite enjoy it."

That was true, even if the politics of the job sometimes wore on her.

"How did you get into it?" Clay asked with interest. "Does your family still live in Denquay? How do they handle you being gone overseas so much?"

Usually, Reine preferred not to talk about her parents. And if pressed, she then kept the summary of her past woes as brief and succinct as possible.

She opened her mouth to give him this brief history...but instead found herself saying, "My father was the Ambassador to Brazil. My mother and I traveled with him everywhere. When I was ten, we took a trip back to Denquay for the holidays."

Old emotion rose inside her; she tamped it down. "Some members of a political faction that disagreed with our president at the time's current foreign policies bombed the house where we were staying." She smiled, but there was nothing mirthful about the expression. "I survived. My parents did not."

"I'm sorry."

Reine allowed herself to meet Clay's eyes, expecting to find pity. That was what she usually encountered when this subject came up. Instead, she found compassion and understanding. A knot of unexpected emotion swelled in her chest.

She pressed her lips into a thin line while she composed herself. When she thought she could speak without her voice breaking, she said, "I joined the diplomatic corps when I was eighteen." She smiled again, this time with real warmth. "I wanted to help make a difference for our country."

"Like your parents," Clay said with a nod. His fingers tightened momentarily on hers.

"Something like that."

"And have you?"

Reine's breath caught in her threat. This man and his questions... She couldn't remember the last time anyone had taken the time to talk to her like this. Usually, she was the one probing for information.

Belatedly, she realized he was waiting for an answer. "I would like to think I have. But, honestly, some days I just don't know." She took her hand off his shoulder to gesture to the ballroom around them. "Probably every single person in this room would claim that they're working to make the world a better place. But have we?"

"Doesn't feel like it some days, does it?" Clay asked wryly.

"No."

Silence fell over them, filled with laughter and the buzz of a dozen different conversations, overlaid with beautiful strains of music.

"You know," Clay said, his voice soft and low. "There are people who don't like the military. They think people like me who want to serve our country are nuts, think that we're being used to prop up the American government on a global scale."

Reine lifted her eyebrows in silent curiosity. Where was he going with this, exactly?

"But those people haven't been the places I've been, seen the things that I've seen." Clay shook his head, the shadows returning to his hazel eyes again. "There *is* evil in this world, and it's not relegated to any one country or part of the planet. It's everywhere." He shook his head again. "Some places it's just a little more obvious."

Reine felt the truth of those words settle in her chest. "This is true," she said, equally quietly.

"The thing is—" Clay held her gaze, the look in his green-brown eyes intense, "—if we don't stand up for the people who can't stand up for themselves, who will?" He swallowed. "That's why I fought."

Reine nodded slowly, feeling threads of kinship weave themselves around the pair of them. *Me too,* she wanted to say. That was why she'd joined the Intelligence Division when they recruited her.

That was partly why she was here tonight, preparing to investigate her own Ambassador's First Secretary.

She couldn't tell Clay any of that, however. Instead, she simply said, "I understand."

And she did—more than Clay Dawson would probably ever know.

Chapter Seven

Clay felt a somber mood settle over them, like someone had thrown a heavy black veil over their heads, dimming the light from the chandelier and the music and noise of the party. It pressed down on him, weighing more than he ever remembered his pack weighing. Forcing a smile, he cast about for something to say that would lighten the mood again.

His words—in all five languages he spoke—seemed to have temporarily abandoned him. He couldn't think of anything to say that didn't sound completely stupid and inane. A bubble of panic rose in his chest, sending sharp pangs shooting through him.

If he didn't find a way to keep things going, this would be the part where she thanked him for the dance and moved on to better waters. Clay had to force himself to relax. The last thing he wanted right now was to lose track of Reine for the evening.

In that moment, he admitted to himself that he was *highly* attracted to this woman and he wasn't afraid who knew it.

In the back of his mind, he knew he had a job to do here tonight, but he couldn't quite bring himself to care. It had been a long time since he'd met a woman who made him forget what he was doing.

Reine saved him by asking, "You said you have never been to South America, *non?*"

Clay grabbed this for the life preserver it was. "That's right." He shook his head, relief curling through him. "Haven't made it there yet, but someday I'd like to."

"Do you know anything about my country?" Reine arched a challenging eyebrow at him, but smiled to let him know she was teasing.

"Actually, I do." Clay maneuvered them around a couple who had stopped short in the middle of the ballroom for some unknown reason. He wondered if they were already a little too inebriated. "I know that Denquay is about the size of New Hampshire, and it's bordered by Suriname, Guyana, and Venezuela. Your main language is French, you have a President, and you have a ton of tropical rainforest."

Reine laughed again, and Clay felt a flush of pride. "Not bad, not bad. I take it you read a brief?" Her dark eyes danced at him.

"Yes, I did." Naomi had prepared it, but Clay would have looked Denquay up regardless. He smiled. "Have to be prepared for an event like tonight. Wouldn't want to be ignorant of our gracious host country."

"That's very wise of you." Reine's fingers traced a pattern on the shoulder of his tuxedo jacket as she held his gaze. "There are some people who don't have enough sense for that."

That attitude, Clay had never understood. He shook his head. "You'd think it would be common sense."

Reine's lovely mouth pursed into a frown. "You would be surprised how uncommon common sense is these days."

"Oh, you have that problem in Denquay too?"

She laughed again, and he grinned. Mission success.

They continued to slowly sway around the dance floor, and the world—the universe itself—seemed to narrow down and disappear until it was just the two of them, in their own little bubble. Because of his training, part of Clay's brain was still on the alert, but this beautiful, amazing woman held most of his attention.

He continued to ask questions about Denquay, and Reine answered them enthusiastically. Yes, the French had originally settled Denquay, before losing the colony to the British for a time. The French had eventually reclaimed it, but over time Denquay had gained their independence.

"As you can imagine, we have a very diverse population. Very colorful." Reine waved a hand to indicate the ballroom. "All those people from France and Great Britain on top of the indigenous people, as well as people who were brought in from the West Indies."

"How many languages do you speak?" Clay asked out of interest. He was willing to bet she spoke at least three.

Reine shrugged, a little self-consciously. "Five, counting one of the lesser-known indigenous dialects."

"That's impressive."

"Eh. I happen to be good at languages. I'm told it runs in the family. What about you?"

It was Clay's turn to shrug. "I speak a few."

Reine arched an eyebrow. "How many is a few?"

"Five, same as you." He shrugged again. "I was working on learning another dialect when my tour ended."

"Wow." Reine looked impressed. "Most Americans I've met are not bilingual, let alone multilingual."

"I'm a rare breed." Embarrassed, Clay steered the conversation in a different direction. Noticing that black-and-white clad waiters were beginning to circulate with trays of hors d'oeuvres, he tipped his head toward the edge of the ballroom. "Are you hungry? Looks like they're serving food now."

To his surprise, Reine's eyes lit up. "Ooh. Yes, I am." She glanced from side to side and then leaned toward him, dropping her voice. "I've been hoping they have shrimp puffs. I do love those."

Another wave of warmth curled through Clay. A woman who didn't pretend that she wasn't interested in mundane things like food? He loved it.

He smiled down at her. "Not sure I've had those, but they sound good."

"Oh, they are." Reine took his hand, craning her neck slightly to get a good glimpse of the contents of the two trays closest to them. "Ooh. This way."

They left the dance floor and she proceeded to lead him through the crowd. At one point, Clay thought he caught sight of Rob looking after them, but he ignored him. They wanted him to network, right? Well, here he was, networking.

It was the most fun Clay'd had at one of these events in a long time.

Chapter Eight

The second hors d'oeuvres tray did have shrimp puffs. Reine let go of Clay's hand and took two as the waiter navigated the crowded edges of the dance floor. Turning back to the American, she handed him one of the small breaded balls.

"I don't know how they make them, but they are amazing." She watched as he popped the entire thing into his mouth and ate it.

His eyes widened. "Wow. Those *are* good."

Reine beamed at him. "I thought you would like them." She ate her own shrimp puff in two bites—even all these years later she hadn't forgotten her mother's etiquette training—and eyed the next passing tray. It held several types of cheeses, held together by fancy toothpicks, as well as a tiny sandwich she recognized as vegetarian, but couldn't recall the name of.

For the next few minutes, they grazed the various hors d'oeuvres, casually meandering around the ballroom. Every once in a while, Reine made eye contact with someone she knew and nodded politely. In a few cases, conversation was unavoidable.

She wasn't high enough up in the hierarchy that anyone cared much if she spent the evening dancing with an American, but now and again she noticed they were garnering a few judgmental looks. She ignored these.

The conversations...were a little trickier, but she was pleased by how well Clay handled them. He was polite and complimented Denquayan hospitality where appropriate.

"You are better at navigating all this than you give yourself credit," she said eventually, when they were back on the dance floor again.

Clay ducked his head. "Not really, but thanks."

"Modest, too."

"That part's not hard." He chuckled, and the husky rumble sent butterflies spinning around in Reine's insides again. "I'm out of my element here."

"You're doing well." She smiled at him, wondering suddenly what it would feel like to run her fingers through the curling hair at the nape of his neck. The thought drew her up short internally. When was the last time she'd thought that about a man?

"Only because I'm with you." Clay smiled at her, but beneath the flirtation, his hazel eyes held a serious note. "I don't believe I've ever met anyone quite like you, Reine Delgado."

Oh, he didn't even know the half of it. Reine bit down on the inside of her lip. What would he say if he knew what the *other* half of her job entailed?

She had a sudden, mad urge to tell him—to let a few hints drop. The sensible part of her brain immediately squashed those thoughts. In the four years she'd worked for the Intelligence Division, she'd never told a single person what she really did.

She couldn't abandon her training and blow her mission now, just because she'd met a man who interested her in ways she'd never thought she could be interested.

Her mission...

Reine's breath caught in her throat. She'd been so absorbed in getting to know Clay, she'd almost lost track of the real reason she was even here tonight. What time was it?

Her internal clock told her it was close to 10pm, but she needed to check. To that end, she opened her clutch and tapped her cell phone. The screen flashed white numbers.

9:52pm.

It was almost time.

"Everything okay?"

Reine glanced up to find Clay looking at her, his expression keen and interested. His words were light, but she sensed something behind them. In that moment, she had the strangest sensation. Somehow, she knew without being told in words that if she was in trouble, this man would do his best to help her.

She offered him a sunny smile. "It is nothing." She snapped her clutch closed. "Merely checking to make sure my boss hasn't decided to make me work tonight and sent me instructions on someone specific to talk to." Her smile turned wry. "That happens, sometimes."

"I can imagine." Clay glanced over his shoulder. Reine suspected he was probably checking for his partners in Blackthorn Security.

A little thrill shot through her. It was nice, for a change, to have a man's full attention instead of knowing he was only interested in talking to her until someone more important came along. She didn't have much experience with that.

Unfortunately, she could feel time slipping past. She had work to do.

Reine looked up into Clay's face, regret blossoming in her chest. For the first time in a long time, she hated to leave one of these parties. It was strange—Clay's company had turned a nearly two-hour slog into a chunk of her evening that had vanished in an eyeblink.

She was so glad to have met him—

—but now she had to figure out how to leave him without letting him know she was leaving him.

Her heart wrenched. Whether she wanted to or not.

Her country came first.

Letting her smile turn a little shy around the edges, Reine lightly touched his arm and then nodded toward the exit. "If you'll excuse me, I need to powder my nose."

Chapter Nine

As he watched Reine's beautiful, purple-clad form disappear behind a knot of guests, Clay's smile slowly faded. A thoughtful heaviness formed in his chest. Something told him she wasn't coming back.

He didn't understand how he knew that, he just…did. Something between them had changed after Reine checked her phone. He'd never claimed to be especially attuned to the way a woman's mind worked, but he'd grown attuned to *her* over the past two hours, and she was…different…after that.

It felt like an invisible shield had gone up between them, like she was trying to figure out how to politely extricate herself from his company.

Clay took a deep breath. Maybe he was reading more into the situation than was warranted. Nothing more than that.

But…he still couldn't shake the feeling that something wasn't right.

He'd always been had a good sense about people. He was naturally observant and was used to keeping track of what was going on around him. In the military, you didn't make it outside the wire if you wandered around oblivious to everything.

That instinct had saved his life on more than one occasion.

Now, Clay wished he was a little more clueless. If he wasn't quite so observant, he could spend the next hour telling himself that Reine would come back, that she'd only gotten pulled into a conversation with someone else and would reappear at any moment. He'd tell himself that they'd laugh about it when she came back, and then she'd spend the rest of the night in his arms.

His instincts knew better.

He'd gotten a glimpse of her phone display when she'd checked it, and there hadn't been any texts, emails, or other notifications. But something *had* changed.

Was it the time? Did she have an appointment with somebody? Clay suppressed a snort. If he was anywhere else, the thought of somebody having a political appointment at ten o'clock at night would have been laughable, but they *were* in Washington D.C. and Reine *was* in politics.

Once again, he resisted the urge to scrub a hand through his hair. It figured. He finally met a woman he wanted to spend more time with, and she pulled a Cinderella on him.

His lips twitched in a rueful smile. Minus the glass slipper.

The second that thought crossed his mind, he wanted to groan. He was crazy. Worse, *she* was going to think he was crazy.

The room suddenly seemed to shrink around him, the air growing close and stale. The combined sound of the music and dozens of conversations grated on his nerves, making him wish he could clap his hands over his ears and shut it all out. He wanted to leave the Embassy, wanted to escape out into D.C.'s night air. It might be muggy as hell, but it had to be better than staying in here.

Clay took another breath, willing himself to stay frosty. Mentally, he shook his head. Oh, if Rob got wind of this, he'd never let Clay hear the end of it.

Head over heels for a woman he'd only just met—a woman he'd probably never see again after tonight? Rob would get mileage out of that for *months*.

A hand clapped him roughly on the shoulder. Clay started, his hands automatically forming fists as he turned, but then he realized it was Rob. He forced himself to relax before they drew attention.

"Rob." He shot his friend a warning look. *Speak of the devil.*

"Where's your friend?" Rob looked around with interest, his dark eyes scanning the people closest to them. He was tall and wiry, with a thin face and dark hair that was going prematurely gray at the temples. The lankiness of his form threw people off; Rob was much faster and much stronger than he looked. He was also a crack shot and had an aptitude for strategy.

"More importantly," Rob rested an arm on Clay's shoulder, "*who is she?*"

None of your business, Clay wanted to retort, but instead he shrugged carelessly. "One of the Ambassador's secretaries. Good dancer."

There was so much more he wanted to say, but he held it back. Rob wouldn't care about Reine for any of the reasons Clay found her fascinating. Neither would Naomi.

If Reine didn't have the connections to get them a good paying job, neither of them would consider her of any further use. Or worth any more of Clay's time.

"Huh." Rob looked around again, before he straightened and let his arm fall to the side. He pinned Clay with a considering look. "Well, I'm glad you've had a good evening so far, but it's probably just as well you're taking a break." His eyes narrowed slightly as he lowered his voice to add, "Don't forget why we're here, Dawson."

"Perish the thought," Clay said lightly, though the last thing he wanted to do right now was stand here and have this conversation. When Rob's considering expression didn't change, he rolled his eyes. "Rob. Don't worry. I'm focused."

That was probably stretching the truth a little, but... Clay was *always* focused. He didn't relax much, he didn't take much time off from the job. He'd never had a reason to.

Until now.

Not that Rob would appreciate the timing of that realization.

Still... Clay held his friend's gaze until Rob slowly nodded. "Okay, then," he said, before melting back into the crowd of glittering evening gowns and tuxedos.

Clay watched him go out of the corner of his eye and saw a glimpse of a woman in burnt orange moving Rob's direction. Great. He let out an irritated breath. Now Naomi and Rob were conferring. No doubt he'd get an earful later.

Okay, maybe he'd stretched the truth a little, but, whatever. Clay brushed that thought aside. So what if they didn't think he was focused? They both knew how much he hated soirees like these. They weren't his style. Never had been, no matter how many times Naomi told him he'd eventually get used to them.

That wasn't the point right now. The real point was that if he had to choose between work and talking to Reine some more...Clay would choose Reine. Hands down.

He wasn't exactly sure what that said about his future with Blackthorn Security, but at the moment he didn't care. He'd think about that tomorrow.

Right now, he needed to find Reine.

Chapter Ten

The ladies' restroom in the hall outside the ballroom was a fancy affair, all black marble and hardwood and gleaming silver fixtures. A discreetly hidden air-freshener sent a periodic cloud of something that smelled tropical into the air. As Reine slipped inside, she immediately noted that one of the stalls was occupied.

Her eyes narrowed. That would delay her just a bit. Ducking in a stall at the end, she pulled off one of her gloves and waited for the other woman to leave. She had a very narrow window of opportunity.

As soon as she heard the faint swish of the door swinging open, Reine bolted out of the stall. She hurried to the left side of the ornate black marble sink. Her eyes flicked to her reflection in the large oval mirror that stretched sideways along the length of the black counter. She looked calm, a little pale around the edges, but calm.

For a split second, she wondered what Clay saw when he looked at her. Then she promptly banished that thought. She didn't have time to worry about anything like that.

Instead, she plunged her ungloved hand into the round hole that had been carved into the marble sink top for trash and felt around on the underside of the counter. Her questing fingers encountered soft fabric and electrical tape and relief surged through her. Yes—there it was.

Exactly where she'd hidden it the day before.

Reine ripped the little package off the underside of the sink where she'd fastened it and pulled it out. She held a small black bag with strips of black electrical tape on it. She'd fastened the bag in a corner of the sink's underside, where the cleaning staff would be unlikely to see it in the shadows when they emptied the trash.

Opening her clutch, Reine dumped the bag's contents inside. She now possessed a small burner cell, a small Y-shaped USB connector with a micro-SD card reader on one side and a USB-C connector on the other, and a couple of other small items she might need for tonight's mission. She then dropped the empty bag into the trash. She couldn't risk coming back for it.

That done, it was the work of seconds to tug her elbow-length glove back on. She checked her reflection once more in the mirror. Good. Not a hair out of place. Coolly, she glided out of ladies' restroom and back into the hall.

Reine started toward the doors to the ballroom, but stopped partway, shaking her head as though she'd just remembered something. She abruptly turned around and hurried over to the staircase that led up to the next floor. It was roped off with red velvet cords, to warn the birthday party guests they were not allowed to go that way.

One of Ambassador Ambrose's security men should have been posted here, but he was nowhere to be seen. Reine suppressed a frown, glancing up and down the hall. She'd had a story prepared to feed him, but it looked like she wouldn't need it.

The hair on the back of her neck prickled uneasily. Strangely fortuitous, that. Why was Gregorio not at his post?

For a nanosecond, she wondered if she should write tonight's mission off. This was an unforeseen wrinkle and she didn't know what it meant. Maybe it would be better to try again another time instead of risking it.

In the next nanosecond, Reine dismissed that idea. Too much rode on tonight's mission, and there was nothing that overtly indicated she might be walking into a trap.

No, she needed to stay the course. She was more or less invisible. That was why the Intelligence Division had recruited her in the first place.

She was the only person at the Embassy tonight who could do this job.

With one last glance over her shoulder, Reine ducked under the velvet rope, hurried up the thick carpeted stairs and turned the corner at the landing. She took the remaining stairs at the same brisk pace—no need to draw any unnecessary attention to herself on the building's internal security cameras by doing anything out of the ordinary—and emerged into the darkness of the wide hall that connected the offices on the top floor.

Frames containing some of the Ambassador's favorite pieces of Denquayan art lined either side of the hall. In the faint light from the stairwell, the frames cast strange shadows along the cream walls. Reine walked the hall from memory, heading for the second door on the left, the office she shared with several other members of Ambassador Ambrose's staff for the duration of her stay at the D.C. Embassy.

Ultimately, she needed to get into Ariane Montoya's office at the other end of the hall, but to keep her cover intact, she'd have to start here. She could claim she was checking on a reply to an important email she'd sent earlier to one of the diplomats back in Denquay. That wasn't a lie—she did need to make sure that response came through.

Reine had cultivated a reputation for being quiet, careful, and thorough. She did her best to handle all aspects of her job seamlessly. If anyone—from the Ambassador and the First Secretary all the way down to the Embassy's security—checked security footage later, they'd just roll their eyes at her compulsive need to be thorough. No one would think anything of her leaving the birthday party for a few minutes.

Even so, Reine's heart beat a little faster in her chest as she booted up her computer, and then opened up her secure email client to check on the status of that email. Once she did this, she would need to get into the Embassy's security cameras.

Nothing happened. Frowning, Reine hit the login button again.

Still, nothing.

She blinked once, twice, and then checked whether or not the internet was working. A faint wave of shock coursed through her when she realized it was out.

That had never happened before. Not at this Embassy. Actually, she couldn't recall the internet ever being out at any of the Denquayan embassies or consulates she'd ever served at.

In this modern world of global communications, Denquay prided itself on ensuring all its citizens had access to fast, cheap, reliable internet access. That included their embassies and consulates world-wide.

This was new.

A wave of frustration rolled through her, so intense that she actually ground her teeth together. She wanted to stamp her foot on the carpet like her best friend back in Denquay's three year-old daughter had done the last time she visited. All this planning, all this anticipation, and now the stupid internet went out right before she needed it?

Insufferable, she thought. *Absolutely insufferable.*

And then her mind flashed back to the missing security guard at the bottom of the stairs. Reine breathed in through her nose, pressing her lips into a thin line. *It's probably a coincidence.*

The fact that the internet was out and Gregorio wasn't where he was supposed to be were *probably* unrelated.

Probably.

Reine bit down on the inside of her lip, staring at the pale glow of her unresponsive email client on her computer screen. She didn't believe that, however. Something twisted uneasily in the pit of her stomach.

This wasn't right. She didn't know what it was, exactly, but something was definitely off.

She resisted the urge to glance at the security camera she knew was hidden in a corner of the office. The camera was all but invisible during the day and didn't give off any light at night.

The Ambassador had pushed for—and received—a digital upgrade to the Embassy's CCTV system a couple of years earlier. Reine couldn't claim to know the intimate details of how the system worked, but she did know that even if the cameras couldn't sync with their server until the internet came back on, they still recorded everything locally.

Which meant that her mission might be officially kibitzed now.

Disappointment tangled with anxiety in her stomach. On her own, she didn't rank anywhere near high enough to be able to access the Embassy's cameras, but...*she* didn't have to. The burner cell phone in her clutch Erica had provided her, courtesy of the Intelligence Division, contained a copy of the app that interfaced with the security system and they had provided her with login credentials.

Unfortunately, though, without the internet, she couldn't even access the app to do anything with the cameras—and she was almost out of time.

Her window of opportunity had nearly closed. On the security cameras, her presence up here for much longer would be too suspicious.

Unable to restrain a disappointed sigh, Reine closed her email client. She was about to shut her computer down when a shadowy figure suddenly filled the doorway, blocking out light from the hall.

Heart in her throat, Reine looked up just as the office light snapped on, temporarily blinding her.

A familiar male voice asked, "Everything okay?"

Reine's voice hit a high note in her surprise. "*Clay?*"

Chapter Eleven

Clay watched Reine stop in the hall and turn around, as though she'd forgotten something, but he still couldn't shake the feeling that something about her was off. What was she doing? Frowning, he edged out of the men's restroom as he watched her vanish up the staircase that led to the Embassy's top floor.

He glanced from side to side along the hall, but it was still empty and quiet, save for the noise from the ballroom. Everyone else in the Embassy seemed to be enjoying the party. He crossed the hall to the stairs, his footfalls making barely a sound against the lush pile of the carpet. Ducking under the red velvet rope just as Reine had done, he slowly followed her upstairs.

Clay swallowed uneasily. He'd done plenty of surveillance before, in his career as a Marine, but this was...different. Following Reine like this made him question his own motives.

I feel like a stalker, he realized belatedly.

Granted, it was out of a desire to help, but... He smiled ruefully to himself. Reine might not see it that way.

Still... He'd made it this far—and he *still* couldn't shake a gut sense that something was wrong. Maybe it was better to ask forgiveness than permission, in this particular situation.

And if Reine didn't want to ever see him again after this... Clay clenched his jaw, then forced himself to relax. Well, it was a small price to pay for his peace of mind. At least he'd have the satisfaction of knowing she was okay.

When he reached the top of the stairs, part of him expected to hear warning shouts from below. He wasn't supposed to be up here —and a place like this most definitely had security cameras. Any minute, someone would sound an alarm and a guard would be dispatched to quietly escort him back to the party.

Clay's lips twitched again. Or he'd be kicked out of the Embassy entirely. Wouldn't Rob and Naomi *love* that? He could just imagine the lecture Rob would give him on the business he might have cost them.

He pushed thoughts of his fellow members of Blackthorn Security aside to focus on the situation at hand. The hall was quiet and empty—and dark.

Clay narrowed his eyes. Reine hadn't turned on any lights. That was...strange.

He edged down the wide hall, moving quietly along the dark carpet. The tropical scent of the Embassy's air-freshener seemed a little stronger up here. The pale walls were covered in framed pictures, though in the semi-darkness he couldn't make out if they were art or photographs.

Doors led off of the hall at staggered intervals—probably offices. Most of them were closed, but there were two open. One was toward the far end of the hall, and the other was a yard away on his left. Clay listened for movement to indicate which direction Reine had gone.

He didn't hear anything.

His confusion deepened. What was she *doing* up here? His eyes tracked from the open door to his left to the one at the end of the hall and resolve hardened in his chest. He'd have to check both of them.

He considered the closed doors, but dismissed them off-hand. He hadn't heard a door shut—and unless these doors were *insanely* quiet, he'd have heard that.

Clay took a breath, his training kicking in and helping him regulate his heartbeat and his breathing. *You're just checking rooms to see where an attractive woman went,* he told himself. *It's not like you're facing possibly getting shot at when you poke your head around the doorway.*

At least, he *hoped* not.

Given that he really didn't know what was going on here, there was a probably a tiny chance that he *was* about to be shot at.

In the back of his mind, Clay thought wryly that if the guys manning the security cams weren't on their way to him yet, they would be. He knew how suspicious he looked.

But, he wasn't dumb enough to just blindly walk into a dark room, either.

Flattening himself up against the wall, Clay edged close to the doorway. He peeked around the doorframe—just far enough to see inside—and felt a knot inside him unwind.

Reine leaned over a desk, her face lit with the pale, unearthly white glow of a computer screen. Her entire body radiated irritation, but she was otherwise alone and seemed perfectly fine.

She's fine.

Clay wasn't sure if it was relief or courage or insanity—or some combination of the three—that precipitated his next movement.

He stepped into the doorway, right hand reaching instinctively for the light switch that was probably right there. Reine looked up just as his fingers touched a light switch panel. Warm golden light flooded the room.

"Are you okay?" he asked, remaining in the doorway so as not to startle her further.

It took a second for his eyes to adjust, but he saw the moment

Reine's eyes adjusted and she recognized him. Her mouth fell open in astonishment. "Clay?"

She looked and sounded so surprised and taken aback, standing there in that shimmering purple gown that made her look like a goddess, that guilt flickered in the pit of Clay's stomach. He opened his mouth to say something—what, he wasn't sure—but Reine beat him to it.

Drawing herself up to her full height, she propped her hands on her hips and regarded him sternly. "What are you doing up here? Unauthorized personnel are *not* allowed up that staircase." She nodded firmly in the direction of the stairs.

Clay swallowed, even as his stomach sank. Yep, this had definitely been a bad idea. The nascent, half-formed ideas he'd entertained this evening of seeing Reine after tonight popped like so many fragile soap bubbles.

"I just wanted to make sure you were all right." He lifted a hand to the back of his neck, feeling sheepish. If he been afraid earlier that he'd reverted to his awkward teenage self, he felt like he'd gone all the way back to a silly little boy now. His phone buzzed in his pocket, but he ignored it.

"Reine, I—" Clay broke off as a burst of distant gunfire shattered the stillness that permeated this floor of the Embassy.

Chapter Twelve

Reine froze in place standing behind her mahogany desk, her eyes wide with shock. She felt as though someone had just thrown a bucket of icy water over her head. Gunfire? In the *Embassy?*

The familiar environs of the rather luxurious office she shared with several other of the Ambassador's staff members took on an alien cast. The gold curtains draping the windows, the bright artwork on the cream walls, the shiny computers, flatscreen monitors, and other assorted paraphernalia cluttering all three desks—it all suddenly looked otherworldly. The edges were too sharp, the colors too bright.

The scent of the sandalwood incense that Clara, Ariane's secretary, kept on her desk threatened to make Reine's stomach revolt.

Another burst of gunfire sounded, followed by distant shouts and screams, and her knees almost buckled. She grabbed for the edge of her desk, gripping it so tightly her knuckles turned white. Her eyes sought Clay's.

For one crazy second, she wondered if he knew what was going on. He was a former soldier. Gunfire was his thing, after all.

But Clay's hazel eyes were just as wide and surprised as her own. Realization slapped Reine with the force of a real blow. She was being ridiculous. Of *course* he didn't know what was going on either. He was a guest at the Embassy tonight, for Pete's sake.

She took a breath, trying to get a grip on herself, and opened her mouth. Words died in her throat as another series of shouts pummeled the air, these sounding a little closer.

That was when Clay exploded into motion.

In one breathtakingly smooth motion, he slapped the light switch panel to kill the overhead light and bounded across the office to the desk where she stood. Wrapping an arm around her shoulders, he pulled her down behind the desk beside him.

"Kill your computer," he said in her ear, his voice barely audible.

His body was a warm, solid presence beside her. Reine felt the heat from him soaking into her side. When had she gotten so cold?

With shaking fingers, she reached up over the edge of the desk and pressed the button to turn her monitor off. Then she grabbed her clutch from where she'd laid it on the desk's surface and sank back down behind her desk, crouched on the thick carpeted floor next to Clay in her high-heeled shoes. Darkness flooded the room, save for a swathe of faint illumination that fell through the doorway from the distant lights in the hall at the bottom of the stairs.

Reine was amazingly hyperaware of Clay. She could feel every inch where the hard planes of his body pressed up against her side. She felt the strength in the muscled arm wrapped protectively around her shoulders. Sparks seemed to radiate out from wherever he touched her.

A shuddery breath escaped her lips. She should probably feel annoyed that he'd followed her up here, but in this moment, all she felt was relief and a profound sense of gratitude that she wasn't alone.

For a nanosecond, Reine let herself imagine what it would be like to be up here by herself, facing whatever was happening tonight completely cut off from everyone else in the Embassy. A fine shiver worked its way down her spine.

It wasn't a pretty picture.

"Any idea what's going on?" Clay asked quietly, breath warm against her ear.

Reine shook her head, before belatedly remembering that he couldn't see the movement in the dark room. "No."

She thought of Ambassador Ambrose and his wife, of all the people she'd come to know during her stints traveling back and forth between Denquay's various embassies and consulates. Dread roiled inside her. Fear pressed clammy hands against her chest, making her heart hammer.

Was anyone dead? Were they hurt? What was—

"Breathe." Clay's arm tightened around her shoulders. "Just breathe. Nice and slow. It's going to be okay."

His words were little more than a whisper, but they sank into Reine like raindrops on parched ground. She drew in a shaky breath, trying to calm herself.

Clay's clean, comforting scent surrounded her, making her feel safe. That was a little surprising, given that they'd only known each other for a couple of hours, but Reine wasn't about to question it. For the span of several heartbeats, she let herself lean against him.

Clay briefly rested his cheek on the top of her head, lending her strength, before he straightened. Alert. Ready for whatever would happen next.

Reine's heartbeat was so loud in her own ears she wondered if Clay could hear it. She inhaled again, slowly expanding her lungs in an effort to stave off hyperventilation. She needed to *think*.

Someone—some sort of terrorist group—was trying to take over the Embassy. Reine pressed a hand to her heart. Maybe even had *succeeded* in taking over the Embassy.

But why? And why tonight? Because it was Karina Ambrose's birthday, a high-profile event?

Beside her, Clay shifted position slightly. "Do you have any idea who's down there?"

"No."

"Does the Ambassador have any enemies capable of pulling off something like this?"

"I don't know." Reine tried to think back, closing her eyes as she cycled back through hundreds of memories from the past couple of years. "Maybe?"

"What about politics back home?"

Reine stilled, drawing in another deep breath. Now *that* was a distinct possibility.

She couldn't tell Clay about the investigation that had been launched into Ambrose's staff. Or her part in it. But now she couldn't help wondering if they were related.

Of course, there were other issues too. She swallowed. "The President has...implemented a few rather unpopular policies concerning renewable resources and some of Denquay's rainforests."

And he'd declared a crackdown on the production of illegal drugs. That hadn't gone over well either. In some quarters of the world, drugs made certain individuals even more money than controlling renewable resources.

Reine couldn't tell Clay that either, even though she suspected he was probably already familiar with that particular fact.

"Environmental crazies with guns?" Clay sounded doubtful. She couldn't blame him. "Always thought chaining themselves to trees or gluing themselves to paintings was more their style."

"It's complicated." That was probably the understatement of the year. "There is a lot of money involved on either side."

Another series of faint screams carried up the staircase and down the hall to them. Reine trembled. If it weren't for her mission, she'd be down there right now. She glanced sideways through the darkness at Clay. They'd probably still have been dancing.

Her mission. She tightened her grip on her purple clutch, which was nestled in her lap. Embassy takeover or no, she still had a mission to accomplish.

Erica and the rest of the Intelligence Division would expect no less. She could almost hear her handler's voice in her ear. *It's a dangerous situation, but it's an excellent distraction. Take advantage of it.*

Reine breathed in and then breathed out, imagining her fear flowing out of her like early morning mist burning away as the sun grew brighter.

Her eyes widened as another disturbing thought struck her. "Do you think anybody outside the Embassy knows what's happened yet?"

"No idea," Clay said grimly, his voice still a barely audible. "Depends on whether or not anybody's managed to call 911 or get a text out." He shifted a little closer to her. "What's Embassy protocol for a terrorist attack?"

A hot flush of embarrassment suddenly flared in her cheeks. That...was an excellent question. What *was* the protocol? She couldn't remember.

"I'm not sure," she said sheepishly. "One of the security chiefs gave a presentation a few months ago, but I don't remember much of it. He didn't say much other than for us to get to a secure room and barricade ourselves in. Seemed to think that in the event something *did* happen, Embassy security would be able to handle it."

They'd gotten complacent—and now they were paying for it.

"This one of those offices?"

Reine shook her head out of habit. "No. The Ambassador's office and the First Secretary's office."

She fumbled in her clutch for her cell phone. Hers, not the burner she'd been given. If she was going to call for help, it had to come through the correct channels.

Just as she unlocked her phone, a low rumble of male voices carried down the hall. She and Clay both froze.

Reine instinctively flipped her phone upside down on her lap, hiding the glow of the screen in her skirt while she hit the power button to shut the screen off again.

Her heart hammered in her chest. The thick carpet throughout this floor made it almost impossible to hear footsteps.

Was someone coming? Were they searching the offices?

She almost couldn't breathe. If the terrorists *were* searching the offices, was it because they knew she, specifically, was missing, or was it just a general sweep?

Clay removed his arm from around her shoulders and straightened. Reine immediately missed his warmth. He pressed a hand to her shoulder, warning her with a touch to stay down.

Then, with a faint rustle of his tuxedo, he rose to his feet and crept around her desk.

From her position on the floor, Reine watched his shadowy form through the thick legs of the desk. Clay picked his way around the office, staying in the black shadows to one side of faint wedge of light coming through the doorway. When he reached the wall beside the door, he flattened himself against it.

Reine pressed a hand to her mouth. Was he doing what she *thought* he was doing?

Her heart leaped into her throat as, for the second time that night, a shadow loomed in the doorway.

Chapter Thirteen

Clay pressed his shoulders to the wall just far enough away from the light switch that a questing hand wouldn't accidentally brush up against him. Turning his head sideways so he could watch the door, he waited.

The terrorists were coming for them. Didn't matter if they knew anybody was up here or not. Anyone with the guts and smarts to execute a takeover of an embassy like this would have their people sweep the place for strays.

The only question was how much time he and Reine had.

Turned out it wasn't long.

Less than a minute later, a shadowy figure loomed in the doorway. A hand reached around the doorframe, searching for the light switch.

Clay grabbed that wrist before the person found the light and hauled the shadowy figure inside the office. The man—it was a man—hadn't been expecting *that*.

Clay used that second's worth of surprise to his advantage. Jabbing the man in the throat with his free hand, he stripped the man's rifle out of his hands before he could squeeze off a shot and tossed it aside into the black shadows at their feet.

Gasping and gagging, the man tried to put up a fight.

Clay kicked him in the knee and then grabbed him in a headlock, but not before the man slammed his head into the doorframe. Stars burst across Clay's vision, but he gritted his teeth end held on.

They grappled for a handful of seconds that felt like hours. The man clawed at Clay, trying to reach his face and gouge his eyes out. Grimacing, Clay squeezed harder, putting inexorable pressure on the man's carotid artery.

His opponent kicked and thrashed, but he'd been caught off-guard and Clay was *strong*

In a moment, it was over. The man went limp in Clay's grip. Clay remained frozen in place, however, straining his ears for any sign that the sound of their struggle had drawn attention from someone else out in the hall.

Nothing but the sound of his own pounding heartbeat met his ears.

Quickly, he dragged the man to one side of the dark office and lowered him to the carpet. Out of the corner of his eye, he glimpsed movement through the darkness, but it was only Reine. Ignoring her for a second, Clay knelt and rifled through the man's pockets.

He emerged with a wicked-looking fold-out knife, a cell phone, and a handful of zip ties. No wallet.

Clay narrowed his eyes. That meant no ID, which meant there was no way this man had gotten into the Embassy the normal way. He set the knife and the cell phone aside and quickly used the zip ties to bind his unconscious opponent's hands and feet together.

"Does he have ID?" Reine asked in a whisper.

"Not that I can find." Clay pressed a button on the cell phone, but of course the screen was locked. He turned its light on the unconscious man's face. "Do you recognize him?"

The cell phone screen's bright light illuminated a man of

Hispanic origins, with a thin nose, a black goatee, and neatly trimmed black hair. He was dressed in evening wear, just like everyone else at the birthday party.

He heard Reine swallow. "I've never seen him before in my life."

"Not surprised. He's an underling. Can't believe they only sent one guy up here. Sloppy, that." Clay slipped the man's cell phone into his left pocket so he wouldn't get it confused with his own phone and then recovered the rifle. "AK-47." He shook his head, slinging it over his shoulder. "I swear, the bad guys *always* have these."

In the darkness, Reine's eyes looked huge in her face. "I don't understand."

"It's okay. Just know that I'd be more concerned if this guy was toting something American-made."

Swiftly, Clay stripped off one of the man's shoes—expensive dress shoes, by the feel of them—and one of his socks. He stuffed the sock into the man's mouth as a makeshift gag and then reached down and grabbed his zip-tied ankles. He dragged the man over to one of the other desks and stowed him behind it.

"We can't stay here," he said softly, when he returned to Reine's side. "You said your security protocols call for you to hole up some-place else?"

She stared at him for a few seconds, long enough that he wondered if this beautiful, amazing woman had finally gone into shock on him.

"Reine?"

Reine blinked. "Yes. The office toward the end of the hall. We can go there."

Clay reached out his left hand and clasped her right hand in his. Even through the gloves she still wore, her fingers felt cold. "Okay, then. Follow me."

Chapter Fourteen

The hall outside Reine's office was mercifully empty. Clay shepherded her out of the office and quietly closed the door to her office. Then he escorted her to the other end of the hall, keeping his body as a protective shield between her and any potential attackers who might appear from the stairs.

Reine couldn't help notice that he moved with a smooth grace that told her he had long practice with operations like this. Clearly, whatever Clay had once been in the United States Marines, he'd been good at it.

She'd secured her clutch to her wrist again, but she gripped it tightly anyway. If only Clay knew what was inside that tiny little bag…He'd have questions. Lots of questions.

Anxiety and fear swirled together inside her, making her stomach churn. Ariane's office was exactly where she needed to be right now…but Reine had *not* anticipated having an audience along for the ride. She felt Clay's quiet, solid presence behind her and guilt mixed with the fear and anxiety.

She wasn't stupid. The odds of her breaking into Ariane's

computer and cloning her hard drive without Clay realizing something was up were extremely low.

They reached the dark doorway of the office. In one smooth motion, Clay whisked her inside and pushed her down to the carpeted floor. He shut the door with a quiet 'click' and then hit the lights.

They both winced as their eyes adjusted. Reine crouched low, her eyes wide, her mouth dry, and her heart hammering in her chest. The lingering cloying scent of Ariane's perfume filled her nostrils.

Clay swept the barrel of his acquired rifle in an arc through the room, searching for potential targets, but the ornate office was empty.

Just like Reine had hoped.

She sagged in relief, but Clay's alert posture didn't change. Lowering the rifle, he sought her with his gaze. "Can you lock the door?"

It was only then that she realized he was bleeding. A stream of blood covered one side of his face from a gash at his temple. Probably where the terrorist had slammed him into the doorframe.

Reine's fingers itched to touch him. "You're bleeding."

Clay blinked, one hand rising to his temple. His fingers came away slick with blood. He inspected them, then shook his head. "We'll worry about that in a minute. Can you lock the door?"

"Yes." Reine rose to her feet, nearly stepping on the hem of her purple evening gown in the process, and stumbled over to the discreet, fancy security panel mounted into the dark wood paneling beside the heavy wooden door. Her knees felt like they were made of water again. She keyed in her emergency code—she did remember *that*—and listened as the door locked with a rather ominous-sounding 'snickt'.

She started to lean against the door, but Clay shook his head.

"No, no. Come away from the door. In case somebody tries to shoot through it," he explained, but she was already moving.

They both looked around at the luxurious office they now found themselves in. A brown leather couch stood along one wall below the windows that faced the street below. The emerald green curtains were currently drawn, covering the windows. An ornate low-slung mahogany filing cabinet stretched along the wall to their right, beside a door that Reine knew led into a private bathroom.

An assortment of picture frames and a crystal tray with a crystal decanter of rum and matching shot glasses stood atop the smooth, glossy surface of the filing cabinet. On the other side of the office stood a small bookcase. Colorful paintings of Denquay's mountains and rainforests were scattered on the walls.

Clay lifted his eyebrows. "Wow." He nodded to the large mahogany desk in the center of the office, with its shiny Mac computer and equally shiny desk paraphernalia. "This the Ambassador's office?"

"No, it belongs to the First Secretary, Ariane Montoya."

Clay turned in a slow circle in the middle of the floor, inspecting the office's corners. Reine knew what he was looking for even before he asked, "Any cameras in here?"

She shook her head. "There are a few places in the Embassy that are more private than others. This is one of them."

She'd been banking on that fact. She'd just needed to tinker with the cameras that covered her office and the hall so that she could get into Ariane Montoya's office undetected. Now, it didn't matter.

Reine flattened a hand against her churning stomach, looking around. Ariane was an excellent First Secretary. She was intelligent, efficient at running the Embassy for the Ambassador, and cool under pressure. She wasn't a cuddly person, or especially inviting, but Reine had come to like her quite a bit.

Maybe that was part of the reason she was having such a hard time with this mission. It was hard to imagine this woman selling out her country for financial gain.

"We need to shut the lights off."

Reine snapped her attention to Clay. He was looking at her, his expression almost apologetic. The weapon in his hand looked incongruous against his now-slight-wrinkled tuxedo, and yet…it fit him somehow. "What?"

"The lights." He gestured to the ornate light fixture in the ceiling, before jerking his chin toward the curtained windows. "We don't want to draw unnecessary attention right now. They might have eyes outside."

"And they might see the light under the door." Reine nodded in understanding, her gaze turning to the door. "I agree." She paused, tilting her head to one side. "I think there's a small nightlight in the restroom. Can we—can we leave the door open?"

She looked at Clay, hoping he understood. She didn't want to sit in complete darkness for the next however many hours until they were rescued…or someone came after them again.

Something in his hazel eyes softened. "I think that would be all right."

"Thank you."

Clay found the light switch and killed the lights, plunging the office into darkness. Reine remained where she was, letting her eyes adjust. A slice of dim light appeared on one side of the room; Clay had cracked the bathroom door.

Reine focused on that light, taking a deep breath and trying to marshal her racing thoughts. What did she do now? What *could* she do?

911, she decided abruptly. *I need to call the police.*

The terrorists had taken out the Embassy's internet and she'd bet everything she owned that they were currently confiscating cell phones from every guest in attendance tonight—as well as everyone else in the building. It was the smartest course of action—no sense letting anyone get out any more information than necessary.

But here she and Clay were, locked safely in Ariane Montoya's office…and they both had their cell phones.

Aloud, she said, "I'm going to call the police."

"Great idea," Clay said as he crossed the dim office to stand by her side again. "Probably better coming from you." He pulled his own cell phone from his pocket and frowned.

"What is it?" Reine tried to keep her voice level.

Clay glanced up at her, a deep frown still etched on his features. "My buddy texted me a few minutes ago to say that armed men stormed into the ballroom."

Reine resisted the urge to flatten a hand against her chest. "As if we need more confirmation."

"I'd text him back, but…" He trailed off, pressing his lips into a thin line and shaking his head.

It was too dangerous. For them *and* for his friend.

Their best bet was to call the local authorities.

Reine dug in her clutch for her cell phone, experiencing a brief flash of panic when she nearly pulled out the burner phone by accident. Swallowing, she withdrew her own phone and dialed 911. Her fingers shook a little more than she would have liked.

On the other end, the phone rang once, twice, and then a cool, crisp female voice said, "911, what's your emergency?"

"I am at the Denquay Embassy. Armed shooters have invaded the building and are holding everyone in the ballroom hostage, including Ambassador Ambrose and his wife." Reine took a breath and then gave the operator their address.

"What's your name?"

Reine shook her head. "I cannot give you that."

"Can you stay on the line?"

Reine's gaze darted to Clay. He shook his head, tapping one ear.

She bit down on her lip, hard. He was right. They didn't know if whoever was behind this could listen in.

"No." She let her voice break a little. "I'm sorry."

The 911 operator asked a few more questions, but Reine only said, "I am sorry. I cannot tell you anything more. Please send help."

She ended the call and pressed her cell phone to her chest.

"You did good." Clay rested his hand on her shoulder for a second. The gesture gave her more comfort than she would have thought possible. "If Rob managed to text me, you can't be the only person to call for help. Maybe somebody else can tell them more."

Reine nodded wordlessly, already scrolling through the contacts in her phone. There had to be somebody else who could help get the word out to the Denquayan government...and by extension, the Intelligence Division.

Even as she left half a dozen voicemails (a wry part of her mind noting it was a shame no one would answer her calls, even if it *was* late), Reine calculated how long it would take the Intelligence Division to learn the Embassy was under attack. In the years she'd worked for them, she'd felt at times that they almost seemed to know about certain events before they occurred. She could only hope that would be the case tonight.

Fleetingly, she wished she could contact Erica, let her handler know what was happening. But that was impossible. She didn't have Erica's number in her personal cell phone and—for all kinds of security reasons—the burner phone safely tucked away in her clutch contained no contacts.

Though Reine had memorized a special number in case of extreme emergencies, this particular emergency did not quite meet the rather stringent specifications she'd been given for using it.

She pressed her lips into a thin line. *Although you'd think something like this* would *count as an extreme emergency.*

Still...orders were orders.

Taking a deep breath, Reine tried to imagine her fear burning away like mist in the early morning sun. She was partly successful. It was only then that she belatedly remembered that Clay was still bleeding.

"Oh! You're still bleeding." Stuffing her phone back into her clutch, she reached for his free hand. Even through her gloves, she felt that spark of electricity, but she pushed it away. "Come with me. There should be a first-aid kit in the restroom."

Chapter Fifteen

Without a doubt, the Denquayan First Secretary's bathroom had to be one of the fanciest Clay had ever seen. It was all silver and turquoise and gleaming white, with glistening sinks and counters and a glossy dark wood storage cabinet with decorative silver fixtures. A stand-up shower stood next to a door that opened up on a toilet and a bidet. The air smelled of the same cloying perfume that permeated the rest of the office.

Clay leaned against the shiny turquoise counter in the dim glow of the nightlight plugged into the wall and let Reine patch him up. The gash in his head wasn't bad, but it had bled a lot, making him look like he'd been hurt worse than he had. Before they'd come in here, he'd shucked his black tuxedo jacket and laid it over one arm of the brown leather couch.

He watched Reine as she cleaned up the worst of the still-wet blood on his face with tissues, and then gently wiped away the rest with alcohol wipes. Her expression was serious. As she moved, he noticed that the purple fabric of her gown shimmered under even this dim light too.

Clearing his throat, he remarked lightly, "You're good under pressure, Miss Delgado. A lot of women—and some men too—would have turned into sobbing messes after going through everything you just did."

Reine's fingers stilled their ministrations as her gaze flicked up to his. "I'm in the diplomatic corps," she said, as though that explained everything.

Clay nodded, but inwardly he thought it was more than that. Some people just naturally handled crises better than others. She was one of those people.

"Tip your head back, please. This may sting a bit," Reine said presently.

Clay complied, and she cleaned the gash out with hydrogen peroxide. He winced as the liquid bubbled over his open wound, but the sting soon passed. Reine patted his skin dry, applied some antibiotic ointment, and then used a couple of butterfly Band-Aids to close the gash.

"I hope those stay," she said, eying the butterflies as though she wasn't entirely convinced they'd behave.

"I'm sure they will." Clay glanced over his shoulder at his reflection in the mirror. "Looks like you did a good job."

"Thank you." Reine nodded gravely and set about cleaning up all of the trash she'd created. She dumped it all into the trashcan under the sink and then put away the first aid kit and other supplies she'd used.

She washed her hands, but turned to look at him halfway through drying them. "I can't believe I haven't asked this before now, but do you have a gun?"

"You mean besides this one?" Clay indicated the rifle he'd confiscated from the terrorist.

"Yes."

"No."

Even in the semi-darkness, Reine's surprise was so palpable that it made Clay chuckle. "What, you expected me to be packing just because I work for a security firm?"

Was that a *blush* rising in her cheeks? She waved a hand. "Well, you must admit you Americans have a certain…stereotype. Everyone knows that Americans love their guns."

"Some of us do." Clay was still smiling. "Some people hate them, and others abuse them. But here?" He spread his hands. "Your embassy has its rules and I respected them."

Reine pursed her lips in a wry frown. "It goes without saying that whoever has attacked the embassy did not."

"That's why the bad guys are the bad guys." Clay shrugged. "They don't respect the law."

Reine inclined her head in a nod. "I can't argue with that."

Chapter Sixteen

As soon as she and Clay exited the restroom to return to the office, Reine hurried over to the brown leather couch. She knelt on the middle cushion, taking care to keep her head low, and carefully—very carefully—peeked through the slit where the two halves of the emerald green curtains met in the middle of the window frame. She gasped.

She couldn't see much, but she *could* see flashing red and blue lights coming from the street far below. Relief and hope battled her fear and anxiety.

She turned back to Clay. "Capitol police are here."

"That's great." He came up beside her and leaned on the back of the couch to see for himself. Then he looked down at her. "We'd better get away from the windows. Just in case."

They both slid off the couch to the thick carpeted floor and Clay reached over to take her gloved hand. "Don't let your guard down." He cast a grim nod in the direction of the locked door. "There's no telling how long it'll take them to either negotiate their way out of this situation, or else put an end to it."

Reine felt cold again. "And we're trapped up here."

"Yes, we are. For now, at least." Clay fished in his trousers pocket for his cell phone and glanced at the display. Then he hissed through his teeth and shoved it back where it had come from.

Reine bit down on the inside of her lip. "Have you heard anything from your friends?"

Clay shook his head, before scrubbing a hand through his hair. It left him looking even more handsome than before, which was hilarious, because Reine knew if she'd tried the same maneuver, she'd have come out looking like she got hit by a rogue blow-dryer.

"They were in the ballroom, last I saw, and if these terrorists have any sense, they went around and confiscated everyone's phones." He smiled painfully. "It'd be too dangerous to try to contact them."

Reine nodded. She understood that only too well.

Tipping her head back against the couch, she stared up through the semi-darkness at the ceiling. Her thoughts were too loud. The silence in this office was almost oppressive, but the noise in her head made her feel like she was on the verge of over-stimulation.

One thought struggled out of the chaos. She froze, feeling a wave of horror trickle over her. She turned to Clay. "You don't think they have a list of everyone who is here tonight, do you?"

"And they're matching guests to the list to see if everyone is accounted for?"

"Yes."

Clay sucked in a breath through his teeth, running a hand through his hair again. "I should have thought of that." He shook his head. "I have no idea. They've already proved that they could bypass the Embassy's security, so it's possible they have access to a guest list too." He hesitated, then added, "If that's the case, then it's only a matter of time before they come looking for you."

Reine swallowed. "And you."

"I was a last-minute addition." Clay shrugged. "I think Rob had to pull a couple of strings to get me in. So they might not know about me."

Reine nodded, focusing on keeping her breathing steady. Focusing on not letting him know how much the idea of an additional time constraint stressed her out. "There's also the man we left zip-tied and gagged in my office," she pointed out. "They'll miss him eventually."

"There's that." Clay reached over to wrap his fingers around her gloved hand. The warmth of his skin seeped through the sheer fabric. "Let's hope the Capitol police can get the job done quickly."

Reine nodded, and they subsided into silence again.

She could *feel* time slipping through her fingers. It thrummed inside her, the knowledge that she was going to fail. Through no fault of her own, granted, but still…

The Intelligence Division had trusted her, and now she was going to blow it.

Reine drew her knees up to her chest, the folds of her shimmery purple gown draping over her legs. She had no idea how beautiful she looked sitting there in the soft glow spilling out from the night-light in the restroom; she certainly didn't feel it. What were the odds that someone would attempt to take over the Embassy the same night as her mission? It was mind-boggling.

She wanted to drum her fingers on her knees, tap her feet on the floor, but she restrained herself. No need to make Clay think even less of her.

He sat beside her on the floor, back against the leather couch, long legs stretched out in front of him. The confiscated rifle lay on the floor beside him within easy reach. They'd both pulled out their phones and were searching for news reports, but even in the semi-darkness she could see the faraway look in his eyes. His thoughts were elsewhere.

Reine swallowed, a nascent plan coalescing in her mind. Maybe everything *wasn't* lost. Maybe she could still accomplish her mission.

Her fingers tightened on her clutch in her lap. Even if the Capitol police were here already, it could be hours before they resolved the situation. What she was contemplating was dangerous. For both her and Clay. But…

The alternative was that she failed her mission. And far more lives were at stake than just hers. Or even Clay's.

As insane as the current hostage situation was, the reality was that it afforded Reine an unprecedented opportunity. She just had to get Clay out of the way—and, thanks to Erica and the Intelligence Division, she had the perfect means to do it.

Reine glanced at his handsome profile out of the corner of her eye. Her grip on her clutch tightened to the point of the clasp hurting her fingers. She needed him to be unconscious while she did her job.

Could she really do that? Could she knock him out?

He'd hate her afterward. But…again… Did she really have another option?

Clay needed plausible deniability. He couldn't know what had happened here tonight. For his own sake, and for hers.

No. She swallowed, looking down at the *Breaking News* headlines scrolling across her own news app. This was the best option.

"I wish we knew what was going on down there," Clay said suddenly, breaking the stillness that had fallen over them. "Not knowing is killing me."

"Agreed," Reine said. She took a deep breath, let it out slowly. Her heart started hammering in her chest again. "I can't find anything other than a report that the Embassy is under attack."

"Me neither." Clay dropped his phone to the carpet beside his leg and changed the subject. "Do you have family back in Denquay?"

Reine blinked, surprised by the sudden change in subject, but she said, "Some extended family." She shrugged. "I was an only child, and my parents weren't from large families. So I grew up mostly alone."

"I'm sorry," Clay said softly. He reached over and wrapped his arms around her shoulders, squeezing gently.

Reine let herself close her eyes, soaking in the comfort he provided. *Better take it now,* a stray corner of her mind said grimly. *He may not want anything else to do with you when this is all over.*

"What about you?" she found herself asking.

Clay was silent for a moment, and then he let out a soft chuckle. "I'm the middle of six children. Four boys and two girls. My family lives in Northern Kentucky."

Reine smiled. "You would fit in well in Denquay. We love large families." Her smile turned wistful as, not for the first time, she imagined what it would be like to have that many siblings. "I imagine your house was noisy growing up."

"Oh, definitely." Clay smiled reminiscently. "We had our share of scuffles, but at the end of the day I always knew they had my back." He shrugged, a little self-consciously. "Kind of like my team, back when I was active duty."

Reine shifted a little on the floor to angle herself toward him so she could see his face better. Beside her, Clay did the same. Around them, Ariane's office seemed to take on an intimate air, like the problems and the dangers beyond the locked door had faded away and all that remained was a little bubble around the two of them.

Reine found herself yearning to know more about this man, to get to know him better before she ruined everything. Maybe it was masochistic on her part, maybe she'd have been better off trying to distance herself, but she couldn't help it. Clay drew her with a powerful attraction like they were two magnets. They could circle each other for a while, but inevitably, that inexorable force would pull them together.

"Why did you join your friend's security firm instead of going back home to Kentucky?"

Clay shrugged, shaking his head. He looked away, and in the faint glow of the nightlight spilling out of the open restroom door, Reine watched a muscle in his jaw twitch. She realized in this moment that she had touched a deeply painful subject.

Instinctively, she put a hand on his arm. "You don't have to answer if you would prefer not to."

He looked at her then, his eyes dark, and sighed. Slowly at first, he said, "I've seen too much, been through too much, to be able to go home and get on with a 'normal'—" he made air quotes with his fingers, "—life. The town I grew up in seems so…small." He shook his head, his right hand opening and closing into a fist where it rested on his lap. "I know there's more to the world, and I know I'm a different person than I was when I enlisted. I just—I can't go back. I've got to do something else with my life."

Reine digested that for a few heartbeats, turning his words over in his mind. That was an eminently sensible way of looking at things. "I can't see anything wrong with that."

"You'd be the first."

"I'm sorry," she said simply.

The understanding in Reine's voice soothed a rough spot in Clay's heart. He hadn't realized how badly he'd needed to talk to someone about this. He rubbed a thumb over the back of her hand, wishing her gloves weren't in the way. It would have been nice to feel her skin.

"Anyway," he forced a smile, "my parents don't understand. They weren't real keen on me joining the Marines in the first place, although they came around eventually. But now?" He lifted a shoulder in a deliberately careless shrug and left it at that.

"What about your siblings?" Reine leaned a little closer to him, her bare arm pressing into his, with only the sleeve of his white dress shirt between them.

"Mixed bag. It's hard."

"Sounds like it."

Clay glanced at her and found Reine looking at him, understanding and empathy written all over the beautiful lines of her face. The dim light enhanced her features, making her dark eyes positively luminous. His mouth went dry.

His gaze darted to her lips. She was close enough that he could kiss her. All he had to do was lean in just a hair and…

No. He swallowed, unconsciously leaning a little away from her. Downstairs a bunch of people—including his friends—were being held hostage. He couldn't be up here making out with Reine, no matter how amazing and beautiful she was.

Even if there was absolutely nothing he could do to help resolve the current situation, he still had standards.

Clay swallowed again and glanced down at his feet. Kissing her would have to wait until this was all over.

If they got out of this. And if Reine wanted him to kiss her.

He hoped she did. Clay rested his neck against the back of the couch and stared up at the ceiling. He *really* hoped she did.

Chapter Eighteen

Clay wanted to kiss her.

Reine didn't consider herself an expert on such things, but she wasn't completely oblivious. The look on his face, the way his eyes had dropped to her mouth… He wanted to kiss her.

That knowledge filled her with a heady giddiness. In that moment, the anxiety and the fear and the stress of their current situation temporarily fell away, leaving just Reine—a woman who was delighted that this man she found so attractive was just as attracted to her.

A slender needle of reality popped her giddy balloon. But he hadn't kissed her. *Why* hadn't he kissed her?

Don't be an idiot, a wry voice whispered inside her. *You are currently holed up in here hiding from armed terrorists.*

And then another thought occurred to her, and Reine's spirits sank all the way to the Embassy's basement. She could use the fact that Clay wanted to kiss her. This was the perfect opportunity.

All of a sudden, she wanted to cry. Because she still had her mission, and now the perfect opportunity to complete it had presented itself. And when it was done, when it was over, Clay would hate her even more.

The back of her throat felt tight, but Reine forced the emotion away. *You're saving lives*, she told herself, as she opened her little clutch and pulled out a black tube of lip gloss. Popping the lid off, she applied a quick, careful coat to her lips. She then flipped the tube around, unscrewed the hidden lid, and applied an even quicker coat of the substance at the other end.

"Really?" Clay asked dryly from beside her.

Reine's heart jumped into her throat. There was no way he knew what this was. No way.

She widened her eyes in what she hoped was innocent curiosity. "What?"

Clay looked amused. "Sorry, it's just…" He gestured to her tube of lip gloss. "Always thought that was a stereotype." He waved to their surroundings. "We've got a dire situation on our hands and you're worried about lipstick?"

He was observant, too. Reine liked him even more…even if the fact that he was so observant was a bit of a problem at the moment.

She flashed him a weak smile, stowing the lip gloss back in her clutch. "Nervous habit. My lips feel dry."

He just smiled, shaking his head again, but she didn't miss the way his pulse in his throat jumped at the mention of her lips.

Reine inhaled slowly, despite the way her own heartbeat had quickened. For the next moment or two, she'd have to be very, very careful not to lick her lips. Otherwise, it'd be lights out for her instead of Clay.

That…would be a problem. She'd never used knock-out lip gloss before, but Erica had given her a thorough explanation of the dangers.

She touched Clay's arm. Words rose inside her—everything she wanted to say before it was too late. "I know everything is crazy, but —" emotion swelled in her breast; she let it color her voice, "—I'm really glad we met tonight. I enjoyed our evening earlier, and—" she laughed a little, gesturing helplessly to their surroundings, "—if I was going to be hiding from armed terrorists in the Embassy, I'm glad you're here with me."

Clay smiled at her, and in the dim light from the barely-open bathroom door, he looked even more handsome than he had standing in the middle of the ballroom downstairs.

He took a breath, pressing his lips together, a strange vulnerability in his hazel eyes. "I'm glad we met, too." He hesitated, and then nodded to the door. "Maybe, when this is all over, we can go out for dinner or something? I'd—I'd really like to see you again."

Reine smiled at him, bittersweet emotion coursing through her. She put her hand on the side of his face, holding his gaze. "I would love that."

And then she kissed him.

Chapter Nineteen

Clay felt like the luckiest man on the planet. His eyes slid shut automatically as Reine's lips touched his, hope burgeoning inside his chest. He had his standards, but it was good to know she wanted him too.

The kiss was sweet and chaste and over far too quickly, but it was glorious. Her lips were as soft as they looked.

Clay smiled at her as she pulled away. She looked a little nervous, but her gloved hand still cupped the side of his face. He couldn't resist the urge to nuzzle her palm. Her lip gloss tasted like cherries.

Slowly, Reine let her hand fall. Clay reached out and caught her gloved fingers, tangling them with his. His smile widened into a teasing grin. "How very modern of you, Miss Delgado, initiating the first kiss."

He watched her breath hitch in her throat, and then she shrugged, tossing her head. She was smiling though, shyly. "Someone had to do it."

"On a serious note," Clay said, rubbing his thumb over the back of her gloved hand. "It's a good thing we live in more modern times. A while back something like this could have ruined your reputation, spending a couple of hours locked in an office with a man like me." He waggled his eyebrows at her suggestively.

Reine laughed, thankfully, but then her shoulders slumped. "Honestly, it still might," she admitted. "Not to that extent, thank God, but…" She sighed and then laughed once. "I will probably never be able to convince anyone this was perfectly innocent." She waved her hand between the two of them.

Well, Clay thought, *maybe not* perfectly *innocent*. But he knew what she meant.

Reine's shy smile suddenly turned wicked. She leaned in a little closer to him, raising an eyebrow, and he caught the scent of her perfume again. "What about you? Will your friends believe that you were in here with me for hours and never laid a finger on me?"

Clay opened his mouth to answer, and then shut it. Ruefully, he shook his head. "No. Unfortunately, I'll probably never hear the end of it."

He started to say something else, but at that moment the world grew fuzzy around the edges. He felt like he was floating away, darkness encroaching on his peripheral vision. Clay tried to raise his hand, tried to speak, but his mouth was full of cotton and his limbs weighed five hundred pounds.

The last thing he saw before blackness took him was Reine, her dark eyes wide and mournful in the semi-darkness.

Chapter Twenty

The knock-out lip gloss took longer to work than Reine expected. She almost wondered if she'd done something wrong, but at the same time, she cherished every second she had with Clay. Their time together was limited, precious.

Even if he didn't know that yet.

When he finally lost consciousness, his head slumping back against the seat of the brown leather couch, something inside her relaxed. She could complete her mission now.

At the same time, guilt churned her stomach. He really was an amazing man.

Reaching over, Reine shook Clay's shoulder lightly and said his name a couple of times, just to be sure, but he did not stir. He was out. She swallowed, and then rose to her feet. Erica had said the lip gloss caused a loss of consciousness for anywhere from forty-five minutes to three hours, depending on body mass and dosage.

The clock was ticking.

First step was to get this stuff off her lips before she accidentally knocked *herself* out. Reine hurried into the restroom and quickly wiped her mouth with several thick squares of toilet paper she pulled from a fresh roll in the little dark wooden cabinet next to the toilet. She discarded the toilet paper and hid it underneath the bloody alcohol wipes and other trash from cleaning Clay's head injury instead of flushing it down the toilet and possibly alerting someone downstairs to their presence.

That done, Reine hurried back out into the office. She did not move Ariane's chair—she wouldn't put it past the woman to have positioned it precisely so she could tell if anybody interfered in her office—but instead leaned over the desk and turned on the First Secretary's Mac with her gloved finger.

While it booted up, Reine dumped the contents of her clutch on the desk. Her own cell phone, the lip gloss, her small wallet, and a couple of other things went back into the clutch. The rest remained.

Step one of Phase One: check for bugs. Reine doubted anybody else could have bugged Ariane's office without the First Secretary's knowledge, but the Intelligence Division believed it was possible that the woman might bug her own office to keep tabs on things when she wasn't around.

Picking up a small black rectangular that reminded her of a TV remote, Reine spent a couple of minutes walking around Ariane's office waving it over everything. To her everlasting relief, she found nothing. The office was clean

Its job finished, that device went back into her clutch, and Reine then picked up her Y-shaped USB cord. She plugged the standard USB end into Ariane's computer and then plugged the USB-C plug into the burner cell phone she'd been given. Her elbow-length gloves made this process a little more unwieldy than normal, but she'd spent time practicing this.

She couldn't leave fingerprints.

That done, she unlocked the phone with a complicated PIN and opened the app that was supposed to crack Ariane's password. She tapped the 'start' button, praying that it worked. A little status bar popped up, flashing through letters, numbers, and symbols too quickly for the eye to see.

While she waited for the app to finish cracking Ariane's password, Reine detached a tiny plastic square containing two micro-SD cards that had been stuck to the card reader. She carefully extracted one micro-SD card and partly inserted it into the small card reader on the other side of the Y-shaped USB cord in preparation for Phase Two. The other micro-SD card was a backup, in case something went haywire with this one.

Her hands were steady, even if her heart thundered in her chest, part of her anticipating either Clay to wake up unexpectedly or else someone to bang on the office door. She knew computers. This part, she could do with her eyes closed.

On her burner cell's screen, the little status bar filled up and flashed green, indicating that the app had indeed cracked the password.

Reine pulled the keyboard tray just far enough out from the desk that she could touch the mouse. She hit 'enter', and watched as she was logged into the computer. Ariane's desktop background was a serene picture of the northern Denquayan coast where she had been born.

Phase One complete, Reine thought grimly. *Two more to go.*

Unplugging the burner cell from the USB connector, Reine pushed the micro-SD card in the rest of the way into the card reader. Once it was mounted, she poked around the insides of Ariane's computer.

That was when she discovered that the First Secretary had a secondary hard drive as well—not standard issue for the Embassy's computers.

You've got to be kidding me. Reine shut her eyes in consternation. Then she opened her eyes and stared at the icon for that secondary hard drive, something twisting unpleasantly in her gut. *Why does Ariane have this?*

Reine abruptly shook her head, gritting her teeth. *Focus.* She didn't have time for this. *First things first.*

She needed to clone the main hard drive. Then she could deal with the other one. Erica *had* said the Intelligence Division wanted everything they could get their hands on.

Reine cast a grim eye at the other micro-SD card sitting on the desk's glossy surface. *You better work.*

Cloning the main hard drive took an agonizing twenty minutes. Reine spent part of that time alternating between glancing from the computer screen to Clay to the door and back, and part of that time reading live updates from Washington D.C.'s main news stations on their situation. Nobody really knew what was going on yet; the terrorists had yet to release any statements themselves.

The second the clone of the main hard drive finished, Reine scrambled up from her spot on the carpeted floor behind the desk and turned her attention to the secondary hard drive. She swapped out the micro-SD cards and set about cloning the second drive.

A warning dialogue box immediately popped up: the secondary drive was encrypted. She'd need to input a password before she could access it.

Still leaning awkwardly over the desk, Reine dropped her head to her chest in frustration and suppressed a growl. Of *course* it was encrypted. Had she forgotten who she was supposed to be dealing with?

She bit down on the inside of her cheek. She was running out of time. If Clay leaned more toward the forty-five minute end of the spectrum, it wouldn't be long before he regained consciousness.

Fighting a sudden burst of panic, Reine plugged her burner phone back into the USB connector and pulled up the password-cracking app. This time, the process seemed to take forever. Not surprisingly, this password was apparently a lot more complicated.

"Come on, come on," Reine muttered under her breath in her native French, watching the progress bar slowly fill. "You can do it."

Anxious tension corded the muscles in her shoulders and neck. Reine straightened and rolled her shoulders before leaning over the desk again. She'd need a good massage after this.

If we make it, whispered a dour voice in her mind.

We'll make it, she thought fiercely. There wasn't room for any other outcome.

She almost wilted in relief when the progress bar finally turned green.

"Yes," she hissed, clicking the 'enter' button.

Seconds later, Reine straightened with a shuddery breath. The cloning process was successfully underway. This hard drive was smaller than the main one, so in theory the process should be quicker.

Phase Two was almost complete.

All she had to do was make it another fifteen or so minutes.

Reine started to sink back down on the carpet beside the desk, but hesitated. The whole time she'd been investigating Ariane for the Intelligence Division, she'd never come across anything concrete to indicate the First Secretary was involved in anything shady. She didn't doubt her handler—if the Intelligence Division had traced the corruption to the staff at this Embassy, then it must be there somewhere—but part of her had wondered.

A non-standard issue secondary hard drive, however… As far as Reine knew, there wasn't any reason for Ariane to have that on her computer.

She bit down on the inside of her lip, her gloved hand hovering over the mouse. She'd cracked the encryption. She could access the contents if she wanted to.

And, oh, did she want to. Curiosity burned in her, like she'd suddenly developed a raging itching allergic reaction to something she'd encountered on a walk through the rainforest back home.

Reine cast a glance over her shoulder at Clay's unconscious form. He was still out cold—no need to worry about him yet. She pressed her lips into a thin line. The real issue was plausible liability. She'd lose hers—at least partly—if she poked around Ariane's hard drive.

Trust your instincts, Reine. Erica's voice floated through her mind again. *We've trained you well and you've got a knack for this. There's a time and a place for going with your gut.*

Taking a deep, bracing breath, Reine double-clicked the icon for the secondary hard drive.

Chapter Twenty-One

To Reine's surprise, the contents of Ariane's secret secondary hard drive mostly consisted of folders labeled with strings of numbers that made no sense. She squinted at them, her mind working through possible explanations.

Not dates or coordinates. She frowned. *Must be some sort of private filing system.*

As she drilled down further into the hard drive, she discovered that all of the folders were also encrypted and password-protected. She didn't hesitate to hook her burner phone back up and crack the code on one of the folders. Thankfully, this one took less time than cracking the encryption on the hard drive itself.

While she waited, Reine poked around the hard drive again—and this time she hit the jackpot. Buried at the bottom of all those folders was a shortcut to an email client—and it was *not* the secure client used across the Embassy.

Reine had never heard of this particular client—and she couldn't think of a single legitimate reason for it to be on the First Secretary's computer.

Unsure what to expect, she opened the client. Dozens of emails met her gaze. Reine blinked in surprise. *Ariane is most definitely actively using this, then.*

Reine scrolled down. The emails stretched back months, if not longer, and just like the folder names, their subject lines bore those strange code names.

When she clicked on an email from just a few days earlier, she was met with what appeared to be an order form in French. The wording was so vague she had absolutely no idea what it was for.

She opened a couple of other emails and found more of the same, interposed with what appeared to be meeting places and instructions for packages to be dropped off, also in French. The churning sensation in her stomach grew stronger.

Belatedly, Reine realized her burner phone had finished cracking the folder's encryption. Closing the email client, she opened a folder at random and found herself looking at a handful of text documents and image files.

Nothing too, strange, I suppose, she thought dubiously.

She selected a random image file and an aerial view of what looked like a section of the rainforest by a river filled her screen. Reine squinted thoughtfully. *Probably taken by a drone.*

She didn't recognize the location, but that was to be expected. Without comparing it to a topographical map, there was no way to tell if this was part of a Denquayan rainforest or somewhere else in South America.

Her brow furrowed. Why did Ariane have these? What made them so important they were buried in an encrypted hard drive the First Secretary wasn't even supposed to have?

Reine drummed her gloved fingers lightly against the surface of the desk, her mind still racing. For that matter, why was Ariane receiving copies of invoices for some indeterminable product or service? The fact that everything was in French told Reine this probably had more to do with Denquay than the United States, but it didn't explain what was going on.

Still frowning, she clicked on another image file—

—and recoiled in horror.

She *knew* this picture. It had been all over Denquayan and international news two years earlier. It depicted a terrified young man and woman, both gagged and bound, on their knees on a dirt floor inside a hut, being held at gunpoint by four masked men armed with AK-47s.

The daughter of one of Denquay's mid-sized tech companies and her new husband had been kidnapped while on their honeymoon. Nobody had outright claimed responsibility, but the rumors running through Denquay's political echelons whispered that it was related to a drug cartel. Somehow, this couple or someone in either of their families had run afoul of a cartel.

Reine couldn't recall all the details, but she did remember one important fact: the daughter had been returned to her father. Her new husband hadn't been so fortunate.

Heart hammering in her chest, Reine opened the rest of the image files. They were various shots of the couple, apparently at different points in their captivity. The last one made her blood run cold.

A picture of the young man slumped in the chair to which he'd been tied, a bullet hole in his forehead.

Reine pressed a gloved hand to her mouth. Denquayan authorities might have been sent this photo as proof that the young man was indeed dead, but if they had, they'd never made it public.

Why in the name of all that is holy does Ariane have these?

Rapidly, Reine chose two of the newest folders and scanned through their contents. One contained nothing more than an invoice and another aerial view of the rainforest and a river, but the second...

The second contained pictures from another kidnapping. One that had occurred just three months earlier. This time, the middle-aged son of a wealthy private citizen.

The son had lived, but he'd returned to his father minus his right hand.

Reine didn't want to go through the rest of the pictures, but she forced herself to look at them anyway. The last one made her put a hand to her mouth in horror again. *That* picture most definitely had not been circulated by the media.

Bowing her head, Reine braced herself against the edge of the desk with both hands, taking a deep breath to quell a sudden bout of nausea. All at once, the enormity of the situation slammed into her. She could think of only two real explanations.

One involved the burgeoning Denquayan drug trade, and the other involved the ongoing political issues with Denquay's rain-forests.

A laugh bubbled in her throat, just-this-side-of-overwhelmed. *And there's no way to know if any of it is connected to whatever is happening downstairs.*

Reine shook her head abruptly, drawing in another deep breath. *Focus,* she told herself again. *You've come this far, risked this much. It has to work.*

None of this would ever get sorted out if she didn't get this information to the Intelligence Division.

Swiftly, she closed everything out until the only thing remaining on Ariane's desktop was the small progress bar counting down the remaining minutes until the process of cloning the secondary hard drive was complete.

Reine swallowed, gritting her teeth together. *We're almost there.*

Ten minutes and thirty-four seconds left.

Carefully gathering her skirts, she sank back down on the carpet beside the desk. She was shielded from view from the door here, and she could easily reach the computer. That was important—if Clay regained consciousness before the cloning process was finished, she should be able to kill everything and shut the computer off in time to keep him from suspecting anything.

Her mouth twisted into a grimace. Emphasis on the *should*. In the event that happened, the Intelligence Division would have to be content with what they could get.

Hopefully it would be enough.

Closing her eyes, Reine scrunched her fingers into the thick pile of the carpet. The silence of the office seemed to press around her like a tangible weight. Heavy as it was, it was nothing compared to the weight of the information she'd discovered.

Without anything to distract her, the torture of waiting this last handful of minutes was almost unbearable. Reine kept imagining she heard Clay stir, or that she heard footsteps and shouts from beyond the secure, locked office door. Every time, she told herself it was nothing.

It *was* nothing, and yet her discovery coupled with the terrorists downstairs combined to stretch her nerves to almost the breaking point.

When someone banged on the door a few minutes later, Reine nearly jumped out of her skin.

Chapter Twenty-Two

Fear and horror rushing through her, Reine huddled in place behind the First Secretary's desk. Even though she had been anticipating something like this, the angry banging still caught her off-guard. It was so loud and brutal.

Angry, muffled shouts in French followed.

She swallowed, hardly daring to breathe.

Had they found the missing terrorist and concluded the people who bested him were in here?

Or had they finally worked their way through the guest list and determined that she, specifically, was in here?

The brutal pounding on the door continued unabated, along with the shouts.

Reine pressed her lips together so hard that it hurt. *Not now. Oh, God, please not now. Don't let them get in here now.*

Not when Clay was lying on the floor a few feet away, unconscious. Not when she was so close to finishing her mission.

They can't break down the door, she assured herself. *And even if they do drag the Ambassador or Ariane up here to unlock the door, it'll take time.*

She'd be able to finish her mission first, whatever else happened after that.

The shouting and beating on the door suddenly stopped.

Reine strained her ears, listening as hard as she could. Had they given up? Or were they just regrouping?

A minute crawled by, followed by another. Nothing happened.

Reine let a slow, shuddering breath, some of the tension in her muscles releasing. Whoever it was had apparently given up.

For now, anyway.

She wanted to slump to the floor in relief, but forced herself to hold steady and turned her attention back to the progress bar.

Only a few minutes left.

She closed her eyes. It was selfish, but she really hoped that Clay was conscious again before the terrorists returned.

She opened her eyes. Three minutes and counting.

Reine spent those last three minutes watching the progress meter, unable to look away. She was so close. So close.

When the cloning process finally finished, she lunged for the mouse and immediately unmounted the micro-SD card from Ariane's computer. She then pulled the tiny card from the card reader, slipped it back into the tiny plastic square case with its sister, and slipped *that* behind the little pocket flattened against her sternum created by the underwires in her bra.

Her fingers only shook a little.

Next, she unplugged the USB connector and shut Ariane's computer down. Those were the two most important components of Phase Three: safely hide the micro-SD cards on her person, and make sure the computer was in the same state as it had been when Ariane left the office.

Just as Reine swept the burner cell and the USB connector back into her clutch, she heard a groan behind her.

Clay was coming to.

A million butterflies erupted in her stomach, but she didn't lose her focus. *Finish the mission.*

The final touch was to push the keyboard tray back into place. That done, Reine scrambled back over to Clay as quietly as she could.

She'd just sunk down on the carpet beside him when he groaned again and opened his eyes. They were unfocused at first, and he blinked a lot, but he seemed to regain control of his faculties rather quickly. He sat up a little, taking in his surroundings, before he turned to look at her.

Reine watched recognition flood those gorgeous hazel eyes and felt guilt and grief mix inside her.

"Hi." She braved a concerned smile. "You're awake."

"Wha—what happened?" Wincing, Clay put a hand to his head.

"You passed out." Reine infused as much innocent concern into those words as she could. She put a hand on his arm, even though it felt dishonest. "I'm glad you're okay."

And she was. That part was probably one of the truest things she'd said to him tonight.

It was just too bad that from here on out she'd have to lie to him.

Chapter Twenty-Three

He'd passed out? Clay blinked in the semi-darkness permeating the First Secretary's office, trying to clear the cobwebs fogging up his mind. Why? What had happened?

"I must have hit my head on that doorframe harder than I thought." He winced; his head was pounding. "I see we haven't been rescued yet."

"No." Reine shook her head.

Clay regarded her a little woozily. The way she was looking at him, her eyes dark and worried, as though it was somehow her fault, prompted a smile. Of course it wasn't her fault. How could it be?

His smile turned teasing. "The last thing I remember is you kissing me."

Those words echoed in his mind. The last thing he remembered…

Clay went very still. Slowly, he rested his head against the seat of the brown leather couch, regarding Reine through hooded eyes. Nah. It was a crazy thought. There was no way it could be true.

And yet…

His mind, though still a little fuzzy around the edges, flashed through the evening's events. Reine had left the ballroom just before the attack went down, conveniently removing herself from immediate danger. She'd been up on this floor in her office, ostensibly trying to work, but…was *she* responsible for the security cameras going down?

Was it *possible*?

Something wrenched in Clay's chest. He didn't want to believe it. Didn't want to fathom that this beautiful, witty, intelligent woman could be involved with the madness happening downstairs.

But she'd lost her parents to political unrest in Denquay. He knew too well how a loss like that could drive someone to seek vengeance. A hurt that deep and a vendetta could create a vicious, never-ending cycle of destruction.

Confusion poked through the scenario playing out inside his head. If that was true, why had she knocked him out? What could she have possibly hoped to gain?

If in fact she *was* responsible for his sudden loss of consciousness.

It niggled at him though, a sense of wrongness. He hadn't thought his head injury was severe enough to have caused him to lose consciousness. He'd taken hits like that in the field before and kept fighting without any issues.

"What?" Reine sounded a little unnerved. "Why are you looking at me like that?"

"You're not involved with those terrorists, are you?"

The words slipped out before Clay realized that was what he was going to say. He didn't take them back, however, he just kept looking at her.

"What?" She reared back, her eyes widening in shock.

Genuine shock, Clay thought. He'd caught her off-guard. He lifted an eyebrow. "You sure?"

"No!" Reine was suddenly on her feet, her gloved hands clenched into fists at her sides and her chest heaving with anger. "I mean, yes! I'm sure. I would never—" She shook her head, as though the mere suggestion was too much to bear. "How could you think that of me?"

Clay continued to regard her steadily. He thought he glimpsed tears sparkling in her eyes. Part of him felt guilty for making her cry, but the other part, the part that had kept him alive outside the wire, had to be sure.

Bonds formed quickly in extreme situations like this, but it didn't change the fact that trust was a fragile, precious thing. Easily broken, and difficult to regain.

He wanted so badly to trust her.

Reine swallowed, visibly composing herself, and then she sank back down on the carpet in front of the couch by his side. She spent a moment arranging the purple folds of her gown around her knees before she met his gaze again. Her brown eyes still sparkled with unshed tears, but that sudden anger had dissipated.

Her shoulders shuddered as she drew in a deep breath, and then she lifted her chin. "What makes you think I could possibly be working with those—those monsters?"

"I didn't say you were. I just asked." Clay wanted to reach out and take her hand, but he restrained himself. Now was not the time. His head was still pounding, though it had started to subside.

Reine just looked at him. Waiting. Like she was on trial and he was about to hand down the verdict. It was a weird vibe.

Clay mustered a wry smile. "You have to admit, your timing is a little coincidental." He shook his head. "You leave the ballroom just before a terrorist takeover? Anybody with half a brain is going to ask that question."

Dead silence greeted these words, and then he watched recognition dawn in her eyes, followed immediately by horror.

Reine buried her face in her hands. "Oh, my God. That's terrible."

Clay waited for a moment, but when she said nothing further, he reached over to poke her in the knee. Gently. "So… Are you a political terrorist, Miss Delgado? Did you stick me with a needle when you were bandaging me up earlier to knock me out?"

He kept his voice somber, but one corner of his mouth twitched in a semblance of a smile. Her reactions were genuine. He still couldn't shake the certainty that *something* was going on with her, but…he didn't think she'd had a hand in this evening's terrible events.

Still…that old adage floated across his mind: Trust but verify.

/ Chapter Twenty-Four /

Disbelief, horror, and a strange kind of morbid amusement swirled around inside Reine's head. She pressed her gloved hands to her face, squeezing her eyes shut. Her cheeks felt hot, even through the sheer purple fabric. How had all of this gotten so complicated?

Clay was an intelligent man. He'd taken circumstantial evidence and the evening's sequence of events and put them together to form a narrative. He'd put them together *wrong*, of course, but that was beside the point.

No one could have foreseen the terrorist attack on the Embassy tonight. Not unless they were in on it.

A helpless laugh escaped Reine. *Oh, this is such a mess.*

If someone like Clay could paint a picture that made her out to be a terrorist, then her colleagues here at the Embassy—with all of their combined years of experience with politics and intrigue and backstabbing—most certainly could paint the same picture. They might even find a few details Clay missed.

Would anybody believe she was innocent? Would the Intelligence Division and Denquay's Department of Defense admit that she'd been operating on their instructions, or would they let her be swept up along with the terrorists in order to keep the investigation from being blown?

Reine honestly didn't know the answer to that—and not knowing terrified her.

She struggled to keep her breathing even, trying to keep Clay from sensing the fear rising inside her like lava from a volcano. *What do I do?*

From out of the distant past, a memory of her father came to her. She heard his voice saying, *Lies are poison that tastes sweet, little one. The truth is always best, no matter how painful.*

Her breath hitched. She had been seven or eight at the time, and she had broken an expensive sculpture while playing with some of the other children at the Embassy. Frightened, she'd lied about it. Her father had gone down on one knee, drawn her to him, and talked with her gently.

She still remembered the earnest look on his face. *Lies are poison that tastes sweet, little one.* She'd forgotten about that.

She knew from her study of his Ambassadorship that her father had never wavered on that front, though stretching the truth here and there would have benefited him greatly at times.

It's a wonder he survived in politics as long as he did, she thought wryly. The old pang of grief came, but she let it glide through her like water through a lazy river. *Thank you, Papa.*

Resolve flooded her, calming her fear. The Intelligence Division had chosen her not only because they believed she was brave enough and strong enough to accomplish the missions they gave her, but also because they believed she could adapt to unforeseen situations.

Well, she thought, dropping her hands from her face and opening her eyes, *this is me adapting.*

She looked Clay full in the face. "What I'm about to tell you cannot leave this room." She waited for him to nod once in understanding before continuing, "I'm not a terrorist. I had nothing to do with tonight's attack. But I did have a mission to accomplish tonight, and you weren't supposed to be here." She flashed him a grateful smile. "I am very glad you *were* here tonight, or that man in my office would have gotten me. But…"

Her heart started pounding in her chest again. "You need plausible deniability. Trust me, you don't want to be a foreigner tangled up in Denquayan politics."

"What exactly is *that* supposed to mean?" Clay narrowed his eyes at her.

She squared her shoulders. *Be brave, Reine.* Her mother's voice, this time.

"It means that I had to drug you." Reine didn't wait to see the shock register on his face, but kept going. Best to get it all over with at once. "I know that doing that put your life in danger, given our current situation." Her voice wavered. "I'm really sorry. But if I had to do it again, I would."

If her heart beat any faster, it would probably beat itself right out of her chest. Clay was staring at her like she had suddenly morphed into an alien creature from an old American science fiction horror movie. If she had ever had a conversation harder than this one, she couldn't remember what it was.

Reine swallowed a painful knot in her throat and spread her hands. "There is something rotten in this embassy, and I was tasked to help investigate. I can't tell you anything more than that." She shook her head. "You have no idea how many of my peoples' lives are at stake. My life, even your life, is a raindrop in a lake in comparison."

Pressing her lips into a thin line, she looked away. She couldn't bring herself to meet his eyes for this next part; it was too intimate. "I…I understand if you would rather not go out for dinner with me after this is all over."

A pregnant pause ensued. Clay said nothing; he merely sat

frozen. She'd expected anger, perhaps an outburst, but this calm silence was far worse.

Hot tears pricked the back of her eyes; she held them back. She'd done the best she could with the hand she'd been dealt. That was all anybody could do.

The truth *was* painful. A corner of her heart felt like it had shattered into a thousand tiny shards, and all of them were currently stabbing her. But...she'd still be able to sleep at night, if they made it out of this.

Pulling her diplomatic training around herself like a shield, she forced herself to look Clay in the eye. "I know you don't have any reason to trust me, but, please...no one can know about this. For both our sakes."

Still, Clay remained silent. He studied her, his expression inscrutable. They were close enough to touch, and yet Reine felt a chasm had opened up between them. Awkward, uncomfortable tension filled the luxurious office, sticking to her skin like an almost tangible film.

At last, Clay blew out a breath and raised both hands to rub his temples. "Let me get this straight." His voice was terse. "You're not a terrorist, but you left the ballroom because you're investigating your colleagues here at the Embassy?" He shook his head, his expression confused and suspicious. "What are you, some kind of spy?"

Under different circumstances, Reine would have laughed. It sounded so ridiculous on the surface. She knew for a fact that nobody except her recruiters at the Intelligence Division thought she was spy material. There was nothing glamorous or exciting about her life or her work.

As it was, she only lifted one shoulder in a shrug. "Something like that."

Chapter Twenty-Five

Until tonight, Clay had never found himself in a position where one of his grandmother's favorite expressions —'you could have knocked me over with a feather'—was so apropos. He was reeling, and he felt like the tiniest nudge would send him flying. Information zipped through his mind, realization after realization.

His instinct that something was up with Reine had been correct. His instinct—crazy though he'd thought it had been—that she'd had something to do with him passing out had *also* been correct.

The worst of it was that he'd never seen that part coming. How had she done it?

Clay drilled Reine with a hard look. "How'd you drug me?" He tipped his head toward her clutch. "If I dump out everything you've got in there, will I find evidence to corroborate what you've told me?"

"You'll lose your plausible deniability." Reine's voice was calm, but her beautiful face was so pale Clay began to wonder if *she* was about to pass out. "I didn't use a needle, but I can't tell you anything more than that."

Maybe it *was* her lip gloss. Clay eyed her clutch again, a wild laugh bubbling up in his chest. That was crazy spy stuff, right?

He swallowed the laugh. If he let that loose, he'd probably scare her, and even after everything he'd just heard, he didn't want to do that.

Instead, he frowned. "You're damn lucky that nobody broke through that door while I was out." He shook his head, his stomach twisting in horror. "If that had happened…"

Reine ducked her head, looking guilty. "Somebody did bang on the door about fifteen minutes ago," she said in small voice. "But they couldn't get in. They went away after a few minutes and they haven't come back yet."

"What?" Clay sat bolt upright, adrenaline spiking through his veins. His hand instinctively reached for the AK-47 rifle still lying beside him. "And you're just now telling me this?"

Reine just gave him a look that said they hadn't gotten to it until now. "They won't be able to get in without using the Ambassador or the First Secretary to manually override our emergency protocols."

Clay looked at the door, and then back at Reine. His mouth worked, but no words emerged. Just about everything about this night had gone sideways.

What could he even say at this point?

He understood duty to one's country and the greater good. He also understood impossible choices.

He scanned Reine's face in the faint glow provided by the night-light gleaming from the cracked bathroom door. Anxiety and stress were written all over her face, but the expression in her brown eyes was sorrowful.

Those moments right before she'd kissed him floated through his mind's eye. The words she'd said…the way she'd looked at him…

She'd meant every bit of it.

Clay looked away, feeling laughter bubble up in his chest again. Wry, this time, and tinged with a hint of hopelessness. With everything else that had happened tonight, it figured that even a potential romance would sprout complications.

Words rose to the tip of his tongue, and he didn't hold them back. After tonight, he figured he deserved to know. Pinning Reine with a steely look, he raised an eyebrow. "How much of what you told me tonight was true?"

He wasn't sure if he expected her to be truthful or not. Part of him doubted if he'd even be able to tell if she was lying to him. But his instincts—and the part of him that had experienced that amazing connection with her—knew that he would know.

"Everything." Reine twitched her shoulders in a hopeless little shrug. She wasn't crying, but her expression was so sad that he expected to see tears start dripping down her cheeks at any moment.

"Including your family? And your job?" Clay couldn't help the sharp note that slid into his voice. She *had* drugged him, after all.

"All of it." The faintest of sad smiles curved her lips before it was gone. "Everything except the fact that I also work for the Denquayan Intelligence Division."

Clay held her gaze for a long moment, searching those brown eyes for any shred of dishonesty. He wanted to believe her.

Reine took a deep breath and swallowed, before dropping her gaze to her lap. She twisted her gloved fingers together, biting her lip as though struggling with words.

The look on her face made Clay want to take her into his arms and kiss her until it went away, but he remained where he was, a man who could have been made from stone.

The reality that she'd rendered him unconscious with a kiss left him feeling violated and itchy all over, like he'd developed a sudden case of hives. He'd never quite experienced anything like it before.

"I didn't expect to meet you tonight," Reine said at last. She glanced up at him, and a soft smile poked through her sadness. "I was just trying to get through the evening until I had to be up here, and…" She shrugged again, her fingers stilling in her lap. "And then you asked me to dance."

She looked so tragically beautiful, sitting there in the faint light from the barely-cracked bathroom door, that Clay's breath caught in his throat. He nodded slowly. That one request—and her answer—had changed the trajectory of both their evenings.

Reine dropped her gaze, busying herself with pulling her cell phone from her clutch. The dim light from the display lit her face, which was taut with a dozen different emotions. She spent a moment checking a couple of things and then dropped her phone to the carpet beside her.

"Nobody knows anything new."

Clay nodded again. That didn't surprise him.

Silence descended on them, heavy with the weight of things unspoken and the knowledge that whoever had been banging on the door could return at any moment.

Reine stared back down at her gloved fingers, which she had entwined in her lap again. Clay could almost feel her withdrawing, retreating into a shell.

In that instant, he realized that he didn't want her to shut down. He wanted… He swallowed painfully.

He wanted to close the distance between them and kiss her.

His mouth went dry; he swallowed again. Wasn't that crazy? Wanting to kiss her again no matter what she'd just done to him?

You've done crazier things, said a wry voice inside his head. *And it's not like she's not plenty remorseful for the deception.*

Her words from earlier floated to the forefront of his mind. *I understand if you would rather not go out to dinner with me when this is all over.*

Clay considered that option. Really considered it. In the silence of the First Secretary's office, with nowhere to go and nothing else to do except wait either for the terrorists to return or else someone to miraculously rescue them, it wasn't like he had anything *else* to think about.

He studied Reine through half-hooded eyes, weighing the events of the evening against each other. She'd deceived him once. Could he trust her not to do it again?

Could he trust her in his personal space again?

Impossible choices, remember?

Clay shifted slightly on the thick carpet, adjusting the position of his back against the brown leather couch. The real question was: could he walk out of the Embassy tonight and be content never setting eyes on Reine Delgado again?

He breathed in, and the truth hit him like a knife to the chest. No. No, he couldn't.

Regardless of how the remainder of this night played out, he did *not* want this evening to be the last—and only—time he ever saw her.

Clay wet his lips, which had suddenly gone dry. Clearly, Reine was preparing herself for that possibility. It was obvious in the way she'd withdrawn.

His heart began hammering in his chest, a thread of adrenaline starting to dump into his system. This could be dangerous. He knew that. He could be opening himself up to all kinds of trouble. And yet...

He straightened up. "I don't regret it," he said abruptly.

"What?" Reine's gaze flicked to him, just this side of startled.

"Asking you to dance." Clay shook his head. "I don't regret it."

Her eyes widened, her lips parting in surprise. "You don't?"

"Nah." He shook his head. "Can't say I'm crazy about the part where you drugged me, but the rest of it?" He let that dangle in the air and then lifted one shoulder in a shrug. "What would you have done if I hadn't been here?"

A wry smile twisted her lips. "Probably failed my mission." The smile faded. "And then I'd be back downstairs with everybody else right now." She lifted a hand from her lap to jerk a thumb in the general direction of the door.

Clay nodded again. "You and me both."

They shared a look. Reine's expression had lost some of its sadness; in the dim light her beautiful brown eyes looked almost hopeful. The urge to kiss her rose again, stronger, but Clay suppressed it once more.

Still not the time or the place.

Deliberately, he glanced towards the door and pursed his lips in a thoughtful frown. "Whoever was banging on the door will be back."

"Oh, I'm sure they will."

It was Clay's turn to glance at Reine in surprise. Her voice was suddenly light, as though they were talking about a waiter returning with a tray of hors d'oeuvres instead of armed terrorists hunting down stragglers.

She raised her eyebrows at him, though her mouth had taken on a resolute firmness. "They might have shut down the Embassy's internet, but they'll assume we have cell phones."

"True. They'll want to confiscate those."

Reine blew out a sudden breath. "I wish I knew what was going on," she said tightly. She shifted her position next to the couch a little, as though suddenly restless.

"I know what you mean." Clay considered a moment and then eased himself up onto the leather couch, careful to keep below the window. He eased the curtain aside, just enough to peek out, and then slid back down to the floor, a little closer to Reine this time. "Capital police are still out there."

"I suppose that's a good sign."

Clay reached over and put a hand over one of her gloved hands. When she glanced up at him, her eyes wide in the dim light, he offered her an encouraging smile. "It's going to be okay."

She held his gaze for a long moment, before she finally inclined her head in a silent nod.

Clay removed his hand, though part of him was loath to let her go, and they sat side by side in renewed silence. Despite the underlying tension of their situation, this time the silence felt lighter. More companionable.

Clay swallowed, the fingers of his left hand unconsciously drumming on the carpeted floor. For the second time, Reine's words floated through his mind. *I understand if you don't want to go out to dinner with me when this is all over.*

He cleared his throat. "Reine, I—"

At that moment, a cell phone close by began to vibrate.

Clay froze, all his senses going alert. As far as he knew, neither of them had received a text or call from anyone since the terrorists took over the ballroom. Beside him, Reine froze too, and their eyes instinctively found each other. Clay saw the same thought running through his head reflected in her eyes.

This was either fantastic news...or else things were about to hit the fan.

Chapter Twenty-Six

Someone was calling her. Reine could feel the vibration from one of the cell phones inside her clutch, which lay on the carpet next to her thigh. Her heart leaped into her throat.

Beside her, Clay was busy checking his pockets. "Not mine. Or the burner we confiscated from that guy in your office." He looked up at her expectantly, and even in the dim light she could see that his hazel eyes were full of questions she didn't have time to answer.

Seizing her clutch, Reine fumbled inside with gloved fingers that were a tad shaky. She half-expected to discover someone from the Intelligence Division was calling the burner they'd given her, but to her surprise, she saw it was *her* cell phone.

She extracted it and the dim light of her screen temporarily banished some of the late-night darkness permeating the First Secretary's office. Another jolt shot through Reine as she took in the caller ID.

Ariane Montoya.

Reine froze again, her blood turning to ice, but there wasn't time to consider the possible implications of this.

She swiped the phone to answer just before the call went to voicemail. "Bonjour?"

She was proud of herself—she only sounded a little shaky.

"Reine?" the First Secretary demanded in French, and then a torrent of words tumbled out of the older woman in a staccato rush. "Where *are* you? Are you all right? Everyone is accounted for except you."

Reine blinked. The First Secretary's usually calm, cool voice sounded rather frayed around the edges. *I suppose being held hostage for hours will do that to a person,* she thought wryly.

Unless of course she's in on the whole thing, whispered a quiet voice in the back of her mind.

Reine ignored that voice. *Had* to ignore that voice. If the First Secretary was innocent, she owed her that much. If she was not... well...the last thing Reine wanted to do was tip her off that she knew something she shouldn't.

"I'm fine, Ms. Montoya." Reine infused as much calm as she could into her voice, even though nervousness fluttered wings in the pit of her stomach. "I'm actually locked in your office."

She didn't wait for a response, but glanced sideways at Clay. "With one of our American guests," she continued, still speaking French. "He saved my life tonight."

Surprised silence met these statements.

Beside her, Clay listened quietly. Reine had the distinct impression that French was one of his five languages. Under different circumstances, that would have pleased her, but she didn't have time to think about it now.

Again, she did not wait for Ariane to find words. "Are the Ambassador and his wife all right? Is everyone else all right? What *happened?*"

On the other end of the phone, the First Secretary finally seemed to gather herself together. "Everyone is fine. And I do mean everyone."

"What happened?" Reine repeated quickly. She didn't think she could wait any longer to find out—and it would be a shame if she had to learn what had happened in her own country's embassy from an American news station.

"It's quite a long story, but suffice to say, Ambassador Ambrose was able to reach a compromise with the…terrorist ringleader. It has to do with the rainforest deal back home." Ariana paused, and Reine could picture her pursing her thin lips together. "John Renault is under arrest for assisting with tonight's debacle. He confessed to using diplomatic pouches to smuggle illegal weapons into the Embassy."

"Renault?" Reine gasped. John was an attaché to the Trade Secretary. Only a few years older than Reine herself, he was charming and well-spoken. She hadn't considered him a political hothead.

"I am sure there will be more to the story," Ariane said dryly. She paused, then said in an even drier tone, "Just as I am sure there is more to your story."

Any other day, Reine might have been alarmed by this. It might have indicated that the First Secretary knew something she wasn't supposed to. As it was, that shoe was entirely on the other foot.

Reine narrowed her eyes, though she kept her tone meek and eager to please. "Yes, ma'am."

"What possessed you to leave the ballroom tonight?"

The cover story she'd prepared rose easily to her lips. "I needed to make sure that Monsieur Vetne responded to the email about the trade summit next month."

"Of course you did." A hint of resignation tinged Ariane's dry tone.

Reine suppressed a flash of triumph. Developing that somewhat anal work habit had been worth it.

She almost jumped when Clay's voice rumbled softly beside her.

"You might," he said quietly, "tell her that there is a man locked in your office and that I have his weapon."

Reine had almost forgotten about that. She quickly relayed this message to Ariane, who absorbed it in stride.

"Very well," the First Secretary said. "We will send a security detail up to collect you and bring you down to the ballroom." She paused. "I'm glad you're all right, Reine. We were...worried."

This time, Reine's response was genuine. "Thank you, Ms. Montoya."

The call ended and she dropped her phone to her lap. After a second, the screen switched off, plunging them back into the semi-darkness again.

Reine struggled to make sense of the conversation. The initial burst of relief she had felt dissolved into confusion and a faint sense of panic that crept along her skin like a fine mist.

It sounded good. It *all* sounded good. The terrorist attack was over, the Ambassador and everyone else were safe, and Renault was under arrest.

And yet...

It *couldn't* be that easy, could it?

From what she knew of similar types of situations involving terrorists and their demands, these things tended to last hours.

"What's wrong?"

Clay's voice, soft, but sharp, cut through her internal discombobulation.

Reine turned to find him regarding her with keen interest, the set of his shoulders radiating tension. She blinked once, twice, trying to work out exactly how much to say. What could she tell him without either jeopardizing her mission or potentially putting him in more hot water?

"I don't know." She shrugged helplessly. "In theory, nothing."

"But something's telling you otherwise."

Clay's voice was matter-of-fact, as though the fact she was

mistrusting the intel she'd just been given by a superior was completely normal. It was strangely reassuring.

Reine shrugged again, her face tight. "I don't know how to explain it." A thought struck her; she narrowed her eyes at him. "I thought you military types are all about the importance of obeying the chain of command."

"Oh, we are." A faint smile tugged at one corner of Clay's mouth. "Obedience and trust are everything. But at the same time…" He shrugged, a trifle self-consciously. "I know what it is to have a strong gut feeling about something." He paused, and then added, "Sometimes boots on the ground see things the eye in the sky can't."

That was a true statement if Reine had ever heard one.

They both fell silent for a few seconds, and then Clay cleared his throat. "If you don't mind me saying, that conversation was…oddly specific."

Reine glanced sharply at him, raising an eyebrow. His words echoed the thoughts now running through her brain. How had he done that?

Her surprise must have been visible on her face, because he shrugged and held up both hands. "I don't know your First Secretary, obviously, but that seems like an awful lot of information to give you over the phone when you're getting ready to come down and talk to her in person."

Suppressing a frown, Reine parsed through her conversation with Ariane again. "She's…probably trying to reassure me that everything's okay and that it's safe to open the door."

"Is it?"

That was an excellent question. Too bad she wasn't totally sure of the answer.

Not that she could tell Clay that.

"It should be fine." Reine tried—and failed—to smile. Her face felt brittle. "I don't have any *proof* something is wrong." She shook her head. "I'm just a lowly attaché. It's not my job to question the First Secretary. Everything *should* be fine."

"That's very reassuring." Clay glanced down at the rifle lying on the carpet beside him and heaved a sigh. "Part of me hates to give this up, but...okay." Rising to his feet, he bent to scoop the AK-47 up off the carpet. "I'll put this where they can see it as soon as they walk in."

He set the rifle on the First Secretary's desk and then returned to settle down on the floor next to Reine again. "Now what?"

"They're sending somebody to collect us." Reine twisted her hands together, tension tightening her shoulder muscles until they felt taut enough to snap.

"Is that normal?"

"Yes."

"How long do we have?"

"Not long." Reine shook her head, that fine sense of creeping panic heightening. Time. She was running out of *time*. "They'll secure my office first and then come here."

Unconsciously, her gaze flicked to the door. Best case scenario, everything was fine, just as the First Secretary had assured her. Worst case scenario....

She couldn't be caught with that burner phone and the Y-cable on her person.

The solution hit her in a bright flash of inspiration.

Chapter Twenty-Seven

Clay watched Reine out of the corner of his eye, trying to interpret the range of emotions playing across her half-shadowed face. Something was bothering her still—something *other* than the fact that she wasn't quite sure she could trust her First Secretary.

What, he didn't know, but...he'd be willing to bet it had something to do with her clandestine mission for...whichever faction of her government she was working for.

The tension rolling off of her slim form was palatable. She'd twisted her gloved hands together so tightly in her lap that he was positive her knuckles were white beneath the almost sheer purple material.

Clay bit down on the inside of his cheek. He wanted to reach over and settle his hand over hers, or even wrap his arm around her shoulders, but he held back.

There were some battles you had to fight alone.

And whatever was going on in her pretty head right now, it wasn't a battle he could help her decide.

His admiration for her deepened. Working with Rob and Naomi

to form Blackthorn Security had given him a glimpse into the complicated world of politics and the wheeling and dealing that accompanied it, but Clay knew Reine was playing on an entirely different field. The stakes, as she'd told him in so many words earlier, were much higher.

Wry amusement welled up inside him. He shook his head slightly, resisting the urge to lean back against the soft brown leather of the couch. *You sure know how to pick 'em, Dawson.*

Leave it to him to meet—and find highly attractive—a woman at this shindig who just so happened to be involved in espionage.

When she scrambled to her feet a few seconds later, he wasn't surprised.

Chapter Twenty-Eight

Tape. Reine shot to her feet and rushed into the bathroom, nearly tripping over the hem of her purple gown in the process. She needed tape.

She thought she recalled seeing some in the first aid kit. Seizing the kit from its shelf in a closet with gloved fingers that only trembled a little, she quickly rummaged through it. A jolt of triumph shot through her when she spotted the little roll of white adhesive tape, but she didn't dwell on it.

Clutching the tape in one gloved hand so that it wasn't visible, she hurried back out into the dark office.

Clay hadn't moved from his spot on the floor in front of the couch, but even through the darkness, Reine could feel his curious look. She took a deep breath, trying to steady her hammering heart. "Clay, I need you to go into the bathroom for a moment. It's important." She bit her lip. "Please. Quickly."

To his credit, Clay neither questioned her nor argued. He simply nodded once, climbed to his feet, and strode into the bathroom.

Once he pushed the door shut until it was barely cracked, Reine sprang into action. Grabbing her clutch, she dropped to her knees on the floor in front of the couch. Grimly, she pulled out the burner phone, the Y-cable, and the little package that had held the microSD cards.

In a few quick motions, she wound the white adhesive tape around the three items to hold them together. Then she ripped off a couple of strips of tape and affixed them to the bundle. That done, she flattened herself on the floor and shoved the whole thing under the middle seat of the brown leather couch as far as she could reach.

It was an awkward angle and hurt her arm, but Reine was reasonably sure her little bundle would be safe there for the time being. Thankfully, this section of the couch did not have a recliner. She used her other hand to smooth the strips of adhesive into place, securing the bundle to the underside of the couch.

That done, she scrambled awkwardly to her feet, snagging her clutch and the roll of white adhesive tape along the way. Heart pounding in her throat, she moved quickly away from the couch.

She hated to leave her equipment in Ariane's office, but...it was better this way. If the First Secretary *was* lying and something was really wrong, Reine couldn't afford to be connected with the Intelligence Division tonight.

Letting out a shaky breath, she shoved the roll of tape into her clutch and called out softly, "Okay, Clay. You can come back out now."

The office momentarily filled with light from the bathroom as Clay stepped out. His expression was calm, though tinged slightly with bemusement.

Reine flashed him a grateful look and then slid past him into the bathroom to discreetly replace the adhesive tape in the first-aid kit. When she returned to the office, leaving the bathroom door just barely cracked again, Clay had reclaimed his spot on the floor.

He was leaning back against the leather couch, frowning at his phone, but glanced up at her and raised an eyebrow. "We good?"

Reine started to nod, then realized he might not be able to see the movement clearly, backlit as she was by the dim strip of light from the bathroom door. "Yes." She tried to smile. "Now we wait."

Clay held up his phone. His browser was open to a local D.C. news station. "Nothing announced on the news yet."

"There might not be, if everything only just got resolved."

It was Clay's turn to nod. He patted the carpet next him. "C'mere."

Reine crossed to the couch and sank down on the carpet beside him. Her heart was still pounding in her chest.

Clay rested a hand on her shoulder. "It's going to be okay."

A swell of emotion rose in Reine, temporarily clogging her throat. His fingers were warm, and his touch sent little sparks shooting through her nerves.

She pressed her lips together briefly to compose herself before saying, "I'm sorry. I'm sure everything is fine."

Clay shook his head, one corner of his mouth tilting in a smile. He caught her gaze and held it. "Don't ever apologize for trusting your gut. Like you said, everything is probably resolved. But if it's not..." he paused, his hazel eyes boring into hers. "I'm right here."

The look in his eyes...the calm sincerity in his voice... Even as they soothed something inside Reine, they both combined with his touch to cause butterflies to erupt in the pit of her stomach.

She looked back at Clay, held in the moment by the strength of his gaze. She wanted desperately to think that he was still interested in her, but she couldn't let herself believe it. *Regardless of what I did, this man is a born protector. He can't help himself.*

Instead of kissing him, like she wanted, she nodded wordlessly.

Something in Clay's hazel eyes shifted. He opened his mouth to speak, but at that moment a sharp, authoritative knock sounded on the door.

Chapter Twenty-Nine

Clay had to hand it to the Denquayan Embassy's security detail—they had moment-shattering timing. For the second time in the last fifteen minutes, the words he had intended to tell Reine vanished from his mind. As they both turned to stare at the door, he heard Reine's breath catch in her throat.

"Show time," he said quietly, dropping his hand from her shoulder and climbing to his feet. He extended a hand to her and Reine allowed him to help her up.

She looked at him, and in the dim light her brown eyes seemed huge in her pretty face. "I've got to open the door." She nodded to the couch. "You'd probably better stay here." She briefly flattened a gloved hand in the center of his chest. "They won't know you by sight."

Even through his dress shirt, her touch set his nerves on fire. Clay wanted to catch her hand and never let go, but he nodded. "Understood."

He didn't like it at all. *He* should be the one standing in front of that door to protect her, but he did understand. Denquayan Embassy, Denquayan rules.

The authoritative knock sounded again.

"I'm coming," Reine called in French as she glided across the dark expanse of the office to the door. She sent Clay a warning glance over her shoulder and switched to English. "Clay, I'm turning the light on."

"That's fine." Clay remained standing in front of the couch. He kept both hands slightly away from his body, so it was immediately and glaringly obvious that he was not an armed threat.

After everything else this evening, he *really* did not want to be shot by mistake.

The First Secretary's office flooded with warm golden light and Clay winced, suppressing the urge to shield his eyes. Instead, he stared fixedly at Reine as she entered an elaborate code into the lock panel. Then, with one last quick glance over her shoulder at him, she opened the door.

Clay braced himself, but even he wasn't quite prepared for the blur of activity that followed.

No sooner had the door started to open than a man started barking orders in rapid-fire French.

"Hands up where we can see them. Now!"

Even if Clay hadn't understood French, it would have been crystal clear what the man wanted. Raising his hands in the air, he stood perfectly still as a team of Embassy security personnel clad in royal blue uniforms poured into the room, most of them aiming their rifles in his direction.

Reine raised her hands as well, though one hand still held her purple clutch. She nodded behind her toward the desk. "The rifle we told you about is over there."

One of the blue-clad security personnel swarmed in that direction and seized it, before retreating to the back of the group, which split apart to allow one man to enter the office. He was a little older than the others, with a wiry frame beneath his uniform and skin a few shades darker than Reine's. His black hair was slicked back from his forehead, making his face seem even narrower than it already was. He carried a rifle, but it hung against his chest from a sling.

Clay narrowed his eyes slightly. *This guy's the boss.*

The narrow-faced man directed his attention to Reine. "You are Reine Delgado?" His voice marked him as the barker of orders.

"I am," Reine answered calmly, though her tone held a hint of annoyance. Clay wasn't sure if that was on purpose or not. "You should be able to match my face to my Embassy ID."

The man extended a hand to her. "Purse."

"Excuse me?" Reine drew herself up sharply, her voice growing cold.

"Purse. Now."

Across the room, Clay watched Reine glare at the man, who was a little shorter than she was in her heels. That told him she hadn't really expected a search to be part of this particular procedure. *Interesting.*

He wondered what she'd hidden in the office while he waited in the bathroom—and found himself suddenly glad that she'd had the foresight to do it.

"You should have a list of Embassy personnel on your phone," Reine chided him.

"This is better," the man said coolly.

Rein eyed him a second longer, before glancing around the office at the armed men watching them warily. Only then did she deign to hand her clutch over to the man. "I don't believe I've seen you before."

"Not surprising." The man snorted as he riffled through the contents of her clutch. "Security guards are invisible."

"What's your name?" Reine asked.

"Salvo," the man replied without looking at her. He extracted her wallet and his gaze flicked back and forth between her ID and her face for a few seconds before he nodded once. "Thank you, Mademoiselle Delgado." He handed her clutch back to her and then shifted to stare at Clay. "Who is your companion?"

"Clay Dawson," Clay said as clearly as he could. He held his ground, hands still raised, as the man flicked a finger in his direction and three guards approached him. He would have dearly loved to ask Reine if she knew *all* the security personnel in the Embassy, but that would have certainly caused a problem. "I'm unarmed."

Salvo leveled him with a cool, unfriendly look. "You will forgive us if we verify that."

While two of the blue-clad security personnel kept their weapons trained on him, the third patted him down—none-too-gently. Clay suppressed a grimace. He wasn't thrilled about the treatment, but he supposed they *had* just let terrorists into their Embassy. *Trying to make up for it somehow.*

Reine frowned at Salvo. "It is not necessary to be so rough," she said sternly. "He is a guest of the Ambassador."

"Have to check everybody," Salvo replied, unperturbed.

Clay resisted the urge to grit his teeth as the third man jammed a hand into his pocket and yanked out his wallet. For a split second, he thought for sure he wasn't getting it back, but, no. The man checked his driver's license, comparing it to Clay's face, and then unceremoniously shoved his wallet back into his pocket.

"He's clean," he said in French. "American, like she said."

"*Bon.*" Salvo nodded curtly, then glanced at Reine. "We will take you back downstairs now."

Reine looked at Clay before turning back to Salvo. Clay could have sworn her eyes got bigger, more doe-like as she gestured to the door.

"Did you get the man who tried to attack us in my office?"

"Yes," Salvo said grimly. "We have him." He paused. "You are safe, Mademoiselle Delgado." He cast a hard, appraising look in Clay's direction. "Thanks to your friend over there."

"Fate, don't you think?" Reine's voice was suddenly throaty and full of emotion. "We only just met tonight."

She looked at Clay again, the expression in her brown eyes one of hero worship, and though he was ninety-nine percent sure she was deliberately putting on an act (though he didn't entirely understand *why*), that look *still* threatened to make his chest swell with pride.

Salvo only grunted and spoke into a walkie talkie he pulled from his belt. "We're headed down."

He herded Reine to the door, a hand on her elbow, and the two men flanking Clay indicated he should move forward with the barrel of their rifles.

Clay *hated* that. Bad enough that he—and Reine—were surrounded by armed Embassy security personnel (if they *were* in fact Embassy personnel; he had his doubts, given Reine's reactions) —but he absolutely hated being unarmed and surrounded by armed men.

He maintained his composure, but internally, he gritted his teeth. Nothing else to do but soldier through. Be ice cold.

His gaze rested on the back of Reine's head and the pretty knot she had twisted her glossy dark brown hair into. The best he could do was be prepared to help her somehow if things went sideways.

Just before they passed into the hall, she glanced back at him and caught his eye. Her look held a warning: she had no idea what they were walking into.

That was okay, Clay decided. He didn't know either.

They were about to find out. Together.

It was crazy, given their circumstances, but he liked the sound of that word. Together.

Chapter Thirty

A knot tightened in Reine's stomach as Salvo and his men escorted them from Ariane's office and down the tropical-scented wide hall to the staircase. This wasn't right. One of the first things she did whenever she traveled to a different embassy or consulate was familiarize herself with the staff list. Every name, every face.

Despite the fact that these men wore Embassy security uniforms, she didn't recognize any of their faces.

Even if she didn't work for the Intelligence Division, that would have been enough to set off all of her alarm bells.

No one spoke as they trooped down the stairs. Reine wasn't sure what to say—or if she should say anything at all. Clay maintained a polite silence, and Salvo and his men seemed inclined to follow suit.

All Reine could do was pray that she was mistaken—that these men really worked for the Embassy and that the danger was truly past.

When they reached the bottom of the stairs and spilled out into the main corridor, the first thing she noticed was the silence. The faint strains of music and low hum of conversation that had been there when she left the ballroom were gone.

She swallowed. *You'd think there'd be more conversation now, if everything was over.*

A strong temptation to glance back at Clay hit her, but Reine resisted. As much as she wanted to see what he thought of this situation, she forced herself to look straight ahead. No need to make Salvo and his men think they had a stronger connection than they did.

A tiny part of her brain wailed that they *did* have a connection, but Reine ignored it. She didn't have the bandwidth to deal with that right now.

She eyed the double doors leading into the ballroom as they drew inexorably closer, wondering what, exactly, they would find on the other side. The memory of the gunfire she and Clay had heard earlier returned, jolting her like she'd been hit by a bolt of lightning.

Up in Ariane's office, it had been easier to push aside thoughts of who might have been on the receiving end of those bullets. She hadn't let herself stop to really consider that gunfire—*couldn't* let herself dwell on it when she had her mission to consider—but now?

Now she wondered who'd been hurt and whether or not she knew them. Not that she wanted anyone at Karina's birthday party to be harmed, but it was harder when the potential victims were more than just a name and a face.

Reine mentally braced herself as Salvo gave a quiet command and one of the blue-clad security personnel broke away from the rest of them, letting his rifle hang from its sling as he went. Increasing his pace, the man forged ahead to push one of the ornate ballroom double doors open.

"After you, Mademoiselle," Salvo said courteously, waving Reine forward.

She passed through the open door into the ballroom—and her

stomach gave a sick lurch before sinking all the way down to the toes of her pretty high-heeled shoes.

First Secretary Ariane Montoya had lied to her.

The terrorist situation was most definitely *not* over. Not by any possible stretch of the definition.

Swallowing the fear that rose in her throat, Reine took in the situation in a quick, sweeping glance. She'd been trained to observe, to pay attention, and she put that training to use now.

She saw at once that all of the distinguished—and not so distinguished—guests in attendance at the birthday party tonight were huddled in rows against the far wall of the ballroom, near the now-empty white stage that had held the small orchestra. A few men dressed in tuxedos and armed with AK-47s stood guard over them, apparently waiting for someone to so much as twitch.

Reine's gaze skipped past them to zero in on the knot of people gathered in the center of the ballroom. Someone had dragged chairs over from the spray of tables along the other side of the ballroom, and the Ambassador, his wife, and the First Secretary were seated in them, along with a few of the other top officials in the Embassy. Karina Ambrose looked relatively unharmed, but the Ambassador appeared to have taken a blow to the face.

To Reine's surprise, Ariane Montoya also looked as though she'd been backhanded in the face. The older woman's lip was bleeding and puffy, and her cheek was swollen, but her dark eyes were full of fury and annoyance. Not fear.

Somehow, that didn't surprise Reine.

In front of the Ambassador and the others stood Jean Renault and a couple of men Reine did not know, apart from the fact that she recognized them as invited guests. Renault's usually handsome face was tight with fury, something Reine had never witnessed before.

In that instant, she knew that Ariane had given her all of that information on purpose—and that the First Secretary had paid dearly for it. Renault *was* responsible for tonight (though the clinical part of Reine wondered if he'd confessed to using diplomatic pouches or if Ariane had deduced that part herself) and, whatever the reason, he wasn't finished yet.

Her stomach lurched again as the ersatz blue-clad security personnel unceremoniously shoved her and Clay into the center of the ballroom and Jean Renault turned those cold, angry eyes on them. Unlike his companions, he was not armed.

Reine narrowed her eyes. *He has people for that,* she thought scornfully.

"Ah, here are the troublemakers," Renault said in English. His gaze flicked from Reine to Clay and back before he arched an imperious eyebrow. "Miss Delgado, I wouldn't have expected it of you. A tryst here tonight? And with an American?"

Reine felt her face begin to flame, started to quash it—and decided to let the blush burn. As much as it might affect her personal reputation, at this particular moment, she preferred to let this terrorist think she and Clay were upstairs having a…romantic entanglement…instead of involved in anything else.

Cheeks flushing, she twitched her bare shoulders in a sheepish shrug. "I was hardly expecting anything like this to happen tonight." She glanced around the ballroom, letting fear color her next words. "Whatever *this* is."

Renault held out his hand. "Purse. Wallet. Phones."

Reine did not protest as Salvo stripped her clutch from her hand. Beside her, Clay stood stock-still as they removed his cell phone, his wallet…and the terrorist's burner phone from his other pocket.

"You." Renault regarded Clay with thinly veiled disgust as he thumbed through Clay's wallet. "We've been to a great deal of trouble tonight to identify you." He studied Clay's driver's license, just as the other terrorist had done. "Clay Dawson."

Clay met Renault's frigid gaze without flinching. "Sorry to inconvenience."

Reine glanced sideways at him. His tone was affable, but was she the only one who heard the underlying steel edge?

She was not.

Renault's dark eyes narrowed. His mouth worked as if he wanted to say something, but he restrained himself. Instead, he turned and tossed the wallet to one of his companions. He gave Reine's purse a cursory look and then also tossed it and Clay's phone to the other man.

"Put these with the others." Renault proceeded to pocket the burner phone. "Best not to lose track of this, since Stefan proved so unwise."

Salvo stepped forward, unslinging his rifle, and prodded Clay in the small of the back with the barrel. "Where do you want them?"

Renault considered a second, before waving to the group of frightened guests huddled on the ballroom floor. "Over there. Away from the door. Both of them. And bind his hands. I don't want any further trouble."

His cold gaze raked over Reine again, and she had the distinctly uncomfortable impression that he was undressing her with his eyes, contemplating what he imagined she and Clay had been doing. It made her shiver. She couldn't believe she had ever thought this man was handsome.

Renault then turned an icy smile on the Ambassador. "Now that...everyone...is accounted for, Ambassador, let us return to the business at hand."

Chapter Thirty-One

Clay gritted his teeth as he and Reine were hustled around the knot of chairs containing the Ambassador, his wife, and his top staff. *So that's how they're going to play it. All hostages accounted for, time to finish the deal.*

His hands curled into fists. And if that wasn't bad enough, the way Renault looked at Reine just now set his blood boiling. The sheer, unmitigated gall of the man...

Get a grip, Dawson, he scolded himself. *You don't have time to worry about that now. How are we going to get out of this?*

Even as his mind raced with possible scenarios, the rational part of his mind knew it was no use. One man—one unarmed man and soon-to-be-bound man at that—wasn't going to be much use against an entire group of armed terrorists.

Clay glanced sideways at the tuxedo-clad men guarding the group of hostages huddled against the wall. Probably armed terrorists with itchy trigger fingers.

In his experience, it tended to work out that way.

Behind them, he heard the Ambassador speak. "Renault..." The Ambassador's barely-accented voice was very nearly a sigh. "You know as well as I do that we don't have much time. Capital police will be here soon, if they are not already outside the Embassy walls—"

"They are," Clay said loudly—loud enough to be heard all over the ballroom. "We called 911."

This earned him a vicious blow to the rib cage with the butt of Salvo's rifle. Pain exploded in his side and he grunted, wincing, but he didn't regret it.

Hope was a powerful thing—and he'd just given everyone in this ballroom a shot of it. They needed to know that people outside were aware of their situation.

He didn't mention Reine's phone calls. Probably wasn't necessary, and the last thing he wanted to do was draw unnecessary attention to her.

With one hand, Salvo unceremoniously shoved Reine down to the floor—which made Clay want to deck him—but he'd barely raised a hand before the man promptly slammed the butt of his AK-47 into his stomach. Clay doubled over, all the air leaving his lungs, and then Salvo hit him in the back.

It wasn't hard to let himself fall like a sack of potatoes. Clay collapsed to the floor, wheezing. For a few seconds, the ballroom faded in and out, darkness hovering in his peripheral vision as rough hands bound his wrists behind his back.

He heard a rustle of fabric and felt a presence beside him a second before a small hand touched his shoulder.

Reine.

In the back of his mind, Clay wished she hadn't had to see that, that things could have been a little more dignified. But this was a terrorist situation and ugly things like this—and worse—happened. Wasn't any getting around that fact.

"Are you all right?" Reine asked in a low voice.

"I'm fine." Clay turned his head to find her looking down at him, those beautiful dark eyes full of concern. A pang shot through his chest. He couldn't remember the last time somebody had looked at him like that.

A wry voice in the back of his mind whispered it had probably been his mom, back before he ever joined the Marine Corps.

"No talking!" barked one of the terrorist guards, who had drifted over to them.

Clay and Reine both looked at the man. He was younger than they were—Clay put him in his early twenties—with a mean look in his dark eyes. The rifle in his hands seemed oddly incongruous with his black tuxedo and crisp white shirt. He glared at them and they both looked away to avoid drawing any more negative attention.

Slowly, not wanting to risk another beating, Clay eased himself into a sitting position. Reine sat beside him, just as she had during the past few hours they'd spent up in the First Secretary's office. Her head was lowered, but glancing at her out of the corner of his eye, Clay saw that she was scanning the ballroom from beneath her eyelashes, assessing the room.

A fresh burst of admiration swelled in his chest. *That's my girl.*

Though, technically, she wasn't his girl.

Yet, whispered that voice in the back of his mind again.

Ignoring that voice, Clay also covertly glanced around, assessing the room. He hadn't forgotten that earlier burst of gunfire they'd heard. Nor had he forgotten about Rob and Naomi.

It was probably foolish of him to automatically assume they might be involved with that mess—he knew for a fact they weren't the only security contractors attending this shindig—but he couldn't help himself. They were still part of his team, or he was a part of their team, however it went, and he needed to make sure they were okay.

Rob, in his tuxedo, blended in with just about every other man in attendance tonight, but Naomi's burnt orange dress was easier to spot. Clay glimpsed her at the other end of the line of guests being held hostage. Even from here, he could see the cold fury on her face.

As though feeling his gaze on her, Naomi shifted—and looked straight at him. Their eyes met; she gave him the slightest nod. She'd seen him come in with Reine, obviously. That nod promised him that they would be having a conversation that he might not enjoy later.

Clay didn't care. He wasn't married to Blackthorn Security. If he lived through tonight, who knew what his future might hold?

The important thing was making sure everybody lived through tonight.

He raised his eyebrows at her, tilting his head in a silent question. *Where's Rob?*

Naomi's face darkened further. She dropped her chin in the tiniest of nods, motioning to her lap. *Hurt,* she mouthed.

It was only then that Clay realized the reason he couldn't see Rob was because Rob was apparently stretched out on the floor, his head in Naomi's lap.

Something in Clay's gut twisted. Either his friend had been shot...or he'd been otherwise incapacitated. Mouth drawing in to a grim line, he pushed the sudden rush of anger away.

Getting angry wouldn't help Rob—or Naomi, or Reine, or anyone else, for that matter. It would just cloud his judgement with emotion, make him react instead of act.

Behind his back, out of sight of Renault's terrorist minions, Clay worked his bound wrists as much as he could, attempting to find a little leeway in the zip ties locking them together. It was useless— he knew it was—and yet he tried anyway.

Around them, little whispers of movement came from the other guests. They'd been sitting here for hours, and Clay was sure more than one butt had gone numb. But no one dared to speak, no one risked drawing attention to themselves. He wondered if anyone had attempted it earlier and been rebutted.

Clay caught Reine's eye. Barely moving his lips, he asked quietly, "Think anybody's offered to buy them out?"

He had to strain his ears to hear her response. "Wouldn't surprise me."

Clay studied her out of the corner of his eye. She was pale, but behind the concerned, anxious expression on her lovely face, he thought he glimpsed...anticipation.

Like she was waiting for something—or someone—to come to their aid.

He nudged her gently. "What is it?"

For a second, she didn't answer. Then, very quietly, she said, "Help has to be on the way by now. My government will not stand for this."

Clay stilled, the pain in his gut and back fading as he remembered one very important piece of information: Reine had made a number of calls after her call to 911. Those early moments in Ariane Montoya's office now felt like a lifetime ago instead of just a couple of hours, but at least one of those voicemails had to have borne fruit by now.

Between the news coverage and the fact that she works at the Embassy in question... Clay glanced at Reine out of the corner of his eye, his admiration for her growing.

He would have smiled, despite the situation, but a sudden angry increase in the volume of Renault's voice drew everyone's attention back to the center of the room.

Chapter Thirty-Two

Reine shifted her position minutely. The smooth maple ballroom floor was not nearly as comfortable as the thick carpet in Ariane's office. It was cold, too—she could feel the chill seeping through the thin purple material of her gown. Part of her wished for a chair...but of course in their current environment, occupying a chair meant being in Renault's crosshairs.

She had no particular desire to draw *that* kind of attention.

She instinctively winced as Renault's calm tones abruptly rose to a shout.

"You insult me!" The attaché to the Trade Secretary threw both hands into the air. "Pah! What do you take me for, Ambassador? A simpleton? Even a child knows that the rainforest ecosystem is worth far more than *that*." He shook his head, his expression growing cold again. "It is *priceless*. Cut it down, raze it to the ground and strip all of its resources the way your friends are planning, and what happens?"

"Renault..." Ambassador Ambrose said wearily.

"Our ecosystem will be *destroyed*." Renault cut a hand through the air. "All those plants, all those animals, and insects, and all the oxygen our Denquayan rainforest releases for the world."

It was the Ambassador's turn to spread his hands. "What would you have me do? What kind of power do you think I have?" He shook his head. "I cannot—"

"You can speak to those here in the United States who wish to do business with Denquay." Renault's voice cracked like a whip. "You can stand up for your country in the face of greedy businessmen and greedy corporations with greedy boards behind them."

Reine's breath caught in her throat. Bold words. *Renault doesn't want much,* she thought sarcastically. Not to mention the fact that he was forcing the Ambassador to deal with this in front of all of these guests.

All of these guests…

She scanned the huddled mass of men and women in evening attire. That raised an interesting question. Why *had* Renault chosen tonight? Did he think an event like this was his best opportunity to pull off a stunt like this?

The particulars of the various trade agreements her country was currently negotiating with other countries weren't something she needed to know in the general course of performing her job. (Or her secondary job.) She tried to keep abreast of all things political because it seemed the sensible approach for a diplomat, but…

Her brow furrowed, conflicting thoughts racing through her mind. If Renault was only looking for an opportune moment, surely one of the half dozen other social events in the last few weeks would have sufficed.

Why *tonight*? Why Karina's birthday party?

The answer dawned on Reine with such clarity that she wanted to smack her forehead in a *well, duh* moment. She restrained herself, but only barely.

Somebody from the country or corporation that was part of the rainforest deal must be here *tonight.*

Beside her, Clay noticed the change in her expression. Catching her eye, he raised a questioning eyebrow.

Reine gave her head the tiniest of shakes. There was no way she could explain her revelation to him now.

With that thought in mind, she covertly studied the group of people confined to chairs in the center of the ballroom again. Nothing had changed—every single person there still belonged to the Denquayan Embassy.

She frowned, thinking rapidly. *It's been several hours since Renault took over. If somebody from that group is here tonight, why isn't he talking to them?*

Renault and the Ambassador were speaking again. First Secretary Ariane Montoya threw in a cutting comment that earned her a reminder that she had best keep her mouth shut, but as far as Reine could tell, they remained at a stalemate.

Reine eyed Renault's tall, slim form from beneath her eyelashes. *He's stalling*, she realized. *Arguing in circles and wasting time. But, why? To make people sweat?*

"You're sure you cannot help me, Ambassador?" Renault locked his hands behinds his back, his tone returning to calm, almost conversational.

"I cannot do what you want." Ambassador Ambrose spread his hands again. In the lights from the crystal chandelier above them, sweat glistened on his forehead along his hairline.

"It is a pity." Renault deliberately turned his gaze to Karina, who still retained some of her usual poise, despite the ashen tone beneath her golden brown skin.

This unspoken threat to his wife roused a growl out of the Ambassador. "Renault..."

The attaché ignored him. Instead, he pivoted half a turn and motioned to Salvo. "Bring him."

Reine tensed—and beside her, she felt Clay do the same. They

exchanged a quick glance. In Clay's hazel eyes, she saw confusion…
and a dawning clarity.

She bit her lip. Maybe he'd reached the same conclusion she
had. The thought made something flutter in the pit of her stomach.

Slinging his AK-47 over his back, Salvo strode over to one end of
the group of hostages and pointed to a man Reine couldn't see
clearly from here. "You," he said sharply. "On your feet."

Slowly, the man in question rose to standing. His movements
were a little stiff at first, and once he was on his feet and moving
toward Renault and the center of the ballroom, Reine saw why.

The man had to be in his late fifties. Maybe even his early sixties.
He had silvery hair and an impeccably trimmed gray beard and the tan
Reine had come to expect from rich people with time for leisurely
activities like golf or yachting. It only took a glance to see that the cut of
his tuxedo would not have been out of place at a fancy European event.

The man did not speak as Salvo led him up to Renault, but stood
there a moment, sizing the younger man up with an air of something that was almost boredom.

"You are Jacques Leitstrug," Renault said. It was not a question.

Leitstrug arched an eyebrow at him. "I can hardly deny it." His
voice was cultured and surprisingly pleasant, given that he'd spent
the past few hours being held hostage on the floor under armed
guard.

From her spot on the other side of the group of chairs, Reine
watched this interchange with bated breath. She wasn't alone.
Everyone was watching, waiting to see where this was going.

"Ambassador Ambrose," Renault swept a hand politely toward
the Ambassador. "You know Monsieur Leitstrug, do you not?"

From the way the Ambassador had gone very still, Reine
guessed that he did.

Clearly, Renault knew it too, because he smiled. "Monsieur Leitstrug, of the Atlantis Corporation?"

"Yes." The Ambassador wet his lips. "I am…familiar with the name."

"And you, Monsieur Leitstrug." Renault turned back to the older man. "You know Ambassador Ambrose here. Your corporation is the one currently vying for access to Denquay's rainforests."

Leitstrug offered him a thin-lipped smile. "My corporation has many interests, Mr. Renault."

"Yes, you do." Renault waved a hand in the air. "And most of them involve depriving the earth of our precious natural resources. Oh, no, please don't try to argue with me," he said, when Leitstrug opened his mouth to protest. "It's a matter of both public and private record. But if *he*—" he tipped his head toward the Ambassador, "—does not think he can come to a mutually beneficial arrangement with us, I believe *you* can."

The silence that suddenly filled the ballroom was so complete that Reine was afraid they would hear the thundering of her heart. *Does he* really *think he's going to be able to pull this off?*

Leitstrug seemed supremely unconcerned that every eye in the ballroom was now fastened on him. He twitched his shoulders in a shrug. "Atlantis Corps does not negotiate with terrorists."

To probably everyone's surprise, Renault threw back his head and laughed. It was a good laugh, a hearty laugh. If Reine had heard him under different circumstances, she might have been tempted to laugh along with him.

"Of course not." He continued to chuckle. "Just like the U. S. Government, yes?"

Leitstrug made no answer to this; he merely stood still and watched Renault. Waiting.

"Atlantis Corps may not negotiate with terrorists, but—" Renault swept a hand dramatically toward the Ambassador, "—you can negotiate with our friend here, yes?"

Reine's breath caught in her throat. *There it is.* Despite herself, she was almost awed.

And had to repress a just-this-side-of-hysterical giggle that suddenly threatened to escape her. The First Secretary had been a little closer to the truth in the fabricated story she'd used to convince Reine the danger was over that she could have possibly realized.

There was a chance—however slim—that Renault might succeed in getting what he wanted after all.

Chapter Thirty-Three

You have to admit the man has balls. Clay eyed Renault, torn between admiration and disgust. He had to admire the sheer scope of Renault's plans for this evening, but at the same, taking an entire Embassy hostage and shooting people was hardly the way to go about it.

His gaze flicked sideways to Naomi, who still cradled Rob's head in her lap. For all he knew, his friend was bleeding out on here on the floor while the terrorist, the diplomat, and the businessman played with words. The rational part of him wanted to believe that a man who cared as much about the environment as Renault did wouldn't stand there and let another human being bleed to death, but…

In his time he'd met a few environmentalists who cared more about things like plants, animals, and water sources than they cared about human lives.

Clay's lips tightened into a thin line. *Not anything you can do about it right now, Dawson.*

His hands were tied. Literally.

He wiggled his hands behind his back again, trying once more to find some leeway in the zip ties binding his wrists. Of course there was none. Salvo had done his job too well.

Clay glanced sideways at Reine. She appeared glued to the drama unfolding in the center of the ballroom, just like everyone else in here, but every so often her gaze flicked toward the door. Even—once or twice—to the glass atrium stretching above them.

Now *that* Clay found interesting. Under the guise of shifting his position on the floor, he cast a surreptitious glance up at the atrium. It was impossible to see anything up there other than the reflection from the chandelier on the panes of glass, but...it made him wonder.

Did Reine think that their rescue might come from up there?

Clay pondered that, temporarily losing the thread of the conversation going on between Ambassador Ambrose, Renault, and Leitstrug. From a tactical standpoint, it *might* be possible to scale the Embassy building (you'd have to scale it; they'd all hear a helicopter hovering overhead), cut holes through the glass, and drop men on lines.

Risky. Very risky. But...possible.

Clay pursed his lips, darting a glance toward the double doors. That was their only other means of escape or rescue. *And you know Renault and his crew are fully aware of it.*

A loud, scornful laugh jarred Clay back to the present. He returned his attention to the center of the ballroom.

Leitstrug's laughter trailed off as he shook his head, pityingly. "Ah, to be young and foolish, unaware of how the real world works."

Instead of taking offense at this, Renault merely offered him another thin-lipped smile. "I assure you, Monsieur, I am fully aware of how the real world works."

"Even if Atlantis Corps and your Denquayan government were to come to some kind of agreement," Leitstrug shook his head, "you *do* realize you won't escape this."

"The thought has occurred to me." Renault lifted one shoulder in a blasé shrug.

Leitstrug drilled him with a look hard enough to shatter a diamond. "We *will* be rescued and you *will* be imprisoned."

"Eh. Such is life." Renault shrugged again. "If the rainforest is safe, I can survive anything." He considered Leitstrug and Ambassador Ambrose, his mouth curving in a dangerous smile. "Reach an accord and I will march out those doors—" he pointed toward the double doors, "—and surrender to the American Capitol police myself."

A few shocked gasps rippled along the line of hostages huddled on the floor.

Clay distinctly thought he heard First Secretary Ariane Montoya draw in a sharp breath.

"Renault…" Ambassador Ambrose began, but Leitstrug interrupted him.

"Noble words, young man. But let's examine this from a practical standpoint, shall we?" He turned one hand palm up, his gray eyes glittering coldly. "Were we to reach such an agreement, you have no assurance it would remain standing the moment we left this ballroom." His eyes narrowed. "Just as *we* have no assurance that you would actually keep your word."

"Oh?" Renault locked his hands behind his back again, arching a dark eyebrow at the older man. He canted his head to one side, like a curious bird. "You do not think everyone here could not stand as a witness?"

"It's a deal made under duress," Leitstrug said calmly. "Not enforceable." He tipped his head toward the nearest man with a gun. "You have weapons, we do not." He spread his hands. "Ergo…"

A woman's shrill voice suddenly shattered the otherworldly quiet filling the ballroom. "Make the deal! Save the rainforest and get us out of here!"

Her words roused others to life. A chorus of similar pleas and entreaties filled the air.

Renault lifted his eyebrows at the Ambassador and Leitstrug, a small smile playing about his lips. It was his turn to spread his hands. "You have the power to change everyone's situation, gentlemen."

Renewed cries for Leitstrug and Ambrose to reach some kind of agreement filled the air.

Listening to this, Clay felt the hair on the back of his neck raise as a sudden chill danced down his spine. *Sounds really good.* He had the distinct impression that Renault was a man of his word. He'd give himself up for the cause.

Clay's gaze shifted from side to side, taking in the other members of the trade attaché's team. *But what about* them? *Are they willing to give themselves up too?*

Did they believe as strongly in the cause as Renault did?

This same thought seemed to have sparked in Leitstrug's mind as well. The older businessman narrowed his eyes at Renault.

"I admire your dedication, if not your methods." He waited for Renault to acknowledge the compliment with a minute nod and then went for the jugular. "But what of your comrades? Are *they* as willing to trade their freedom for your cause?"

To his credit, Renault did not flinch. "Of course." He waved a careless hand. "We all undertook this mission with the understanding that one way or another, we would not be walking out of this Embassy as free men."

Clay glanced around the ballroom, taking in the stoic expressions on all of the terrorists' faces. He hadn't been sure before, but he was now. He knew a true believer when he saw one. Afghanistan had taught him that much.

Words escaped him before he had time to think about whether or not speaking was a good idea.

"I'd say they're committed."

Beside him, Reine inhaled sharply.

Clay didn't look at her. He didn't look at anyone, but focused his full attention on Leitstrug and Renault, who both shifted to see who had spoken.

"And you are?" Leitstrug demanded, before Renault could speak.

"Nobody." Clay shrugged from his place on the ballroom. "Just a Marine who served a few tours in Afghanistan."

Leitstrug eyed him coldly. "And what makes you think you are qualified to speak to this situation?"

Clay allowed one side of his mouth to curl up in a smile. "You might say I have some experience dealing with men willing to die for their cause." He nodded toward Renault. "And these guys? I'd say they're serious."

"You cannot possibly know that." Leitstrug's lip curled.

"Oh, really?" Clay lifted his eyebrows, jerked his chin toward Renault. "How about you make your deal and find out?"

Chapter Thirty-Four

I can't believe he's doing this. Reine's gaze bounced back and forth between Clay, Leitstrug, Renault, and the Ambassador like her eyes were ping pong balls. Inside her gloves, her hands went clammy. Her heart started thundering.

What does he think he's doing, getting in the middle of this?

She bit her lip, hard enough to draw blood. Fear licked at her insides. *He's going to get himself beaten—or worse.*

And yet...Reine had to admire his courage. Of all the people in this room—all the money and power and prestige represented here —the only one brave enough to speak out was a relatively lowly former American soldier.

Oh, God, please don't let him pay for his courage with his life.

She had never gotten the sense from Renault that he was a particularly violent man...but then, she'd never dreamed he would do something like take over the Embassy, either.

Another silence filled the ballroom, this one fraught with tension and restless, almost fearful anticipation.

Another laugh built in Reine's throat; she choked it back with an effort. *You've backed yourself right into a corner,* she thought, staring at Leitstrug. *He's got you there.*

The businessman seemed to realize this too. His eyes narrowed to gray slits, his lips pressing into a thin, bloodless line.

"Well, Mr. Leitstrug," Ariane Montoya said unexpectedly, in a tone as dry as the Sahara Desert. "What have you to say to *that?*"

"Ariane—" Ambassador Ambrose darted a wide-eyed glance at his First Secretary. "I hardly think—"

"Oh, no, Ambassador." Ariane held up a hand, her expression as unruffled as if they merely disagreed on some slight matter of etiquette. "This is hardly the time to pretend that everyone from the President down to the common man on the street does not know the rainforest deal is plagued with issues." She looked from Ambrose to Leitstrug. "You can hardly be unaware, Mr. Leitstrug, of the popular unrest in Denquay regarding this matter."

The older man brushed her words aside. "There are always people who protest any sort of change, regardless of the eventual benefits." He sniffed. "I admit this particular…environmental endeavor…" he indicated Renault and his men with another wave of his hand, "is perhaps more dedicated than most, but still." He shook his head. "My corporation does not negotiate with terrorists —or abandon our aims because of pressure from terrorists."

Somewhere behind him, a woman moaned in dismay. The sound was contagious; several other women and, Reine was positive, several men as well made sounds of distress.

She switched her attention to Ambassador Ambrose, her dark brown gaze drilling into the side of his head like a laser. *Be a man,* she urged him mentally, her thoughts inadvertently echoed Renault's earlier enjoinder. *Have courage and stand up for your people and your country.*

For a few heartbeats, Ambrose seemed to melt under the combined scrutiny of every person in the ballroom. His shoulders slumped; the sheen of sweat on his brow seemed to glisten even brighter.

Reine held her breath. This was his moment. His pinch point.

Whether Ambrose realized it or not (and she thought that he did), his ambassadorship would be remembered for this moment.

Words suddenly welled up inside her. Reine released the breath she was holding and called loudly, *"Viva la Denquay!"*

Her voice rang through the ballroom, a lone feminine voice floating in the air—

—and then it was joined by a chorus of other voices repeating the same words in gathering strength. *"Viva la Denquay! Viva la Denquay!"*

Out of the corner of her eye, Reine saw Clay glance at her, what looked like a smile hovering on his lips. She did not take her eyes off the Ambassador but remained focused. Willing him to do the right thing.

The First Secretary was right—the rainforest deal *was* flawed... and everyone knew it.

Ambassador Ambrose wet his lips and then a change came over him. It was almost regal, the way he regained control of the situation. His shoulders straightened and he sat up in his chair as though he was behind his imposing desk in his big office.

A small, satisfied smile tugged at the corners of Leitstrug's mouth.

Reine narrowed her eyes, hope and anticipation warring with misgiving inside her breast. *Oh, God, please let him remember he is a man.*

"Renault, you heard Monsieur Leitstrug." Ambrose turned both hands palm up. "Atlantis Corps does not negotiate with terrorists." He twitched his shoulders in a matter-of-fact shrug. "Neither does the great country of Denquay."

He raised a stern eyebrow at Renault, ignoring the sounds of dismay behind him. "You ought to know as much."

Renault merely shrugged in response, a polite smile on his face. Clearly, he sensed the same thing as Reine and everyone else in this room—they were poised on the brink of something they might not be able to recover from.

"However…" Ambrose deliberately paused a beat, letting the word hang in the now-breathless silence flooding the ballroom. "That does not mean that those of us who serve our country—our beautiful, wonderful country—cannot listen to the pleas of her people and revisit matters that are causing her people great distress and consternation. Is that not our job?"

Reine caught her breath, unable to restrain the smile growing on her face. *Come on*, she urged the Ambassador silently. *Don't stop now.*

Renault's smile widened as well, while Leitstrug's face froze. The businessman's eyes narrowed again while he tried to catch up with the sudden—and unexpected—twist this conversation had taken.

Ignoring the armed men around him, Ambrose abruptly rose to his feet. With his usual suave confidence, he faced Leitstrug. "As of tonight, I am recommending that Denquay pause its negotiations with Atlantis Corps until we can make a more…thorough investigation into the environmental impact this alliance will have on our precious natural resources."

It took a second for these words to penetrate the fearful, overwrought minds of the hostages gathered in this room—a shocked second of silence. Then a roar of approval resounded throughout the ballroom, until the air itself seemed to be made of nothing but soundwaves.

Reine pressed a hand to her chest, her eyes bright and filled with relief. *Thank you, thank you.* This was good. This was an excellent first step.

She looked at Renault, who was still smiling, thought it was tinged with bittersweet relief. *If he is a man of his word, as Clay thinks he is…*

"You can't do this!" Leitstrug's angry, demanding voice sliced through the cheers. An angry red flush had come into his tanned cheeks. "Ambassador!"

Ambrose lifted an imperious hand. "You may make an appointment to revisit the matter at a later date, Monsieur." He glanced at Renault, arching an eyebrow. "Does this satisfy you, young man?"

Renault performed a formal bow. "It does, Ambassador. Thank you."

"I'll thank you then, not to prolong the ruination of my wife's birthday party any further." Ambrose drew himself up to his full height and held out his hand toward his wife. Karina hesitated only a split-second before rising from her chair and placing her hand in his.

Reine had to admire her composure. She was sure the older woman was afraid of what might happen, but Karina maintained a cool, peaceful expression as she took her place by her husband's side.

An uncertain hush fell over the ballroom as everyone ceased their relieved murmurings to anxiously watch the proceedings. Their fate hung in the balance.

It was Renault's turn to draw himself up to his full height. "I am a man of my word, Ambassador." He turned toward his men, raising both hands into the air. "It is over."

Reine's gloved hand tightened against her chest as she looked back and forth between Ambrose and Renault with wide eyes. *Can it really be that easy?*

Would Renault's men *really* cooperate, as Clay thought they would?

For a heartbeat, no one moved.

Salvo tightened his grip on his AK-47, his knuckles briefly going white. Something worked in his face—a brief spasm—and then then he nodded sharply. Unslinging the weapon from around his neck, he marched over to the knot of chairs where Ambrose now stood with his wife (though everyone else still remained glued to their seats out of residual fear and anxiety).

"Ambassador," he said curtly, bowing and casually dropping the rifle at the Ambassador's feet. It made a heavy, clunking sound as it hit the wooden ballroom floor that seemed to echo in the giant room.

One by one, the rest of the members of the environmental terrorist group followed suit.

Reine turned to Clay, a delighted smile lighting her features. He looked back at her, a small smile curving his lips.

It *was* over. Finally.

Chapter Thirty-Five

Clay wasn't too proud to admit that for a moment after he opened his big mouth, he was pretty sure he was about to get beaten—or maybe even shot.

This wouldn't be the first time his inability to keep his mouth shut had gotten him into trouble. Despite his momma's warnings over the years, he'd ended up in plenty of dustups during high school, and even a few during his career in the military. This was just probably one of the direst situations his mouth had gotten him into.

If Renault and his crew wanted to beat him (or shoot him), Clay had little choice but to take it like a man.

And yet...instead of resulting in him being perforated with a bullet hole or two, it appeared his intervention was actually helping to speed things along a little.

When Reine suddenly cried out, *"Viva la Denquay!"* beside him, it startled him, but Clay couldn't help but admire her courage. Still, he tensed, afraid she'd face retribution. He calculated the best way to defend her with his hands still bound as they were.

But instead of drawing Renault's ire, Reine's shout had the

opposite effect. The terrorist leader *agreed* with her. Not only that, but her words seemed to enervate the Ambassador, shoring him up and reminding him that environmental terrorists might have taken everyone in this Embassy hostage, but they couldn't take his best weapon from him: his words.

As Clay listened to the Ambassador speak, he couldn't help but admire the graceful shrewdness with which the diplomat had seized on the opportunity laid at his feet.

An old saying of his father's came to mind. *Smart enough to recognize the answer when told.*

Ambrose had a way out—and Reine had helped give him the courage to step up and take it.

Even as cheers rippled around the ballroom from the exhausted hostages, Clay kept a sharp eye on Renault's men. Just because he was convinced they were true believers didn't mean that one of them wouldn't do something crazy if Renault's plan didn't quite align with whatever reality they believed in their head.

He was more than a little amazed when they all cooperated.

One by one, from Salvo all the way down to the last man standing guard over the hostages, the men dropped their weapons into a pile at the Ambassador and his wife's feet.

"Over there, please." Ambrose directed them to stand on the other side of the ballroom. Grim-faced and solemn, the men gathered into a knot a good distance from their hostages.

"What about the rest of your men, Jean?" First Secretary Ariane Montoya demanded as she also rose to her feet. She propped both hands on her hips, fixing the younger man with a stern look "You have men keeping watch in the security office, don't you?"

"They will stand down as well," Renault assured her.

From their spot on the floor, Clay exchanged a look with Reine. "Let's hope so," Clay said under his breath.

As everyone watched, Renault removed a phone from his tuxedo coat pocket and made a call. After the first few rings, his face took on a quizzical expression. He pulled the phone away from his ear to glance at the display, then put it back to his ear again.

"Let me guess," the First Secretary said in that dry tone again. "No one is answering?"

A sudden premonition made the hair on the back of Clay's neck stand up. He glanced toward the ballroom's double doors in time to watch them fly open.

A dozen Capital police officers in SWAT gear poured inside, weapons drawn.

"Hands in the air!" one of the officers in the lead shouted. "Drop the phone! Now!"

Startled cries echoed throughout the room. Renault frozen, looking stunned.

"Drop the phone now!" the officer commanded again.

Renault obeyed. He let the phone slip from his fingers and it made a shattering sound as it impacted the ballroom floor.

Clay winced (the Denquayan government was sure to want the contents of that phone), but then he had to bite down on the inside of his cheek to control a sudden urge to laugh his head off. These poor police officers were just doing their job—they had no way of knowing the situation they'd come to help fix had already been resolved.

In all the years he'd served in the Marines, Clay had never been on the hostage side of a hostage situation. He'd most definitely never been involved with a hostage situation in which the hostages resolved it before help arrived.

He doubted Capital police had ever dealt with a situation like this before either.

Clay had to hand it to the Denquayan Ambassador. Now that Ambrose had regained control of himself, he took control of the situation with masterful ease.

"Gentlemen," the Ambassador said loudly, drawing the attention of the Capital police officers. "Thank you for coming to our aid, but as you can see," he spread his hands, "the situation has been resolved."

The police officers stood there for a second, looking wary and uncertain. The officer in the lead was the first to lower his weapon. Taking a step forward, he said, "You are Ambassador Ambrose?"

"I am." Ambrose nodded in turn to Renault and the knot of terrorists standing a distance apart. "These are the men who took over our Embassy. I would like you to restrain them and hold them over there for the moment." He motioned to the other side of the ballroom.

"I can do one better, Ambassador." The officer eyed Renault and the rest of his team. "We'll arrest them and get them out of here."

Clay knew what the Ambassador would say before his deep, authoritative voice rang out through the ballroom. *There's no way they're going to let anybody else handle this.*

"No." Ambrose shook his head. "I thank you, but they will not be leaving this Embassy. They are Denquayan and they are under Denquayan authority. They are all under arrest and we will deal with them ourselves."

The officer gave him a long look, and then nodded to his men. They all lowered their weapons and busied themselves with handcuffing Renault and the rest of the men. None of the environmental terrorists resisted.

The Ambassador, Clay thought, was back in his element.

"We have at least one person here who is injured." Ambrose frowned, his gaze sweeping along the other end of the line of hostages, who were now shakily gathering to their feet. "I believe he might be an American citizen."

The police officer nodded. "We have ambulances waiting outside."

Ambrose strode back to the center of the ballroom and raised both hands. "Ladies and gentlemen," he called out in a loud voice. "I do apologize for the turn this evening's events took." A slight smile curved his lips. "This was not how I wished to celebrate my Karina's birthday, nor was it a proper representation of Denquayan hospitality."

A nervous, exhausted titter ran around the room.

"Capital police will no doubt need to take statements, but we will do everything we can to ensure that you are not required to remain here any longer than necessary." Ambrose bowed slightly toward the group of weary guests. "I thank you for your patience." He turned toward the group of police officers and waved them forward. "Gentlemen?"

From his spot on the floor, Clay suppressed a grin. *Capital police don't know what's hit them.*

Beside him, Reine murmured, "What's so funny?"

Clay glanced at her and then tipped his head toward the police officers, who still looked a little off-kilter, like the Ambassador had completely taken the wind out of their sails. "They weren't expecting it to be over when they finally got in here."

He was pleased to see a small smile light Reine's beautiful face. She glanced at Ambrose and the police officers as well, and nodded thoughtfully.

"No, I would say you are correct. But this is better for everyone."

"No argument here," Clay said, with feeling. "Nobody wants the alternative. Trust me."

He held her gaze a moment longer, and something passed between them. An understanding of sorts. Despite the fact that Clay's hands were still bound behind his back and they were still huddled on the floor, the ballroom and the rest of the guests huddled around them seemed to fade away until it was just the two of them.

They'd made it. They'd survived an evening unlike anything either of them had ever anticipated when they walked into this ballroom six hours earlier.

He wanted to kiss her. Oh, how he wanted to kiss her. But first...

For the third time that night, Clay opened his mouth to say something, but at that instant Reine glanced away, her attention caught by a new arrival who had just rushed into the ballroom.

Chapter Thirty-Six

Reine probably should have been a little alarmed at the bond that had formed with this American former soldier over the course of the evening. And at the sheer strength of that bond.

Probably.

She had never felt a connection like this in her entire life. And the funny thing was, mused a thoughtful voice in a stray corner of her mind, it felt completely natural.

Like this was how it was supposed to be.

Clay's hazel eyes were bright and full of fierce joy as he looked at her. A few drops of blood had seeped through the butterfly bandages she'd put on his head earlier. His tuxedo was as rumpled as that of every other man in this ballroom and his hands were still zip-tied behind his back, and yet…

He looked completely comfortable in his own skin. Like surviving environmental terrorist takeovers at fancy Embassy birthday parties in the middle of Washington D.C. was something he did every day.

For an indeterminable number of seconds, the rest of the world seemed to fall away as they stared at each other.

The look in Clay's eyes shifted, the green in his hazel eyes coming to the forefront, and Reine realized with heady expectation that he was probably going to kiss her. His scent seemed to surround her, the faded notes of whatever cologne he used combined with something that must just be pure Clay.

And then a commotion over by the ballroom's double doors broke the spell that had fallen over them.

Reine's gaze flicked automatically in that direction to see what was going on—and her breath froze in her chest. A tiny, middle-aged woman in dove gray slacks and a pink silk blouse had pushed her way past the police officers guarding the door and stormed over to Ambrose, his wife, and First Secretary Montoya.

Reine blinked twice. *I don't believe it.*

She knew that woman. Clarissa Fierier, who worked at the Embassy in New York City. Clarissa also worked with the Intelligence Division.

Reine had reported to her once, about a year and a half ago.

A smile broke across her face, something warm rising in her chest. Whether they'd heard about it through American channels or through one of the people she'd called, the Denquayan government —and the Intelligence Department—had learned about tonight and wasted no time in acting.

She let out a sigh of relief. *Thank God.*

Clarissa made it to Ambassador Ambrose, Katarina, and Ariane Montoya and greeted them all with just the right amount of concerned warmth. She took each of their hands in turn, speaking rapidly. Reine wished she could hear what was being said.

"Who is that?" Clay's voice broke into her thoughts.

Reine glanced back at him, that small smile still hovering over her lips. "Another member of the diplomatic corps. She…works in another embassy here in the U.S., not far from D.C."

Clay's brow scrunched in mild confusion. "Why is she here? Moral support?"

Now *that* was an amusing thought. Reine suppressed a giggle. "No, no, nothing that banal. Capital police needed her here to give them access to the Embassy." She smiled at him and had to restrain a sudden urge to brush a lock of his sandy hair off of his forehead. "You see, Capital police are the ones who respond to any problems here in D.C., but they can't set foot on Embassy soil without the proper authorization."

"Ah." Slow realization dawned on Clay's rugged features. "I should have known." He shook his head. "I wondered how they were able to get in."

"Yes." Reine thought that was a safe assumption. It would have *had* to have been Clarisse—everyone else in the Embassy had been held hostage all night.

Clay looked down at the floor, one corner of his mouth lifting in a wry semblance of a smile. "Not used to all this diplomatic stuff."

The timbre of his voice—low and intimate and husky—sent an unexpected delicious shiver down Reine's spine. She swallowed, a little caught off-guard by her own reaction to this man, and nodded. "It can be confusing at first, but you get used to it." She offered him an understanding smile. "Much like your previous life in the military, I imagine."

Their eyes met and held, and the warmth in Clay's hazel eyes intensified for a second before a shadow passed over his face. He looked away from Reine, peering down at the other end of the room.

She knew he was searching for his friends.

All around them, people were climbing up off of the floor in relief, milling around in little groups while they tried to figure out what they were supposed to do now.

Reine bit the inside of her cheek and then nudged him with her elbow. "Clay."

He glanced down at her, tension written all over his face. "Yeah?"

"You should go find them." She nodded in the direction he'd said he'd seen his wounded friend, and then pursed her lips. "And we need to find somebody to get those off of you." She indicated his bound wrists with another nod.

"That would be nice." Clay's lips quirked in a half smile, but then his expression smoothed back into something serious, touched with a grimness that reminded her he'd spent a good chunk of his life serving as a soldier. "You may have to come with me, though. Somebody might get the wrong idea."

Reine was suddenly quite sure that Clay couldn't have been the *only* man that Renault's group had needed to restrain tonight, but she understood.

"I can do that."

They both climbed to their feet, a little stiffly. Clay started off toward the place where he'd seen Naomi, and Reine matched his pace.

"Reine, I—" Clay began, but then he abruptly broke off, his expression going tight.

Reine didn't have to follow the direction of his gaze to know what had distracted him.

He'd found his friends—and one of them had indeed been shot.

Chapter Thirty-Seven

Later, he'd chalk it up to exhaustion and the head injury he'd sustained, but Clay lost the thread of his conversation with Reine the second he spotted Rob and Naomi. His heart clenched in his chest: Rob had definitely been shot.

Naomi looked up as they approached, her dark eyes widening with first relief and then curiosity as she took in his still-bound hands and the woman trailing beside him.

Clay didn't give her more than a cursory nod, his attention focused on the man lying sprawled on the floor with his head in Naomi's lap. Rob's eyes were closed and his face was pale. His tuxedo jacket had been wadded up underneath his head on Naomi's lap to provide a little bit more cushion, leaving him in his white shirt.

Well, *formerly* white shirt. That once-crisp white shirt was now stained red with Rob's blood.

Clay assessed his coworker with the speed of a soldier in the field. He'd taken a bullet to his right shoulder that had bled a lot. Somebody—one of Renault's terrorists, apparently—had taken the time and effort to find a first-aid kit. Either they'd applied the bandage, or (and Clay thought this scenario more likely) Naomi had taken it from them and staunched the bleeding herself.

Rob's blood stained Naomi's burnt orange dress in places; Clay doubted any of *that* would come out. She'd discarded her matching gloves in a bloody pile on the smooth floor beside them.

Naomi's light brown face bore a pallor of worry, despite the fact that they'd all been rescued. Clay understood that all too well. The threat might be over, but the debris left behind in the aftermath would require a great deal of care.

He knelt beside the two of them. "How is he?"

"Not great," she said tightly. "I'm afraid they've nicked his lung or something. But they gave him something for the pain and it kinda knocked him out." Her lips twisted into a grim semblance of a smile. "Maybe for the best."

Clay met and held her gaze. "How are you?"

A rather unladylike snort escaped her. "I'm fine." She waved her bare free hand. "You know, all things considered." Her dark eyes narrowed as she jerked her chin to Reine, who had politely halted a little ways behind him. "Who's your friend?"

She didn't bother asking why he was tied up; Clay guessed she'd witnessed that part.

"Attaché here at the Embassy." Clay shook his head. "Long story."

"I'll bet." That considering light remained in Naomi's eyes.

"Anybody called for the medics yet?" Clay twisted around to search for paramedics—he'd thought they had already started streaming into the ballroom.

"They're on their way." That tight, tense note hadn't left Naomi's voice.

In her lap, Rob stirred slightly. He tried to open his eyes, but could only manage half-slits. "That you, Clay?" His voice emerged in slurred tones.

"It's me." Clay drew closer, uncaring of the fact that his hands were still bound behind his back.

"Thought ya mighta…got yourself…shot…"

"It was close, but not quite." Clay pressed his lips together. "I see you didn't manage to stay out of trouble."

Rob snorted a laugh, though it immediately turned into a coughing fit that left him gray and pale-faced.

Instantly, Naomi flattened a hand on his good shoulder, her face creasing with concern. "Don't talk, Rob. Not now." She glanced up sharply as movement behind Clay caught her attention. "What's she doing?"

Clay turned in time to see Reine striding boldly over to the nearest knot of police officers, speaking rapidly and waving her hands. "I think she's getting Rob help faster."

"That's kind of her." Naomi watched Reine for a second before turning her attention back to Clay. It was only now that she seemed to notice the butterfly Band-Aids on his temple. She jerked her chin toward him. "What happened to you?"

"Had a little tussle with one of Renault's men earlier." Clay shrugged. "It's a long story."

Despite the worry pinching her features, Naomi's dark eyes narrowed. "You said that earlier." She tilted her head to one side. "Where *were* you? Really?"

"Really?" Clay offered her a wry, lopsided smile. "Holed up in the First Secretary's office with her." He tipped his head toward Reine. "That's the short version."

Naomi's eyebrows had climbed practically into her hairline. "I'll be interested to hear the full version, then."

Clay suppressed the desire to tell her he wasn't looking forward to that and promptly changed the subject. "What happened?" He nodded down at Rob's prone form.

Naomi shook her head, even as her lips tightened. The look she cast down at Rob was equal parts fond and irritated. "He decided to play the hero."

"Did…not…" Rob murmured.

"Oh, yes, you did." Naomi propped her free hand on her hip. "Got a little too aggressive with one of the men who was going around confiscating cell phones." She shook her head again, a bleak note flitting through her dark eyes. "Rob was trying to call 911 after he texted you, but I guess the guy thought Rob had a gun and popped him."

"I was afraid it was something like that." It was Clay's turn to give Rob a look, for all the good it did. The other man's eyes were still closed.

"Could have been worse, but still…" Naomi lifted one bare shoulder in a shrug. "Guess it accomplished one thing—everybody cooperated after that."

"I'll bet they did."

"Head guy, Renault, was it?" Naomi glanced at Clay, who confirmed this with a nod, and she continued, "Anyway, he wasn't happy at all. Said a few strong words to the guy and switched him out with a guy watching the door."

"We heard the gunfire, but we weren't sure what had happened."

"Well, that's what happened."

Movement out of the corner of Clay's eye caught his attention; Reine had turned and was striding back to them. Two paramedics followed her, having split off from the group attending Ambassador Ambrose and making rounds through the ballroom.

Clay stepped aside as the paramedics immediately dropped to their knees and began working on Rob. He caught Naomi's eye. "Call me later."

She nodded, her dark eyes sharpening again, and then she returned her full attention to Rob.

Clay looked at Reine, but before he could open his mouth to thank her, she took him by the elbow.

"Come on. We really do need to get you out of those." She nodded briskly to the zip ties still binding his wrists together behind his back.

Clay half-smiled. "That would be appreciated."

Reine marched him back over toward the knot of people around the Ambassador and approached one of the police officers. "Excuse me," she said politely, but firmly. "We need some help removing these, please."

The man turned immediately, his gaze assessing both of them in an instant. "And you are?"

"I am Reine Delgado, an attaché here at the Embassy, and this is Mr. Dawson, one of our American guests at tonight's party. Jean Renault's men restrained him earlier." Reine allowed her lip to curl in disgust.

"Sure." The police officer obligingly cut through the zip ties, and then put his knife away, nodding to Clay's head. "Do you need medical attention?"

"No. I'm okay." Clay brought his wrists around to his front and rubbed them, thankful to be able to move freely again. "Thanks."

The police officer nodded again. "Well, we'll have to get statements from both of you."

"That's all right." Clay's mouth twisted slightly. "I can point out the guy who hit me."

The officer looked interested. "That'd be helpful."

"Where do you want us to go for now?" Clay glanced around the large ballroom. It seemed that even more people had appeared, seemingly out of nowhere, and they were dragging in chairs and blankets for those of the guests who needed to sit down on a chair. The ballroom no longer resembled a party scene so much as it did an ornate conference room with a fancy glass atrium.

"Over there." The police officer pointed to the right side of the room, where a clump of guests were gathered, looking a little the worse for the wear. Some of the expensive shine and glittered had rubbed off, leaving just people behind. Exhausted people who wanted nothing more than to go home and crawl in their beds.

"Thanks." Clay started in that direction, but stopped, looking down at Reine. "Are you coming, or do you have someplace else you need to be?"

"Honestly?" Reine lifted a shoulder in a prosaic shrug. "I would rather stay with you, but..." She smiled wryly and shrugged again. "I should probably go talk to the First Secretary."

"Yeah, after tonight..." Clay trailed off, unsure what else to say.

They shared a look, an awkward silence falling over them for the first time since Reine had confessed she'd drugged him with a kiss.

A dozen thoughts raced through Clay's head, a dozen possible things to say. They all jumbled into a train wreck before any of them reached his mouth.

Reine's smile turned just the slightest bit sad, and then she was gone, gliding smoothly toward the knot of Embassy officials gathered around the First Secretary.

Clay watched her go, feeling oddly bereft and adrift, like part of him was walking away with her.

Chapter Thirty-Eight

Unexpected tears stung the backs of Reine's eyes as she walked away. The way Clay had looked at her just now… something told her that look would haunt her for the rest of her life.

She wasn't even sure how to describe it. Some strange blend of confusion and longing, though she was afraid to let herself hope that he'd ever want to see her again after tonight. He'd protected her earlier, yes, but she couldn't read anything into that. It was his nature.

He'd have done it for her either way.

Resisting the urge to glance back at him over her shoulder, Reine tightened her grip on her clutch and joined the small group that had formed around Ariane Montoya and Clarissa.

"…redistribute everyone's cell phones to them," Ariane was saying briskly. Unlike the Ambassador, who had clearly showed signs of strain earlier, the First Secretary was still as cool and unruffled as she'd been before the night took a turn for the worse. Her lips twisted into a disapproving frown as she glanced at Clarissa. "Renault's men confiscated them all, you see."

Clarisse shook her head. "That is a lot of phones."

"It won't take that long." Ariane waved a hand briskly, and then she caught sight of Reine. Her expression turned considering.

Here we go. Reine braced herself, meeting the First Secretary's cool gaze without flinching. The microSD cards hidden in her bodice seemed to burn against her skin, as though announcing their presence to the universe.

But instead of launching into a brisk interrogation, Ariane looked her over. "Are you all right?" She nodded past Reine's shoulder without taking her eyes off of her. "The young man they brought in with you—the one you were trapped in my office with?" She raised a questioning eyebrow; Reine confirmed it with a nod. "Well, he looked a little worse for the wear."

"He fought one of the men they sent to look for stragglers." Reine was surprised by how calm her voice sounded. "We left him tied up in my office and then barricaded ourselves in yours." She gave the First Secretary an apologetic look. "I was able to phone for help while I was there."

"That is good." Ariane studied her for a second, eyes narrowed just slightly. "Quite brave, that young man."

"Yes." Reine hesitated, then smiled wryly. "To be honest, I was glad he was there."

"So you're the one who called Pierre." Clarissa propped her hands on her hips, studying Reine.

Reine nodded. "I made a number of calls, trying to get through to someone who could help us." She twitched her bare shoulders in a shrug, uncomfortable with the way everyone was looking at her.

"Well, word got out eventually." Clarisse's gaze slid past Reine to return to the First Secretary. "I got here as fast as I could, Ariane."

"And we are all very grateful for that," Ariane said smoothly.

Reine breathed an internal sigh of relief as everyone's attention left her. *Clarisse doesn't remember me.* She doubted the woman would remember her under normal circumstances, but she might have after that brief assignment from the Intelligence Division.

That she did not was a small mercy.

Reine considered Clarisse out of the corner of her eye. At least, she didn't *think* the older woman remembered her. It was entirely possible Clarisse's diplomatic poker face was just that good.

Reine dismissed that thought with a mental shrug. *Either way, it doesn't matter.*

The important thing was that news of the Embassy takeover had been passed along the right channels to get a Denquayan official to D.C. in order to authorize Capital police to enter the Embassy. How it had happened was irrelevant.

"Reine."

Reine snapped her attention back to the First Secretary. "Yes, ma'am?"

"I need your help getting the cellphone situation straightened out. You and Daphne." Ariane pointed to another attaché who had joined their group. "Also…" she pursed her lips together. "We need to see what happened to the kitchen staff. There should be food left, but whether or not it's salvageable is another—" She broke off as Ambassador Ambrose's voice—cultured, yet commanding—cut through the hum of chatter filling the ballroom.

"Ladies and gentlemen, if I may have your attention?"

Everyone turned toward the center of the ballroom, where the Ambassador had stepped up onto a chair. He swept his gaze around the ballroom to encompass everyone. "Once you have finished giving your statements to the fine members of the Capital police who have come to our aid tonight, we will ensure that the cellphones that were confiscated earlier are returned to you." He spread his hand. "After that, you will be free to depart."

A low murmur greeted this—and not, Reine thought, a pleasant one.

Ambrose sensed this, too. "Yes, yes, I understand." He grimaced politely, spreading his hands out palm up. "None of this is anything any of us signed up for tonight. However, there are...procedures... that must be followed when something of this magnitude occurs."

He glanced toward the chief Capital police officer in charge, who straightened his back and puffed his chest out a little, nodding importantly.

The Ambassador's gaze then swept the ballroom again. "On behalf of Denquay, I thank you for your cooperation."

Ambrose stepped down from his chair, and conversations exploded across the ballroom once more.

Taking a deep, bracing breath, Reine turned to the other attaché, Daphne Hendricks. "Are you ready?"

Daphne scrunched her face into a frown. She wore a strapless rose pink evening gown that accentuated her dark complexion, hourglass figure, and ample bosom. "No, but we don't have much choice." She flicked a lock of glossy black hair out of her face, her expression brightening. "Maybe there will be coffee."

Coffee. Reine swallowed a bitter lump in her throat. Coffee sounded so mundane after everything that had happened tonight.

Still...duty was duty. She swallowed again, her thoughts traveling back to that moment she'd kissed Clay to drug him. *Never let it be said that Reine Delgado shirks her duty.*

She could not, however, resist the urge to glance over her shoulder in search of him as she and Daphne left the ballroom.

Chapter Thirty-Nine

Clay watched Capital police officers, paramedics, and Embassy workers bustle about and it struck him how bizarre his situation really was. His thoughts flitted briefly to his former teammates, imagining their reactions to seeing him on the hostage side of a hostage situation. Unarmed and dressed to the nines in an expensive tuxedo and shoes, no less.

A wry smile tugged at the corners of his mouth. He'd never hear the end of it—once they stopped rolling around on the floor laughing their butts off, that is.

Once everyone had been taken care of medically, Capital police and Embassy officials began taking statements. Clay had no idea how they were deciding who went first, but judging by the first few names they called, he was pretty sure the list wasn't alphabetical.

Frankly, he'd have been shocked if it was. You'd have to blind, deaf, and live under a rock somewhere to *not* know the world was skewed in favor of those with money, power, and influence. He'd known that long before he started working with Rob and Naomi and Blackthorn Security.

The police and Embassy officials would get to him and the other individuals at the bottom of the list when they got to them.

In the meantime, Clay sat at one of the tables arranged in a spray along one side of the ballroom along with everyone else who was waiting to give a statement. Tired waitstaff circled with trays of drinks and hors d'oeuvres—like an exhausted parody of the scene that had taken place hours before. Almost everyone had a drink in hand—be it champagne or coffee.

Clay wasn't entirely sure (it was one of the things he wanted to ask Reine about later), but he thought the kitchen staff had been found locked in the kitchen. Clearly, they'd managed to salvage some of the food, as well as rustle up some coffee (not to mention more alcohol), and the Ambassador had sent them around to tend to his guests until they were lucky enough to be able to leave.

He'd eaten a couple of shrimp puffs, wondering as he chewed if Reine had gotten any. Shrimp puffs and coffee wasn't exactly a flavor combination likely to be a nation-wide hit, but at this point? Clay wasn't complaining.

He was coming down from the adrenaline high that had been this entire evening, and he wasn't too proud to admit he was tired. It reminded him of the aftermath of an op, back in his active duty days.

Clay took another sip of his coffee, which was better than he'd expected, although, to be honest, he really didn't know what to expect from coffee in a foreign Embassy. It reminded him of Colombian coffee, which he supposed made sense, given that Denquay was also located in South America. He drank some more, and then shook his head at himself.

Just because you're sitting in a Denquayan Embassy drinking coffee doesn't mean that they imported the coffee all the way here from Denquay.

For all he knew, they'd bought Colombian coffee at the nearest grocery store.

Swirling his half-drunk coffee in its styrofoam cup, Clay looked around the ballroom again. Beyond the ballroom's windows and domed glass ceiling, Washington D.C.'s skyline remained as dark above the golden glow of streetlights. Pre-dawn light had not started turning the sky to gray.

The other remaining guests seemed to wilt a little more with every passing quarter of an hour. Clay couldn't blame them. This was hardly the evening any of them had signed up for, especially since the tension and dangerous excitement of the actual hostage situation was over.

As he'd done for longer than he cared to think about, his hazel gaze searched the ballroom for Reine, but there was no sign of her. He didn't even catch a glimpse of purple. Whatever her First Secretary had sent her off to do, it did not involve the ballroom in any way, shape, or form.

Draining the last of his coffee, Clay resisted the sudden urge to crush the empty styrofoam cup in frustration. Instead, he blew out a measured breath. *She's still in the Embassy,* he consoled himself. Surely, *surely,* their paths would cross again before he had to leave.

Setting the empty cup on the table in front of him, Clay started to reach into his pocket for his cell phone…before he remembered he didn't have it back yet. He pressed his lips into a thin line to suppress the words that wanted to slip out. *You'd think you'd remember that by now,* he chided himself.

Clay sat back in his chair, a wry smile tugging at the corners of his mouth. How many times over the past few years had he been guilty of making comments about how their society as a whole was glued to their cell phones, and here he was, just as dependent as everyone else?

All around him, the remaining guests were just as antsy as he was. Some, more so, judging by the rapidity with which they drained champagne glasses. Clay resisted the urge to shake his head. *They better get a move on, taking statements, or they won't be getting them from a few people.*

Again, his thoughts turned to Rob and Naomi. He was sure that Rob was probably at a hospital in surgery by now. The tall, spare man would probably be fine.

Probably.

But Clay couldn't text Naomi to find out until he got his phone back. And he wouldn't get his phone back until after he gave his statement and he was cleared to depart the Embassy. Waiting for this was almost as nerve-wracking as waiting in the First Secretary's office had been, though Clay had to admit that he much preferred Reine's company to this lot.

Reine. He released another measured breath, one hand curling and uncurling into a fist. Oh, how he wished he could see her right now.

The yearning was so strong it made something inside his chest ache. He'd never experienced something like this before—separation had never bothered him. But this...*Reine*...was different somehow.

"Clay Dawson?" an authoritative voice broke into the middle of thoughts swirling around Clay's tired brain.

He snapped to attention, the voice triggering his past in the military and all the years he'd spent responding to command voices. Rising to his feet, he turned toward the ornate double doors and held up a hand. "That'd be me."

A restless rustling and murmuring along the tables sounded, just as it did every time someone was called now. Clay resisted the urge to look over his shoulder at his remaining fellow guests. There weren't many, but he was still surprised that he wasn't dead last.

A Denquayan Embassy employee in a rumpled tuxedo stood just inside one of the doors, a tablet in his hand. He gave Clay a sharp once over as he approached. Clay pegged him at a few years older than he himself was.

"This way, please," he said in accented English, indicating Clay should follow him.

They didn't go very far. Just after they exited the ballroom, the short Embassy official directed Clay through a heavy wooden door into what turned out to be a small conference room with glossy, heavy wooden furniture and a shiny flatscreen TV on one wall.

A Capital police officer sat on one side of the table. He was tall, with dark skin and a regulation haircut starting to gray at the temples. He gave Clay a business-like nod and indicated the chair opposite him.

"Mr. Dawson. I'm Officer Hardin."

"Officer Hardin." Clay returned the nod and took the indicated seat. The short Embassy official moved around the table to sit at the chair next to Hardin.

"State your name for the record, please," Hardin said.

"Clay Dawson."

Officer Hardin ran through a few more questions, with occasional input from the Embassy official (who never did give his name, Clay noticed), and then he asked Clay to give them a rundown of the evening's events.

That took a good fifteen minutes, by the time Hardin and the official asked questions to clarify certain points.

Clay told them everything—almost. He confessed he had followed Reine because he'd fallen for her instantly and hadn't wanted to lose her (this raised an eyebrow from the official, though Hardin appeared to take it in stride). He described how they'd heard gunfire and then he'd fought the terrorist sent to search for stragglers. He described how Reine had called 911 and they'd spent hours locked in the First Secretary's office.

The only thing he left out was passing out as a result of Reine drugging him. (Well, that and their resulting conversation about her secret mission, but really, that was all part of the same thing.)

Clay was fairly confident Reine would not be mentioning that either.

He answered a few resulting questions as patiently and as thoroughly as he could, and tried not to breathe an audible sigh of relief when the Embassy official looked at Hardin and said, "I believe we are done with Mr. Dawson."

"I agree." Officer Hardin made another note on the tablet in front of him.

The Embassy official addressed Clay. "You are free to leave. If we have any further questions, Mr. Dawson, we will contact you."

"Thank you." Clay's heart began to pound.

"Your cell phone will be returned to you on your way out," the official continued. He gave Clay a side-eye. "Do try not to roam into other off-limit areas of the Embassy on your way down to the foyer."

"Understood." Clay smiled wryly, rising from his seat. "It will not happen again, sir." With a nod of thanks, he left the conference room behind.

Relief faded into anticipation, thrumming in his veins. Now to find Reine…

Chapter Forty

Reine had to hand it to the Capital police—they were extremely efficient. She had no experience with American police departments and therefore had no idea if this level of expediency was normal or not, but there was no denying that Washington D.C.'s police worked hand in hand with Embassy security to take statements and clear guests to depart for the night at an impressive rate.

She suspected Ambrose would have preferred to pretend nothing of import had occurred tonight and just let everyone leave (though perhaps he simply wished to further inconvenience his wealthier, more influential guests), but protocol would not allow it.

There would be no resuming festivities, of course. Not at this point. Katrina Ambrose's birthday party would go down as an Event, probably memorable for a few weeks longer than other happenings in America's capital simply because of the terrorist angle. But the birthday party itself had been ruined.

Again, Reine couldn't help but wonder if Jean Renault had possessed a particular reason for choosing Katrina's birthday outside of simple expediency. And, yet again, she still failed to think of any reason why the attaché would dislike the Ambassador's wife. *Perhaps this really was just the most opportune occasion.*

Two black bags containing everyone's cell phones had been brought down to the foyer and their contents spread over the large teak reception desk. Reine and Daphne were now seated behind this desk with tablets to record the names of guests who had retrieved their cell phones.

The First Secretary had insisted that everyone sign for their phone.

"After this evening," Ariane had said firmly, "we will not have any incidents involving missing cellular devices."

A few of Katrina's more famous guests protested this procedure, citing the fact that everyone knew who they were, but Reine and Daphne politely held their ground. Rules were rules.

Those rules even applied to Reine and Daphne themselves. Both women had immediately spotted their own phones in the multicolored pile of devices and lost no time retrieving and signing for them. Reine tucked her phone back into her clutch along with her purple gloves, feeling a wave of relief at having the device back in her possession.

She wasn't the only one.

Most of the guests who filtered through the main floor, heading for the exit after they'd given their statements and been cleared to leave, were happy to have their cell phones back.

In her exhausted, coming-down-from-an-adrenaline-dump state, Reine wondered what that said about the state of American society —and Denquay's own society, for that matter—that people were so dependent on these little tiny devices.

Leaning back in her chair, Reine started to rub her tired eyes— remembering at the last second that she'd smudge what remained of her eye makeup. She dropped her hands back to her lap. *Makes you wonder,* she thought with a mental shake of her head, *how human beings ever managed to survive all these decades without cell phones.*

Exhaustion tugged at her limbs, fraying her thoughts, but Reine carried on with a smile and impeccable manners. Some of the departing guests were overwrought and cranky after everything that had happened. She tried not to hold it against them.

Jacques Leitstrug was among the disgruntled. The wealthy businessman selected his cell phone from the many scattered on the glossy teak surface of the reception desk, proved it was his by unlocking it, and departed with a barely-restrained snarl.

Reine was happy to see him leave.

She couldn't wait for this part of the evening to be over. The longer she sat behind the desk next to Daphne, the more the micro-SD chips hidden in her bodice seemed to burn against her breastbone.

Reine resisted the urge to rub the spot. *Thank God nobody is being searched. It'd be hard to explain why I have these.*

Her head hurt just *contemplating* the magnitude of *that* potential headache.

As the night wore on, the pile of cell phones gradually dwindling and the list of names on both Reine's and Daphne's tablets lengthening…butterflies began swooping around in Reine's stomach. Clay was still inside the Embassy. She had no idea which of these phones was his, but he had yet to appear down here to claim one. Any minute now, he would come walking through the foyer.

On the wings of those heady butterflies, anxiety twisted through her. Would this be the last time she saw him? A brief exchange over his cell phone and then he'd depart the Embassy and walk right out of her life?

A pang shot through Reine. *Oh, I hope not.*

Beside her, Daphne drooped forward over the reception desk. Tucking a lock of her glossy black hair behind her ear, she cast a longing glance in the direction of the kitchen. "I need another cup of coffee. And a snack."

"That sounds good." Reine's stomach gave a little grumble at the thought of food. Waitstaff had brought them both coffee and a few remaining hors d'oeuvres earlier, but that had been ages ago. Now that the adrenaline from the night's events was fading, her stomach chose to remind her of its existence.

"Thank God we're down to the last of them." Daphne indicated the remaining cell phones with a flick of her bare finger.

"Agreed." Reine surveyed the remaining cellphones and felt butterflies twist in her stomach for a completely different reason now. She and Daphne still had to give their statements before they would be allowed to leave.

One last hurdle to pass before she could leave these microSD cards—and they held—at the prearranged drop location and complete her mission.

It will be fine, she told herself. *There's no reason for anyone to suspect anything—particularly after tonight.*

Besides, it wasn't like this was her first assignment from the Intelligence Division. She'd done this before. She had experience.

Her mouth twisted into the faintest of wry grimaces. *You've just never investigated anybody at this level before.*

A shadow fell over her side of the reception desk. Automatic smile in place, Reine glanced up from her tablet. "Name, please?"

Her breath caught in her throat, her eyes widening and her heart skipping a beat.

It was Clay.

He smiled down at her, though there were lines of fatigue around his hazel eyes. "Clay Dawson."

In her peripheral vision, Reine saw Daphne perk up. The other attaché straightened in her chair and leaned forward over the reception desk, offering a tantalizing peek at her cleavage.

A dim corner of Reine's mind noted Daphne's disappointment when Clay didn't even glance her direction, but she was too busy staring at him to feel much exultation. (That would come later.)

Clay was still wearing his tuxedo jacket, but he'd loosened the collar of his white dress shirt. With his five o'clock shadow and the butterfly bandage at his temple, his sandy hair curling just a little, he looked even more ruggedly handsome than he had earlier.

Hating herself for being a little tongue-tied, Reine dutifully entered Clay's name into her spreadsheet. Then she motioned to the remaining pile of cell phones spread out across the teak desk. "Is one of these yours?"

Clay was still looking at her. The intensity of his gaze threatened to bring a blush to Reine's cheeks, but at last he dropped his gaze to the collection of mobile devices in front of him.

He nodded to a phone with a plain black case on Reine's left. "That one."

"Would you unlock it, please?" It wasn't what Reine wanted to say, but she had a job to do. Particularly under Daphne's watchful (and more than a little jealous) eye.

Picking the phone up, Clay entered a pin and showed Reine his unlocked screen. His background, she noted, was a beautiful shot of an orange-gold sunset over some dusty brown mountains. (She wondered if he'd taken it in Afghanistan, or someplace else. A pang of grief shot through her; she'd probably never get the chance to ask.)

"Thank you." She made another note on her tablet and looked back up at him. "You are free to depart. On behalf of the Ambassador and the Denquayan Embassy, I thank you for your attendance tonight and apologize for the unpleasantness."

"Thanks." Clay tucked the cell phone into his front tuxedo jacket pocket.

And that was it.

Reine tasted bitterness. She swallowed, forcing it away. Despite the way he'd looked at her, it was nearly dawn. He had no obligation to stay here any longer.

Any sane person would wish to go home.

She wanted to go home, wanted to lock herself in her little studio apartment and take a long, hot shower. Wash the physical effects of the night away.

After she sent the micro-SD cards still tucked into her bodice on their way, of course. Taking care of them was the final step in completing her mission.

She still felt like they burned a little against her skin. It was all in her head, she knew, but…

She'd be glad when she could check this mission off as completed and truly relax.

An ache formed in Reine's chest, right over her heart. Too bad Clay would likely never want to set eyes on her again.

She expected him to say good night and walk away, but, no, he was still standing in front of the reception desk, smiling at her. The corners of his hazel eyes crinkled with something soft Reine would have called fondness, if she'd seen it on anyone else's face.

Hope flared to life; she hardly dared to breathe.

His eyes locked on hers, Clay opened his mouth—

—but at that moment Daphne sighed dramatically and made a show of welcoming the next person behind him, stopping him in his tracks. Clay darted a glance at her and then looked back at Reine. Whatever he'd been about to say was apparently not that important.

Reine would have *loved* to kick Daphne in the ankle with the extremely pointy heel of her shoe, but she restrained herself. Instead, she held out her hand to Clay, willing her voice to remain steady. "It was wonderful to meet you tonight."

His warm, callused fingers closed over hers and that same spark of electricity shot up Reine's arm. A lump formed in her throat. *Surely he feels that, too.*

"It was a pleasure meeting you as well, Miss Delgado." Clay smiled crookedly at her, still holding her fingers. "If I were ever to get caught in a hostage situation again, you're a good person to be stuck with"

A tremulous laugh escaped Reine. "Yes, well, I can't say I want to repeat the experience either, but..." She swallowed the lump in her throat. "Thank you for everything."

For a second, as Clay's fingers tightened on hers, Reine had the fleeting impression that he didn't want to let go either. His eyes were locked on hers and Daphne, the woman she was helping, and the environs of the Embassy's foyer around them faded into the background.

"It was my pleasure."

His low, husky voice sent a tingle down Reine's spine that somehow pooled in her stomach. She could have stayed here all night, staring into this man's warm hazel eyes.

Reality, however, did not care what she thought or wanted. It intruded with the sort of bustling efficiency that steamrollered everything in its path.

Another group of people—ruffled, disgruntled, and thoroughly relieved to finally be allowed to leave—streamed through the foyer toward Reine and Daphne to collect their cellphones. They crowded up to the long desk behind Clay. Their jostling, combined with their not-so-discreetly voiced discussions of the evening, served to effectively jar both him and Reine back to themselves.

And the reality of their situation.

Clay released Reine's fingers. It felt, oddly, as though she'd been dropped off the side of a cliff.

He smiled at her once more. "Good night." Then he was gone, disappearing behind the group of weary guests who were more than ready to call it a night and escape home.

Reine felt his loss keenly, even as she pasted a diplomatic smile on her face and continued her assigned task of dispensing cell phones. Daphne whispered something to her at one point, but she barely registered the words. (Though she *still* wanted to kick the other woman in the ankle.)

Her chest ached, as though her heart had just been carved out and now resided in the pocket of Clay's trousers, headed off who knew where in D.C.

The lump in her throat returned, harder and bigger now, like a piece of Denquayan rock worn smooth by the constant pounding of ocean surf. It made the backs of her eyes prickle with tears again.

He *was* gone now…and she'd never see him again.

The certainty settled in the pit of her stomach, like something as inevitable as the fact that all politics eventually included some form of betrayal.

Clay was gone.

The group of guests dispersed, happy to have their cell phones back and even happier to be able to leave, and Reine busied herself with her tablet. The side of her face seemed to burn under Daphne's curious gaze, but she didn't feel like answering any questions. Wasn't sure she could get coherent words out at all, actually, let alone string them into sentences that made sense.

But then Daphne gave a dramatic little gasp from the chair beside her.

The sound startled Reine; after the evening they'd had, more surprises couldn't be a good thing. She jerked her head up, eyes wide and scanning for any possible danger—and then she realized why Daphne had gasped.

Clay hadn't left, after all. He was striding back to the desk.

Back to her.

Chapter Forty-One

Clay slowly made his way through the Denquayan Embassy's foyer, one thought and one thought alone running through his brain on a continuous loop. He should have asked Reine for her phone number. He'd *meant* to ask her for her number.

Instead, like an idiot, he'd let the noisy group of guests behind him pressure him into getting out of the way. He'd left Reine sitting there, staring after him.

He'd probably never see her again, after tonight.

Their paths weren't likely to cross.

Clay swallowed a lump in his throat. His cell phone felt like it weighed fifty pounds and was red-hot, burning a hole in his pocket. Every step away from Reine felt like a step in the wrong direction.

It had been *years* since he'd experienced anything like that—and never with regards to a woman.

What *was* it about her?

You've only just met, part of his brain tried to argue. *You can't feel this way about somebody you just met. Especially since she drugged you and knocked you out!*

Except…Clay did.

He'd had hours to consider their situation, and he couldn't honestly say that if he had been in Reine's shoes, he wouldn't have done exactly the same thing. Because he probably would have. There were things more important than any one individual. Hadn't he joined the Marines for exactly that reason?

No, he could forgive her for knocking him out with a kiss. She hadn't given him any other reason to mistrust her, and he was dead certain the fact that she'd had to drug him had torn her up.

Clay glanced over his shoulder toward the desk, but the now-dwindling knot of people there prevented him from getting one last glimpse of Reine. Something twisted in the pit of his stomach.

In that moment, he knew, with gut-wrenching certainty, that if he walked out of those ornate double doors ahead of him—if he left the Denquayan Embassy—without at least getting Reine's phone number, he would regret it the rest of his life.

Clay swallowed again, clenching his jaw. God knew he had enough regrets already without adding to them.

It's a phone number, he told himself. *The worst she can do is say no. And you'd already decided to get it anyway.*

Taking a deep breath, he pulled his cell phone from his pocket and turned around. The last of that clump of guests eagerly turned away from the reception desk and hastened across the marble floor toward the door and the freedom of the muggy pre-dawn D.C. air outside.

This was his moment.

Surprisingly, it took little courage to stride back over to Reine and her coworker. The woman in pink perked up, fluttering her eyelashes at him and offering him another glimpse of her cleavage, but Clay only had eyes for Reine.

Reine, who was staring down at the tablet in front of her as though it held all the answers in the universe. Clay thought he glimpsed grief in her stoic expression, and it set hope fluttering wings inside his chest.

Something must have told her to look up (afterward Clay wondered if it was his gaze on her or some sound from the woman beside her). Reine lifted her gaze and he had the distinct satisfaction of watching her eyes widen in shock—

—and hope. There was definitely hope in her dark eyes.

Clay felt that same hope beating its wings inside his own chest. He smiled at her as he approached, unable to help himself.

Reine just watched him, as though she wasn't quite able to believe what she was seeing.

Clay held up his cell phone as he neared the desk. "Forgot something."

He watched Reine swallow and wet her lips before she answered, "And what would that be?"

Clay shook his head soberly. "I almost walked out of here without asking you for your phone number."

The small, delighted smile that broke out on Reine's face was an absolute joy to see. She quashed it—not very successfully—and tilted a dark eyebrow at him. "Oh, really?"

"Yeah." Clay slid his phone across the desk to her. "May I have it?"

Reine tilted her head back to look up at him, that smile still hovering around the corners of her mouth. Then she twitched her bare shoulders in a little shrug. "Oh, I suppose."

Beside her, the woman in pink gave a rather inelegant little snort.

Clay and Reine both ignored her.

Reine entered her details into his phone and slid the device back across the glossy wooden surface of the desk toward him.

"Thank you." Clay picked the phone back up with a smile and tucked it back into his pocket. Out of the corner of his eye, he glimpsed yet another gaggle of tired guests in wrinkled evening wear approaching from an elevator.

Annoyance flickered inside him. *How many more of them* are *there?*

Reine cast a glance sideways and saw them as well. Her expression fell, just a little, and Clay's heart soared. She didn't want this to be the end, either.

"One last thing." The words popped out before he could help himself.

Reine glanced at him, that faint gleam of hope in her dark eyes again. Beside her, the woman in pink gave him her full attention as well.

"I know there's probably a ton of things you'd rather do when you get done here—" Clay motioned to the desk with a wave of his fingers, "—like take a shower and sleep, probably." He chuckled sheepishly. "But would you have breakfast with me?"

"Yes."

"I understand if you're too tired, but there's a cafe about three blocks—" he broke off as her answer finally registered. "Wait, yes?"

"Yes." It was Reine's turn to smile—a smile that lit her entire face, chasing tired shadows away and impacting him almost like a physical blow to the chest. "I would love that." She scrunched her nose, and it was the most adorable thing he'd ever seen. "I would love a cup of coffee right now."

"Okay." Clay blinked, a little dazed that she'd actually said yes and automatically stepped back out of the way of the oncoming stream of people coming to collect the last few cell phones scattered across the desk. He scrubbed a hand through his hair. "Okay."

"I should be off duty shortly. We're nearly done here." Reine cast a considering glance at the woman beside her, who nodded. She looked back at Clay. "Text me the address."

Still a little dazed, he nodded. "I'll do that."

They exchanged smiles once more, and then a man moved in between them, blocking her from his view.

Clay took this as his cue to leave. For real, this time.

Unable to restrain a smile, he strode toward the double doors with a light heart. He repressed the urge to whistle, thinking it might not go over well with the grim-faced security personnel still standing guard.

This evening wasn't the end. Despite the fact that he'd nearly screwed up everything, he'd see her again shortly.

He could hardly wait.

Chapter Forty-Two

A little bell jingled merrily as Reine set foot in the Rosewood Cafe. She spared a thought for her shimmery purple gown before smiling at her own silliness. This was Washington D.C., after all. This morning probably wouldn't be the first time the waitstaff saw customers dressed in fancy evening wear.

Won't be the last, either, Reine thought wryly. Politics and evening galas being what they were in America's capital.

From the outside, the coffee shop didn't look like much, but Reine had learned a long time ago that when it came to eateries, appearances meant nothing. The best food she'd ever eaten—both back home in Denquay and here in the U.S.—had come from hole-in-the-wall places most people didn't even know existed.

She took a deep breath, her eyelids fluttering as she inhaled the heavenly scent of coffee. With it, she smelled a familiar undertone of cinnamon and chocolate—no doubt from the pastries she spotted sitting under glass domes along the counter. The decor was the same trendy, upscale glass and wood combination she'd seen else-where in D.C., though a variety of flowers and trailing vines hanging from planters scattered around the coffee shop provided a natural twist Reine immediately found refreshing.

Outside, Washington D.C.'s streets were still dark, save for the periodic white glow of streetlights. Dawn was on its way, but the eastern sky had not yet begun to lighten. Inside, the Rosewood Cafe was awash with welcoming golden light. Soft American pop music played in the background.

At first glance, Reine counted four people inside the coffee shop —including the sleepy-looking barista behind the front counter. Far too early for anything remotely resembling a morning rush. She bit her lip to hold back an exhausted giggle. *It's not even five in the morning.*

At second glance, Reine spotted Clay, who was tucked into a corner at a little table beside a window. He sat on the side that allowed him to keep his back to the wall, which didn't surprise her. She'd encountered many individuals over the years—police, military, etc.—who preferred to ensure no one could sneak up on them.

Clay had been frowning down at his phone, but his attention snapped to the door the instant she stepped inside. Their eyes met and for a second the rest of the world seemed to fade away again. In his rumpled tuxedo, Clay looked oddly incongruous, sitting at that table, but at the same time…something about him just…fit.

He waved to her, a smile breaking out over his ruggedly handsome face.

As Reine approached him, butterflies dancing in her stomach again, he rose from his chair and stood to greet her. If anything, his smile seemed to widen.

Reine felt an answering smile light her own face, even as the nervous butterflies in her stomach swooped into barrel rolls.

She stopped beside the table, one still-gloved hand holding her clutch, and they smiled at each other for a few seconds.

"Hi," Clay said, his voice a quiet rumble.

"Hi." Even to her own ears, Reine thought she sounded a little breathless. She took a breath, struggling to get a grip on herself. The look in his eyes…

"I'm glad you're here." Clay motioned to the other side of the table, with its glossy warm brown surface, and Reine allowed him to pull her chair out for her.

She sat down and he scooted her in. She set her clutch on the edge of the table by the window while he returned to his seat. Once he was facing her, she met his eyes and offered him a small, almost shy smile.

"I'm glad you invited me." Reine hesitated, then added, "To be honest, I wasn't sure we would ever cross paths again after….everything."

Clay just smiled at her, before tipping his head toward the front counter. "What can I get you? The coffee here is fantastic and they have wonderful breakfast bagels." His smile deepened. "They also have a decent chocolate croissant, if you like chocolate."

Reine arched an eyebrow at him. "You do know that is a stereotype, don't you? That all women love chocolate?"

Clay's hazel eyes danced at her across the table. "But you do, don't you?"

It was impossible to keep a straight face when he was looking at her like *that*. Reine let her smile break through. "Of course I do."

Clay just laughed, shaking his head. "Well, what would you like?"

Reine pursed her lips, considering. Her stomach growled, reminding her that a couple of shrimp puffs and a cup of coffee was all she'd had for hours. "I would like a mocha latte," she said at last. "And whichever of the breakfast bagels you think is the best."

"Ooh." Clay narrowed his eyes playfully at her. "Testing me, are you?"

Reine smiled at him, lifting one shoulder in a shrug. "Perhaps."

"All right. Challenge accepted." He rose from his chair, but paused to cock an eyebrow at her. "Are you *sure* you don't want a croissant?"

Oh, it sounded so tempting. And after the night she'd had… Reine bit down on the inside of her lip, torn.

Clay seemed to sense this. "We could split it," he offered.

Reine felt her resistance crumble. She shrugged again, her smile taking on a shy edge. "If you insist."

"You won't regret it," Clay promised, and then he was gone, striding up to the front counter to place their order.

The delay gave Reine a moment to gather her thoughts, which had scattered like flower petals on the wind the instant she'd set eyes on Clay. The drive here from the Embassy hadn't given her much time to think, with the way her head still spun from the events of the evening.

Once again, she resisted the urge to flatten her fingers over the spot in her bodice where the microSD cards continuing the contents of both of Ariane's hard drives nestled up against her breastbone. *It's probably better this way,* she told herself. *If Ariane—or anyone else from the Embassy—suspects anything and had me followed, I'm not doing anything unusual.*

A smile tugged at the corners of her mouth. *Well, except perhaps for having an exceptionally early breakfast with a former American soldier I just met.*

The sound of the espresso machine behind the counter seemed abnormally loud, but Reine did not let it bother her. Instead, she focused on quelling the nervousness that had risen inside her.

You managed to clone not one but two *of the First Secretary's hard drives,* she told herself. *You successfully knocked somebody out with spy lip gloss, and on top of that, you lived through a terrorist takeover at the Embassy.*

That certainly topped anything else she'd ever done for the Intelligence Division before. Reine shook her head slightly at herself. *Having breakfast with a handsome man should be nothing after all that.*

And yet…

Quiet footsteps drew her gaze sideways in time to see Clay and the barista approaching, both with their hands full. Clay held two cups of coffee in paper to-go cups, while the barista carried two plates heaped with food.

She set them down in the middle of the table and cast a nod in Reine's dress. "I love that dress."

"Thank you," Reine said, and then the barista was gone, back to her place behind the counter.

Clay set one of the coffee cups down on the table in front of Reine and the other in front of his own chair. He nodded to her cup. "You won't be disappointed."

"If it tastes as good as it smells," Reine said as she picked up her cup, "I expect not." She took a careful sip of the hot liquid. It was bliss.

"Oh, that is good," she said, after she swallowed.

"I'm glad you like it." Clay smiled at her again, taking a sip of his own coffee.

Reine then took a bite of her breakfast bagel. It was hot, and the combination of egg, cheddar cheese, and slightly crispy ham blended amazingly well with the crispy edge of the bagel. She made a small sound of appreciation and then glanced at Clay, daring him to comment.

He just grinned at her and reached for his own bagel. "I like a woman with a healthy appetite. Did I pass the test?"

"Yes. I am so hungry." Reine reached for her napkin with one hand and dabbed lightly at the corner of her mouth. "I am grateful for the coffee, too, but..." she shrugged her shoulders, which were still covered in lacy silvery shawl.

"Me, too." Clay shook his head slightly, and it struck Reine then how tired he looked. "It's been a long night."

Setting her bagel down, Reine picked up her coffee again. "How is your friend?"

"Still in surgery, but Naomi—remember her?" When Reine

nodded, Clay continued, "Naomi says the prognosis is hopeful. He should be okay."

"That's good." Reine nodded slowly, before taking another sip of coffee.

For a moment, silence descended on them both as they ate, save for the sounds of the espresso machine behind the counter as the barista prepared coffee for another early customer.

It was only after Reine finished her bagel and picked up a plastic knife to cut the delicious-looking croissant in two that Clay spoke again.

"What will you do now?"

"Beg your pardon?" Reine froze, knife in hand, and stared at him, startled and a little bemused. "What do you mean?"

Clay took a deliberate sip of his coffee before setting the cup down on the table's glossy wooden surface and leveling her with a look. "You know." He waved vaguely toward her. "You had your… thing. Now that it's done, what will you do?"

Oh. Realization dawned on Reine like the sun rising over the horizon. A small corner of her mind noted how carefully he'd avoided saying the word 'mission' and a fresh wave of endearment swept over her.

She smiled slightly, giving a little shrug, and neatly sliced the croissant into two pieces. "Carry on same as usual, I expect. At least until this particular post is finished." When Clay just continued to stare at her, she elaborated. "I can't remember if I told you before, but the Diplomatic Corps sends me to whatever Denquayan Consulate or Embassy requires assistance until they don't need me anymore."

"I see." Clay nodded slowly. "And there's no way of knowing how long that will be?"

"Unfortunately, no." Reine made a wry face as she set half of the croissant on her empty plate. "There are times the not-knowing is quite inconvenient."

Clay nodded again, his hands curling around his cup to cradle it. He was quiet, and Reine hoped that was because he was tired after the night they'd had and not because he'd suddenly realized that asking her to meet him here was a mistake.

Soft pop music filled the silence between them. Reine felt her heartbeat start to pick up. The silence seemed to be stretching, opening up a chasm between them. She needed to say something. She needed to...well, she wasn't quite sure *what* she needed to do, but she had to do *something*.

"I'm sorry again," she blurted out abruptly. "About..." It was her turn to vaguely wave a hand in his direction, "...before. Really."

Reine met his gaze and held it, willing him to understand. She had thought that perhaps he did, but in the hours since they had been escorted from Ariane Montoya's office, tendrils of doubt had crept into her mind and sunk deep roots.

She didn't expect the smile that broke out across Clay's face.

Chapter Forty-Three

Clay smiled across the table at Reine, a warmth spreading through him that had nothing to do with the hot coffee he'd just consumed and everything to do with her. In the cafe's soft golden light, he saw fatigue written across her beautiful face, but he also saw her intelligence and strength.

This woman. This wonderful, brave, amazing woman.

Once more, those moments right before she'd kissed him in that dark office floated through his mind's eye. The words she'd said… the way she'd looked at him…

The warmth in his chest increased.

"You don't have to apologize again." Clay shook his head, his smile widening into a crooked grin. "I get it."

"You do?" Reine stared at him, her head tilting to one side in confusion.

He swore her shoulders drooped a little with relief beneath that silvery shawl. The tension in her face eased as well.

"C'mere." Pushing both his empty plate and her plate with the croissant to one side of the table, Clay reached for Reine's hands. Her fingers were cold, but the second he touched her, he felt that spark of electricity ignite between them again. He hoped she felt it too.

"I had a lot of time to think while I was waiting for you." He wrapped hers fingers around her hands, offering her a lopsided smile even as his heart began thundering in his chest. "And I came to the conclusion that we're going to have a hell of a story to tell the grandkids."

He had the satisfaction of watching Reine's dark eyes widen comically.

"Grandchildren?" she gasped. She blinked several times, hardly able to believe her ears. What was he talking about? How could he —did he—?

"Yeah." Clay rubbed the backs of her hands with the pads of his thumbs. Her skin was so soft and smooth, it made him wonder what the rest of her would feel like.

Whoa, hold up there, buddy. Forcing his thoughts back into proper channels, Clay lifted one shoulder in a shrug. "You know, what with the Embassy and the terrorist attack and everything." His expression turned mock-serious. "No more drugging me, though. Gotta draw the line somewhere. But, yeah. We're going to have an amazing story."

Reine stared at him so long he was afraid he'd scared her. But then she laughed once, in quiet disbelief, and shook her head. "Clay. What are you saying? You're not making any—"

"—sense?" he interrupted. "Sure I am." His smile faded, to be replaced by a serious expression. "I'm glad I met you tonight, Reine Delgado." It was his turn to shake his head. "In fact, I've never met anyone like you."

"Clay…" A hint of rosy pink tinted her cheeks. She shifted in her seat, but she didn't remove her fingers from his.

Clay was glad for that. "I'm serious, Reine." He leaned a little closer to her, uncaring of the way the edge of the table bit into his sternum. "You are amazing, and I realized way before I left the

Embassy tonight—or this morning, or whatever the hell time it was —" He laughed and she laughed with him, "—that if I walked out of there without at least getting your number, I'd regret it for the rest of my life."

Reine's breath hitched in her throat. "Oh, Clay…" She bit her lip. "We've known each other for less than a day. How can you be so sure?"

"Can't explain it." He shook his head. "I just know."

Reine looked at him, and he thought he saw hope dawning in her dark eyes. "Even though I'm Denquayan and you're American?"

"You're in diplomatic relations, aren't you?"

"What about your friends? Your job?"

Clay brushed that aside with a wave of his hand. He'd had time to think about that, too. "It'll be fine." He offered her an assuring smile, settling his hand back over hers again. "If and when I leave D.C., they'll find somebody better suited to mesh with the two of them."

Reine blinked at him, taking this in. Then she shook her head in bewilderment. "But what will you do?"

"What do you mean?" Clay shrugged, grinning. "I've got options. There's a whole world of possibilities for somebody with skill set I've got." He shook his head. "Doesn't have to be security work. I could be a translator or an interpreter."

For a second, he thought Reine was going to cry. Alarm spiked through him; he hadn't wanted to upset her or freak her out, or anything like that.

Before he could say anything, she shook her head and blurted out, "Why? Why would you give all that up for a woman you only just met?"

Oh. That's what had gotten her all emotional. Clay almost sagged in relief, but restrained himself.

Instead, he just shrugged again. "It's pretty simple, actually. I knew when I met you tonight that you were something unique.

What happened this evening just proves it." He cocked a teasing eyebrow at her. "I'm serious about the not knocking me out again part, though."

A tremulous laugh escaped Reine. "No. No, I won't." She shook her head and then met his gaze, lifting her chin. "Not unless I have to."

"Because the fate of the world depends on it?" Clay looked askance at her, long enough to see a flicker of nervousness in her expression before her inner core of steel reasserted itself. That warm glow of pride swelled his chest again. *This amazing woman…*

He pretended to think, before tightening his grip on her fingers and offering her a soft smile. "I suppose I can live with that."

Hazel met brown as he searched her eyes, and then Clay did what he'd been wanting to do all evening. He leaned across the table and kissed her.

Chapter Forty-Four

Up until now, Reine had thought this entire night had been the most surreal experience of her life, but this moment? This moment topped everything else. The coffee shop, the world—the entire universe—fell away until it was just her and Clay.

Her eyes slipped shut as Clay closed the gap between them and kissed her. The touch of his lips against hers—gentle, but confident—sent sparks racing through her, spreading from her mouth to her chest and out through all of her limbs.

Reine kissed him back, her heart swelling with emotion. This time—this time there was no guilt, no ulterior motive, just the gentle slide of his lips against hers.

Clay pulled back long enough to search her face. He must have found what he was looking for, because he leaned in and kissed her again. Reine freed a hand long enough to slide it into the short hair at the nape of his neck as she kissed him back.

For a glorious moment, there were no words.

Reine could have stayed here forever kissing Clay, but the jingle of the bell above the coffee shop's door brought them both back to reality. Clay gave her one more lingering kiss and then sat back in his seat, looking happy and supremely pleased with himself.

She couldn't begrudge him that. Not when her lips were still tingling, she couldn't keep from smiling, and she thought there was a very good chance that she might simply float out of her seat. And especially not when she knew she was the woman responsible for his smile.

On the heels of her giddy elation, his earlier words returned to her. Reine stared at him across the table. "You'd really give up your job and your entire life for me?"

Clay smiled ruefully and reached for his coffee. "It's not really much of a life I've got right now." He lifted one shoulder in a casual shrug. "I don't think I'm the right fit for this job, and like I told you, my family never really understood why I left. Or why I haven't come back to settle down."

He looked at her, sudden vulnerability in his hazel eyes. "I liked seeing the world. I wouldn't mind seeing more of my own country, or visiting yours, for that matter. And—" he hesitated, before plunging ahead. "I'm at a point where I'd like to start thinking about settling down. With the right woman."

He shrugged again, casting a self-conscious glance down at his coffee cup. "If she wanted to settle down with me."

"Clay..." Reine didn't know what to say. She pressed a hand to her chest, which felt like it had expanded to the bursting point. Words swirled around inside her head, but none of them made it out of her mouth.

All she could do was look at him in shy amazement.

Clay met her gaze again. "I meant what I said. You are an amazing woman. I don't want to scare you off or anything, and I'm not jumping into a marriage proposal—" he held up a hand, "— but...I'd really like the chance to get to know you better." That vulnerable look returned to his eyes again. "If you'll let me."

Reine exhaled shakily, that same vulnerability overtaking her in this moment. She felt open and exposed, like Clay could see all the way to her core. She'd kept her guard up for so many years it felt beyond strange to let someone in, and yet...

The connection she felt with this man was so natural, so easy, that after just one night—albeit an intense night—she felt as though they'd known each other far longer.

Reine had never experienced that before.

Looking at Clay, seeing the hope in his eyes, Reine had an epiphany. She couldn't explain *how* she knew, but she knew with a sudden, clear, and intense certainty that if she walked away—if she failed to seize this opportunity to get to know this man better—it would be something *she* would regret for the rest of her life.

Reine drew in a breath, but before she could recover from the magnitude of that realization, the memory of her parents, waltzing together in the living room of their quarters in the Embassy compound, returned to her. Despite their tragic end, they had been happy living life together. Their love had been deep and committed.

In that instant, Reine knew that she and Clay could be that couple, still slow dancing in their living room after who knew how many years together.

The thought left her breathless and a little shaky again, but filled with a kind of hope she'd never experienced before.

It was her turn to reach out to Clay and place a hand over his. Giving him a soft smile, she nodded shakily. "I would like that."

Another look passed between them, a look full of hope and promise and the mutual decision to explore a future together.

Clay raised her hand to his lips and pressed a kiss to her knuckles. His gaze then dropped to her lips and he laughed softly. "I'd *really* like to kiss you again, but..." he nodded to their surroundings. "I don't want to get carried away and get kicked out either. Too early in the morning."

Reine giggled. "That is true. If that happened, our only other option nearby might be a fast food place." She nodded to his rumpled tuxedo. "We might stand out a bit."

Clay laughed again. "Just a bit." His hazel eyes danced at her. "But this *is* D.C.."

"You know, I had that same thought earlier."

They shared another smile, and then Clay tipped his head toward the chocolate croissant still waiting to be eaten. "Ready to try that now?"

"Yes." Reine squeezed his fingers and then let go. She set half of the cut croissant on his plate before pulling her own plate back in front of her.

Her first bite was heaven.

"Oh, my," Reine said, after she'd chewed and swallowed. "That is amazing." She cast an awed expression at the front counter where the barista was making another cup of coffee for someone. "Pastry like this can be tricky—whoever bakes for them did a phenomenal job."

"I don't know where they get 'em, but they're good." Clay grinned at her across the table. "I'm glad you like it."

"I do." Reine smiled back at him, and then proceeded to systematically demolish the rest of her croissant.

When they had finished, and the last of their coffee was gone, Clay cast a considering glance at her. "I think showers and long naps are in both our immediate futures, but would you have dinner with me tonight?"

Warm delight filled Reine, but she maintained a straight face as she leaned back in her chair. "That depends."

"On?" Clay cocked an eyebrow at her.

"Whether or not you think we can avoid any further terrorist encounters." Reine cracked an impish smile, shaking her head. "Really, I haven't the energy for more than one of those a week."

Clay laughed and then leaned forward to take her hand again. He couldn't seem to stop touching her—and Reine couldn't say she minded.

"Well, Miss Delgado," he drawled, "I can't flat-out *promise* we won't run into trouble, but I *can* assure you that our odds of having an amazing evening are pretty good."

Outside the coffee shop, the first rays of early morning sunshine splashed across the street. Inside, Reine felt like she'd been flooded with that same sunshine. She still had a job to finish—at some point today she had to visit the post office and send Erica the microSD cards via Priority Mail, carefully hidden inside a hardback romance novel that was ostensibly a birthday present—but once that was done, she was free.

Free to get some rest and then enjoy dinner with a handsome man she had never expected to meet.

Reine nodded solemnly, though she couldn't restrain her impish smile. "In that case, Mr. Dawson, I accept."

Danger at the Embassy

A NOVELLA

E. R. PASKEY

Chapter One

When Reine Delgado was a child, she'd thought the parties her parents occasionally hosted at the Denquay Embassy in Brazil were the epitome of what it meant to be an adult. Beautiful ladies in glittering evening gowns, handsome men in black tuxedos, and delicious little finger foods that floated through the air on trays held by all-but invisible waiters and waitresses.

She'd pouted when her parents left her for the night, and curled up in her bed, impatiently counting the days and months and years until she was old enough to attend those parties too.

Now that she was an adult, Reine knew better. Oh, the evening gowns were still glittering—in fact, getting dressed up was probably still her favorite part of attending a party—and the sharp-looking tuxedos hadn't changed much. The food was still good. (She adored shrimp puffs and little fruit creations best.)

But the people? She'd learned that in reality the women weren't as beautiful and the men weren't as handsome as they'd been when seen through a dreamy child's eyes.

Especially not now that Reine understood the motivations of most of the people attending these parties…herself included.

Tonight, the ballroom in the atrium that took up half of the top two floors of the Denquay Embassy in Washington, D.C. was resplendent. Made from bulletproof glass, the atrium provided a wonderful view of D.C.'s skyline, the Washington Monument just visible in the distance. A giant crystal chandelier hung from the center of the domed ceiling, providing most of the ballroom's light, though decorative lamps with sconces lined the walls and provided even more illumination.

Reine took a champagne flute off of a passing waiter's tray with a smile of thanks. She made it a point to thank the waitstaff when she could. People at parties like these only noticed waitstaff if something was wrong.

Plus, in her line of work, being kind to waitstaff sometimes came in handy.

Reine pretended to sip her champagne, surveying the room with keen interest. Even through the thin fabric of her deep purple elbow-length gloves, the glass stem felt cold. The steady influx of guests had slowed; she guessed most of the people Ambassador Ambrose had invited to celebrate his wife's birthday were here already.

She turned slowly, and the folds of her purple gown—the same shade as her gloves—swished against her legs with a delightful slide that made her feel like a princess, even now. The fabric shimmered with a subtle sheen in the light from the chandelier overhead. She loved this dress, with its halter neckline and tight bust. The fabric of the skirt draped in such a way that it looked like it hugged her hips, but it was loose enough that she'd be able to run if she had to.

Or if she had to scale the side of a building. (That had happened once, a year and a half ago. She still couldn't believe she'd managed to pull it off.)

On one side of the massive ballroom, a small white stage held an eight-person orchestra in formal black gowns and suits. They played various classical pieces from Mozart to Beethoven, interspersed with modern and classical pieces that were the pride of Denquay. The music was just loud enough to provide good background noise, but not so loud that it overshadowed conversation.

A spray of tables curved along one side of the ballroom, giving partygoers a chance to sit down and converse while they enjoyed the view of America's capital city outside. Most of those tables were empty; everyone here was much too interested in mingling to take a chance on sitting down and missing out on some choice piece of information or chance of a making good deal on something. Sitting down might come later, when the party finally wound down in the early pre-dawn hours.

The world of international relations might look glamorous on the surface, but over the years Reine had learned there were some wicked undercurrents. Her parents had been caught in one of those undercurrents. The aftermath hadn't been pretty.

Now that she was an adult, Reine had found a way to help keep other people from getting caught in those undercurrents.

It wasn't easy. And she'd learned that you couldn't save everybody. Still, she liked to think what she did helped.

At the very least, it meant she slept better at night.

Reine drifted across the ballroom's smooth, polished maple surface, pretending to sip her champagne while she surveyed the glittering crowd of guests. She caught whiffs of at least a dozen different perfumes and colognes along the way, though she knew for a fact that this Embassy building had a top-of-the-line air scrubber system.

Her internal sense of time told her that it was well after 8pm. Any minute, the Ambassador and his wife would make their grand entrance and the party would begin in earnest. When that happened, Reine would have a little time to kill before she set off to accomplish her mission.

She recognized many of the faces in attendance tonight. Some because she knew them personally, from her job traveling back and forth as needed from the Embassy here in D.C. to the Denquayan Consulates scattered in important cities across the United States. Others because she had been briefed on them—and she always studied those briefs thoroughly. There were American politicians and businesspeople here, along with an array of visiting Denquayan politicians and businesspeople, and those from other countries doing business with both Denquay and the United States.

Reine even spotted a couple of Denquayan celebrities in attendance—stars of one of her country's most popular television shows who had traveled from their home country for tonight's event.

In the background, the music suddenly shushed. A thrill of satisfaction curled through Reine. *There they are.*

She turned to face the ballroom entrance along with everyone else as the ornate double doors opened to admit Ambassador Ambrose and his wife, Karina. The middle-aged duo always looked elegant, but tonight they had outdone themselves. The cut of the Ambassador's black tuxedo and crisp white shirt camouflaged his middle-aged paunch, while his wife's slinky, off-the-shoulder mermaid blue gown highlighted her smooth, flawless shoulders.

Karina did a better job of staying in shape than her husband, that was a fact.

Reine had always suspected—and the rumors that swirled around the upper echelons of Denquayan politics echoed this—that the Ambassador had something of a wandering eye. Idly, she wondered how well that was going, giving that the Ambassador was stationed in the heart of American politics. There were plenty of opportunistic women here, she was sure.

The Ambassador held up a hand in welcome; his wife clung to his other arm, an elegant smile curling her pretty red lips. In the respectful silence that filled the ballroom, his cultured voice carried to everyone. "Welcome to the Denquayan Embassy. On behalf of myself and my wife, we would like to thank you for coming tonight to celebrate my Karina's day of birth. We will start the festivities with a dance—my Karina's favorite traditional waltz."

He turned his head to plant a kiss on his wife's dark brown hair, which was swept up into an elegant French twist and studded with glittering diamonds and peridots. She beamed up at him, and then the pair made their way out into the center of the ballroom.

Reine watched along with everyone else as the Ambassador and his wife settled into position. Perfectly on cue, the orchestra started up again. Beautiful strains of a violin and cello tangled together in an enchanting melody.

The song triggered a memory, making Reine's breath catch in her throat. Her mother had loved this song, and no matter how many times she had heard it in the years since, it always struck Reine the same way. She blinked and the memory—of her parents waltzing together and laughing in the large living room of their quarters in the Embassy compound—vanished liked mist.

She raised her champagne to her lips and drank—a real sip, this time. The fizzy liquid burned down her throat. *Focus*, she told herself. *What would Erica say if she knew that stupid song still affected you?*

Cold. Rational. Emotionless.

That was her goal right now. Emotion clouded judgment. The last thing she could afford right now was to make a mistake because of old emotion dredged up by a piece of music, of all things.

Her job might allow her to travel back and forth between the Embassy and various Consulates around the country, but only in prescribed measures. If she failed to complete her mission tonight, it could be weeks or even months before she had another shot—and by then it might be too late.

Lives depended on her. More lives than she cared to consider.

Reine took a deep breath. *Don't think about the pressure.*

She was up to the task.

She had to be.

Chapter Two

Officially, Reine was an attaché, which in her case meant that she was nothing more than a glorified secretary and messenger girl. A slightly cushy job, bestowed out of a lingering sense of guilt on a girl whose parents had given their lives in the service of their country.

Unofficially, she'd been recruited four years earlier by the Intelligence Division of Denquay's Department of Defense. They had used her job as a cover for many covert tasks, but tonight was a new wrinkle.

The Intelligence Division suspected that the First Secretary in the Embassy in D.C., a woman named Ariane Montoya, was arranging the trade of key information for American contracts—and getting paid handsomely for it. Reine's job was to break into Ariane's computer, clone her hard drive, and get the evidence back to her handler, Erica.

It sounded simple, on the face of it, but the job was considerably more complicated than that. Denquay might be only a fraction of the United States' size, with a fraction of their national security budget, but they had good tech. *Really* good tech.

Reine had been secretly training for this for several months. She'd assured her handler she could, well, *handle* things. The party tonight was both her mission and a chance to dress up in fancy clothes. (She'd kept being excited about that part to herself.)

Now, standing here in the ballroom while couples flooded to join the Ambassador and his wife on the dance floor, she casually glanced around for anything out of the ordinary. Anything that might derail her mission.

She didn't expect anything, but of course, the only real rule of spying was to expect the unexpected. At some point tonight, something would probably go wrong. When it did, she'd deal with it just like she dealt with everything else.

Her problem now? She had entirely too much time on her hands until her window of opportunity opened.

A restless sense of energy filled her, curling and swirling through her nerves from her head, out to the tips of her fingers and all the way down to her toes. She did her best to banish it, to send a mental wave of calm through her body, like an imaginary wave of cool ice. Most of the time, this sort of exercise worked pretty well.

Tonight...tonight Reine was having a little trouble. She still felt on edge.

Maybe it was the fact that this was a big mission. Probably one of the biggest she'd been given, in her four years in the Intelligence Division. Everything else she'd ever done had involved a Consulate, and the Ambassador himself had only been there on one of those occasions. She'd never poked around the Embassy like this before.

Or perhaps, she mused, as she let her hips sway in time to the waltz's rhythmic beat, perhaps it was not so much her locale as the politics behind it. She'd been told once by one of her supervisors in the Intelligence Division not to worry about the politics. She was a delicate instrument—an instrument meant to perform an assigned task, not to think on her own.

Those instructions had been politely—but firmly—negated by

that man's supervisor. Marcus was sometimes a dinosaur, Reine had been told. There were areas of life in which he failed to realize that Denquayan culture had marched out of the Old Days and into a new world that required more resources and more finesse.

Politics—both internal and international—*absolutely* colored everything. Politics were the entire reason agents like Reine were necessary in the first place.

Well, that and greed, she thought with a wry smile, letting the glass rim of her champagne flute rest against her lips. Greed colored a great many things as well.

She froze imperceptibly as the hair on the back of her neck prickled. Someone was staring at her. Reine maintained her cool, pleasant expression, but inside all her senses went on full alert.

It was probably one of the older men here. Even though she was usually more of an invisible wallflower, she still couldn't escape. What was it about old people that they thought gave them the right to throw proper etiquette out the window and just openly stare? Or make comments that they'd never in a million years have made if they were two decades younger?

Slowly, Reine turned a little to the left, her hips still swaying to the music. Brown met hazel as her gaze collided with that of a man looking straight at her.

She took the measure of him in a quick once-over. He was perhaps early thirties, probably half a head taller than she was in her heels, with broad shoulders and an athletic build. Though dressed in an expensive black tuxedo and equally expensive Italian shoes, he had a look about him that screamed military. Or perhaps ex-military.

She wasn't entirely sure what nationality he was—European or American, probably, judging by his light skin and sandy brown hair. She *was* sure he was not a politician. His posture was too stiff, and he lacked that suave confidence that oozed out of every pore of every politician she'd ever encountered.

He also had entirely too much scruff for a politician. On him, however, the slightly unkempt facial hair was oddly attractive. Reine pegged him as either a bodyguard, or the brainless muscled arm candy of somebody else more important than he was. Attractive, but probably not much of a conversationalist.

No sense being rude, however. She inclined her head in a polite nod.

The man returned the nod with a smile that lit his entire face, lending a genuine warmth to his hazel eyes.

That smile hit Reine with the force of a small bus. A little shaken, she turned away, lowering her champagne flute as she took a steadying breath. Okay. Perhaps she needed to revise her initial impression of him.

That smile made him surprisingly attractive, in a subtle way that kind of crept up on a woman.

Still not a politician, she thought, resisting the urge to look over her shoulder, *but 'brainless' might have been too harsh.*

She felt a presence come up behind her a second before someone tapped lightly on her bare shoulder and said, "Excuse me."

Reine turned—and felt something flutter in the pit of her stomach as she found herself staring up at the handsome man.

"Hi," he said with another amazing smile that was just a little shy around the edges. "I'm Clay Dawson." His voice was a pleasant, husky rumble that was entirely too attractive.

He held out a hand to her. "May I have this dance?"

Chapter Three

His erstwhile partners had explained it twice, but Clay Dawson still wasn't entire sure what he was doing here at the Denquay Embassy tonight. He took a sip of chilled water from a fancy wine glass, gaze constantly assessing the ballroom, and let the buzz of conversation and the lovely strains of music wash over him.

In the grand scheme of things, attending the Denquayan Ambassador's wife's birthday party didn't seem very important. It was a birthday party, for crying out loud. Surely Blackthorn Security had higher priorities to attend to.

His partners, Naomi Jones and Rob Skelton, begged to differ. A birthday party on this level was *exactly* the sort of thing they needed to attend. As far as either of them was concerned, running a security firm required networking and getting fat contracts from people who knew people.

And here Clay had always thought that word of mouth advertising about them being reliable and good at what they did would be enough.

He kept that thought to himself, however. His opinions weren't very popular, lately. Going into business with his old buddy from the war in Afghanistan and a woman who'd worked in Naval Intelligence had seemed like a good idea at the time, but there were days that made him realize the three of them were lightyears apart in some of their ideologies and business practices.

Tonight was a case in point.

Hence the reason Clay still wasn't entirely sure why he was here. Rob wanted to show him off, wanted prospective employers to see that they could hire security people who were urbane, cultured —and could kick ass when the situation warranted it. Clay wasn't sure small talk at an international birthday party was the best way to get all that across, but what did he know?

He was just an ex-soldier who spoke five languages and could kill a man ten different ways with his bare hands alone.

Clay had to admit the venue was rather stunning, though. The ballroom in the Denquay Embassy was beautiful. He cast an appraising eye up at the domed glass ceiling that rose above them.

Not tactical at all, even if it *was* bulletproof glass, but definitely beautiful. Of course, they were in Washington, D.C. and not Afghanistan or Iraq, so it wasn't like they had to worry about somebody shooting a missile into the building, but his years in the Marines had left an impact.

Clay would probably never be able to walk into a room without immediately assessing the people in it and both its tactical advantages and disadvantages again.

Most of the time, he was okay with that.

He took another sip of his water. Rob teased him about it sometimes, but Clay preferred not to drink on the job. He didn't drink much period, anymore, but most definitely not when they were working.

Besides, he'd never much cared for champagne anyway. It had always struck him as one of those things people liked to say they enjoyed because it was fancy and expensive.

He glanced around the ballroom again. The food here would probably be good, though. Waiters hadn't started circulating with trays of hors d'oeuvres yet, but it was only a matter of time. That was one thing Clay had gained an appreciation for while stationed overseas—he'd tried a number of new foods and had really come to enjoy most of them.

His tie felt too tight around his throat, but he resisted the urge to loosen it. He also resisted the urge to tug at his cuffs. Naomi had pointed out once that when you thought about it, wearing a tuxedo wasn't really that different from wearing a dress uniform, but it felt a *lot* different in Clay's head.

Earlier that evening, Naomi had examined him critically when he'd showed up in the lobby of the hotel they were staying at while they were in D.C. She'd bemoaned his stubborn unwillingness to shave, but otherwise declared that his tuxedo and Italian shoes passed muster. On this stage, looks were just about as important as qualifications.

Deep down, Clay admitted he was a touch scared to find out what Naomi would do to him if he ruined Blackthorn Security's image tonight by looking sloppy. The third member of their trio looked cool and elegant herself, with her riot of dark curls and tasteful burnt orange evening gown, but Clay knew she wasn't above picking the locks on his hotel room and waterboarding him in his sleep. There were days he wondered if her past in the military wasn't just a little more extensive that what she told everybody.

The sudden hush that flooded the ballroom told Clay that Ambassador Ambrose and his wife had finally made their appearance. He dutifully turned to listen to the Ambassador's speech along with everyone else, but while all eyes watched the couple step out on the dance floor, he watched the crowd over the rim of his water glass.

Most of the people here were career politicians—regardless of their nationality. Then there was the usual group of businesspeople, celebrities, and other hangers-on. Here and there, he spotted members of various security details.

They'd been trained to do a good job of blending in, but like recognized like. Clay picked them out easily. It was something in the way these men and women stood—an alertness in their posture and attitude that couldn't completely be disguised.

It was the way the world worked now. Nobody on this level ever felt completely safe. Bodyguards and security details were as normal as meetings and long chats about the world's future over late lunches and dinners.

Some of the women in attendance tonight were beautiful. Some were married, though Clay had learned in the past that that didn't stop them from flirting outrageously at times.

His gaze caught on a young woman dressed in a deep purple gown that highlighted the olive tones of her skin. Thick, glossy dark brown hair was twisted up into a complicated knot on the top of her head, though a few tendrils framed her narrow face. She was watching the crowd too, a half-full flute of champagne in her gloved hand, her hips swaying in time to the music. What he could see of her expression was pleasant, but her eyes held an oddly thoughtful note.

It only took one glance for Clay to know that she exercised regularly. Her arms, which were bare from her shoulders to the top of her purple elbow-length gloves, were lithe and muscular. He wondered who she was.

He didn't remember seeing her face in any of the profiles Rob and Naomi had put together of potential employers at this soiree.

As though feeling his gaze on her, the woman turned slightly and their gazes met. Dangly silver earrings glinted in the light from the chandelier as she gave him a nod.

Clay felt a little shock go through him. Oh, yes, she was definitely beautiful. But there was something *more* about her—something breathtaking he couldn't even figure out how to put into words at the moment.

A little stunned, he smiled at her and nodded back.

After a second that seemed to last forever, she looked away and their connection broke. Clay felt a pang deep in his chest. He inhaled sharply and raised his free hand to scrub it through his hair, remembering at the last second that he couldn't do that right now. What was *that?*

He'd never experienced anything like that before. All she'd done was *look* at him and—

He swallowed. *Focus, Dawson. You're on the clock tonight. Don't get distracted by a pretty face.*

His feet, however, had a mind of their own.

Before Clay quite realized he was moving, he found his feet carrying him toward the woman. Heart thudding in a way that it hadn't even the last time he'd taken point on a field patrol to sweep for IEDs, he reached out a hand and tapped her on the shoulder.

He introduced himself and asked her to dance before he could lose his nerve.

Clay was only mostly shocked when she accepted.

Chapter Four

Hiding the fact that there were butterflies doing a mad dance in her stomach, Reine allowed Clay Dawson to lead her out to the dance floor. Why not? She had time to kill and he might be a good distraction for a while.

On the way, they both set their half-empty glasses on a passing waiter's tray. Reine noticed with interest that Clay had been drinking water. That was unexpected. Either he didn't drink or he had a code of ethics that involved restrictions on alcohol.

That thought disappeared as Clay took her hand in his and settled his other hand at her waist. Even through the filmy fabric of her gown, his touch seemed to radiate heat. Hoping he couldn't hear the way her heartbeat had quickened, Reine placed her left hand on his shoulder, the loop securing her matching purple clutch to her wrist securely in place.

Clay waited a second, as though counting beats in his head, and then seamlessly swept her into the collection of couples swirling around the dance floor at the center of the ballroom.

Only years of experience kept Reine from raising her eyebrows in surprise. She tilted her head to one side, considering her dance partner. What was that old saying her grandfather, God rest his soul, used to say? Never give a sword to a man who couldn't dance?

Well, this man could dance. Reine had danced with better, but for someone who mostly likely had a military background, Clay was not bad at all. He was light on his feet and he didn't grip her too tightly.

This close to him, she noticed that he smelled good. His cologne, which he'd applied lightly, smelled fresh and clean. Through the almost sheer fabric of her gloves, she could tell that his fingers were strong and a little weathered. This was a man who worked with his hands.

Deep down, Reine approved. She could never openly admit it in her line of work, but she liked a man to have hands that were not as smooth—or smoother—than her own.

She looked up into Clay's face just as he looked down at her and lifted an eyebrow with a mischievous smile.

"So, I've told you my name, but you have yet to introduce yourself, Miss…?"

"Delgado. Reine Delgado."

"Miss Delgado." Clay cocked his head. "It *is* 'Miss', right?" He made a show of looking around them. "Don't have to worry about an angry husband coming after me, do I?"

This drew a laugh from Reine. "I don't think anyone has ever asked me if they had to worry about an angry husband before." Over the top of Clay's black-clad shoulder, she glimpsed the Ambassador and his wife waltzing together. Their posture was the easy familiarity of two people who lived their lives together, but there wasn't any obvious passion.

Maybe the rumors were true. Maybe the Ambassador did have a wandering eye and his wife tolerated it. Or perhaps they were simply private people, who kept their emotions and behavior tightly checked in public.

Eight years working in the diplomatic field, and Reine still had yet to figure that out.

She turned her attention back to her dance partner as he asked, "May I call you Reine?"

The sound of his voice saying her name sent a surprising jolt of pleasure through her. She regarded him steadily, a little surprised by his politeness. (Sometimes Americans were entirely too forward.)

Smiling, she inclined her head in a nod. "You may."

The waltz ended and changed to another, a lilting melody with a slightly slower pace that was more conducive to conversation. In the back of her mind, Reine marveled at how even tonight's music had been chosen deliberately with that in mind.

As they settled into a slow dance, Reine canted her head to one side, offering Clay a coy smile. "What brings you to the Embassy tonight, Clay Dawson?"

"Work, I'm afraid."

"Let me guess. Security?"

He pretended to look affronted, before grinning at her, a trifle ruefully. "Is it that obvious?"

Reine found herself smiling back at him, though she tried—and failed—to school her expression into something serious. Even through his tuxedo jacket, she could feel the hard muscles in his shoulder beneath her gloved fingers. "Well, you do have that...military...look about you."

"It's not the hair," he said. "Grew it out on purpose."

"No." Reine scrutinized his sandy brown hair, which curled just a bit around the edges, and her smile widened. "It's not the hair."

Clay spun her around in time to the music. The little girl inside Reine swooned at the way her skirt swirled out and then swished against her legs as he spun her back into position.

A little breathlessly, she said, "It's the way you stand. I've seen it before, in countless men and women who have served in various countries." She freed a hand to wave it in his general direction.

"There is an alertness about you, as though you are always watching everything around you."

"We *are* always watching everything around us," he said seriously, but then he grinned. It lit his entire face, making his hazel eyes sparkle. "Occupational hazard, I'm afraid. Drilled into us right from the start." The sparkle in his eyes abruptly dimmed, something somber flickering through his gaze. "Not sure it ever goes away."

"I'm inclined to agree with you." Reine's smile turned a little softer at the edges. "Have you ever been to South America?"

"No. Not yet. Spent most of my time in the Middle East."

"Ah. May I ask where were you stationed?"

"Afghanistan, mostly. Did a few tours."

That was about what Reine had expected. She nodded, then tilted her head to one side again. "Do you miss it?"

Clay gave her a considering glance, as though debating the best way to answer this. Seeing her genuine curiosity, he shrugged. "I miss having a clear sense of purpose, maybe. This—" he jerked his chin to indicate their surroundings, "—isn't quite the same."

Reine thought of sand and rock and the smell of gunfire on the wind. "No," she said slowly. "I don't see how it could be."

"Don't get me wrong, I'm glad to have something to do." Clay twirled her around again in time to the music, and when he brought her in close again, he gave her a charming smile. "In this job, I get to meet lovely ladies like you."

She acknowledged the compliment with a smile of her own and a flutter of her eyelashes. This American was surprisingly easy to talk to. It would be time for her mission before she knew it.

Curiosity dug little pinprick claws into her again. She studied the bearded contours of Clay's face, noting a couple of faded scars along his hairline on his left side. "Why did you leave the military, if you loved it so much?"

She felt the muscles in his shoulder tense beneath her hand. He looked at her and then looked away, the expression in his hazel eyes going distant. A muscle twitched in his jaw, before he forced himself to relax.

"It was time." Clay turned his gaze back to her, his eyes full of shadows. "Lost a couple of good buddies to an IED. Damn near blew me up too." He shook his head. "When that last tour was up, I decided I'd had enough."

Reine held his gaze, nodding slowly. There was more to it than that, she was sure—there was always more to a story like that—but it would suffice for now. Honestly, it was more than she'd expected him to reveal.

Clay took a breath and the shadows cleared. He smiled, a touch self-deprecatingly. "Enough about me. Tell me about you, Miss Reine Delgado."

"Oh, well, there is not much to tell." Reine took her hand off of his shoulder long enough to wave it casually through the air. It was her turn to offer a self-deprecating smile. "I am basically a glorified diplomatic secretary and messenger girl."

"You're Denquayan, right?"

"Yes. Although I have spent a lot of time in Consulates in various cities here in the United States."

"So you travel around a lot?" Clay's eyes twinkled. "I can relate."

"I'm sure you can."

The music changed as the orchestra shifted to a slow, elegant ballad more suited for standing mostly still and swaying in place. (Not everyone who attended these parties knew how to waltz, and Karina Ambrose was well aware of that.)

Clay shifted his grip slightly, bringing Reine a little closer. Her heartbeat quickened again at this increase in proximity. She inhaled, feeling heat rise to her cheeks. Oh, he smelled amazing.

Something about the way he looked at her made her feel like she was the only woman in the room. She felt like he could *see* her—see straight past her defenses to the real her inside.

She drew in another, slightly shaky, breath. *This is dangerous.* She was a woman on a mission tonight; she didn't have time to get sidetracked by a charming American security contractor, no matter how…attracted…she was to him.

She was going to have to nip this in the bud.

Chapter Five

Clay couldn't remember the last time he'd felt so at ease around a woman he felt such a strong attraction to. It was beyond strange. Part of him felt like he'd reverted to his awkward teenager self again—all thumbs and left feet and hot and bothered under the collar—while at the same time another part of him marveled at how easy it was to talk to Reine.

For a lower middle-class boy from Northern Kentucky, an event like this one was so far out of his comfort zone it might as well have been in the stratosphere. He wasn't used to rubbing elbows with politicians, diplomats, and the extremely wealthy, even in a working capacity. Rob and Naomi kept assuring him he'd get used to it eventually, but most of the time Clay felt like an impostor walking around these parties in a tuxedo.

Right now, though…

Clay looked down at the woman in his arms. The lights from the chandelier gave Reine's dark hair a glossy sheen, and made the fabric of her purple dress shimmer. He wasn't sure if it was her hair or her perfume, but she smelled like cherries. The good kind of cherry scent, not the one that reminded him of nasty cold medicines he'd taken when he was growing up.

Like most of the women here, she was probably wearing heels, which put her head a few inches above his shoulder. Without them, Clay suspected the top of her head would probably be level with his shoulder. He couldn't help thinking that either way she was the perfect height for him.

He looked down at her as they swayed to a classical piece of music he didn't recognize. Unlike some of the other women here tonight, her makeup was tasteful and enhanced her features rather than just being caked on.

His eyes darted to her lips, before he forcibly dragged his gaze back up to her eyes. *Don't go there, Dawson*, he warned himself. She was out of his league and he knew it. (And even if she wasn't, he could practically hear the lecture Rob would give him about getting involved—or wanting to get involved—with somebody at an event they were working.)

To distract himself, he arched a playful sandy brown eyebrow. "I'm not keeping you from any other potential dance partners, am I?"

For an instant, Reine looked startled, and then she laughed. Clay instantly loved the sound of her laugh. It was like music—sweet, tinkling bells. A part of his mind started plotting how he could make her laugh again.

"No," she said, laughter still coloring her voice. She made an exaggerated show of looking around, mimicking his earlier motion. "No, I don't think anyone else is waiting."

"Good. Their loss." A flicker of satisfaction curled through Clay. He didn't want to share her attention with anyone else. Selfishly, he found himself wanting to spend as much time with her as he could at this fancy shindig.

Reine looked at him, and for a second, Clay thought he glimpsed surprise in her dark eyes, as though this sentiment wasn't one she encountered often. He pushed that aside; he'd probably imagined it. A woman as beautiful as she was, working in the diplomatic corps, probably had all kinds of opportunities to meet men.

He was just lucky to be in the right place at the right time tonight.

Chapter Six

"How long have you worked for the Ambassador?"

Clay's voice brought her back to herself. Reine lifted both bare shoulders in a careless little shrug. "Eight years, give or take. On the whole, I quite enjoy it."

That was true, even if the politics of the job sometimes wore on her.

"How did you get into it?" Clay asked with interest. "Does your family still live in Denquay? How do they handle you being gone overseas so much?"

Usually, Reine preferred not to talk about her parents. And if pressed, she then kept the summary of her past woes as brief and succinct as possible.

She opened her mouth to give him this brief history...but instead found herself saying, "My father was the Ambassador to Brazil. My mother and I traveled with him everywhere. When I was ten, we took a trip back to Denquay for the holidays."

Old emotion rose inside her; she tamped it down. "Some members of a political faction that disagreed with our president at the time's current foreign policies bombed the house where we were staying." She smiled, but there was nothing mirthful about the expression. "I survived. My parents did not."

"I'm sorry."

Reine allowed herself to meet Clay's eyes, expecting to find pity. That was what she usually encountered when this subject came up. Instead, she found compassion and understanding. A knot of unexpected emotion swelled in her chest.

She pressed her lips into a thin line while she composed herself. When she thought she could speak without her voice breaking, she said, "I joined the diplomatic corps when I was eighteen." She smiled again, this time with real warmth. "I wanted to help make a difference for our country."

"Like your parents," Clay said with a nod. His fingers tightened momentarily on hers.

"Something like that."

"And have you?"

Reine's breath caught in her threat. This man and his questions... She couldn't remember the last time anyone had taken the time to talk to her like this. Usually, she was the one probing for information.

Belatedly, she realized he was waiting for an answer. "I would like to think I have. But, honestly, some days I just don't know." She took her hand off his shoulder to gesture to the ballroom around them. "Probably every single person in this room would claim that they're working to make the world a better place. But have we?"

"Doesn't feel like it some days, does it?" Clay asked wryly.

"No."

Silence fell over them, filled with laughter and the buzz of a dozen different conversations, overlaid with beautiful strains of music.

"You know," Clay said, his voice soft and low. "There are people who don't like the military. They think people like me who want to serve our country are nuts, think that we're being used to prop up the American government on a global scale."

Reine lifted her eyebrows in silent curiosity. Where was he going with this, exactly?

"But those people haven't been the places I've been, seen the things that I've seen." Clay shook his head, the shadows returning to his hazel eyes again. "There *is* evil in this world, and it's not relegated to any one country or part of the planet. It's everywhere." He shook his head again. "Some places it's just a little more obvious."

Reine felt the truth of those words settle in her chest. "This is true," she said, equally quietly.

"The thing is—" Clay held her gaze, the look in his green-brown eyes intense, "—if we don't stand up for the people who can't stand up for themselves, who will?" He swallowed. "That's why I fought."

Reine nodded slowly, feeling threads of kinship weave themselves around the pair of them. *Me too,* she wanted to say. That was why she'd joined the Intelligence Division when they recruited her.

That was partly why she was here tonight, preparing to investigate her own Ambassador's First Secretary.

She couldn't tell Clay any of that, however. Instead, she simply said, "I understand."

And she did—more than Clay Dawson would probably ever know.

Chapter Seven

Clay felt a somber mood settle over them, like someone had thrown a heavy black veil over their heads, dimming the light from the chandelier and the music and noise of the party. It pressed down on him, weighing more than he ever remembered his pack weighing. Forcing a smile, he cast about for something to say that would lighten the mood again.

His words—in all five languages he spoke—seemed to have temporarily abandoned him. He couldn't think of anything to say that didn't sound completely stupid and inane. A bubble of panic rose in his chest, sending sharp pangs shooting through him.

If he didn't find a way to keep things going, this would be the part where she thanked him for the dance and moved on to better waters. Clay had to force himself to relax. The last thing he wanted right now was to lose track of Reine for the evening.

In that moment, he admitted to himself that he was *highly* attracted to this woman and he wasn't afraid who knew it.

In the back of his mind, he knew he had a job to do here tonight, but he couldn't quite bring himself to care. It had been a long time since he'd met a woman who made him forget what he was doing.

Reine saved him by asking, "Have you ever been to South America?"

Clay grabbed this for the life preserver it was. "No." He shook his head, relief curling through him. "Not yet. I spent most of my time in the Middle East. Afghanistan, mostly," he said, before she could ask.

"Do you know anything about my country?" Reine arched a challenging eyebrow at him, but smiled to let him know she was teasing.

"Actually, I do." Clay maneuvered them around a couple who had stopped short in the middle of the ballroom for some unknown reason. He wondered if they were already a little too inebriated. "I know that Denquay is about the size of New Hampshire, and it's bordered by Suriname, Guyana, and Venezuela. Your main language is French, you have a President, and you have a ton of tropical rainforest."

Reine laughed again, and Clay felt a flush of pride. "Not bad, not bad. I take it you read a brief?" Her dark eyes danced at him.

"Yes, I did." Naomi had prepared it, but Clay would have looked Denquay up regardless. He smiled. "Have to be prepared for an event like tonight. Wouldn't want to be ignorant of our gracious host country."

"That's very wise of you." Reine's fingers traced a pattern on the shoulder of his tuxedo jacket as she held his gaze. "There are some people who don't have enough sense for that."

That attitude, Clay had never understood. He shook his head. "You'd think it would be common sense."

Reine's lovely mouth pursed into a frown. "You would be surprised how uncommon common sense is these days."

"Oh, you have that problem in Denquay too?"

She laughed again, and he grinned. Mission success.

They continued to slowly sway around the dance floor, and the world—the universe itself—seemed to narrow down and disappear until it was just the two of them, in their own little bubble. Because of his training, part of Clay's brain was still on the alert, but this beautiful, amazing woman held most of his attention.

He continued to ask questions about Denquay, and Reine answered them enthusiastically. Yes, the French had originally settled Denquay, before losing the colony to the British for a time. The French had eventually reclaimed it, but over time Denquay had gained their independence.

"As you can imagine, we have a very diverse population. Very colorful." Reine waved a hand to indicate the ballroom. "All those people from France and Great Britain on top of the indigenous people, as well as people who were brought in from the West Indies."

"How many languages do you speak?" Clay asked out of interest. He was willing to bet she spoke at least three.

Reine shrugged, a little self-consciously. "Five, counting one of the lesser-known indigenous dialects."

"That's impressive."

"Eh. I happen to be good at languages. I'm told it runs in the family. What about you?"

It was Clay's turn to shrug. "I speak a few."

Reine arched an eyebrow. "How many is a few?"

"Five, same as you." He shrugged again. "I was working on learning another dialect when my tour ended."

"Wow." Reine looked impressed. "Most Americans I've met are not bilingual, let alone multilingual."

"I'm a rare breed." Embarrassed, Clay steered the conversation in a different direction. Noticing that black-and-white clad waiters were beginning to circulate with trays of hors d'oeuvres, he tipped his head toward the edge of the ballroom. "Are you hungry? Looks like they're serving food now."

To his surprise, Reine's eyes lit up. "Ooh. Yes, I am." She glanced from side to side and then leaned toward him, dropping her voice. "I've been hoping they have shrimp puffs. I do love those."

Another wave of warmth curled through Clay. A woman who didn't pretend that she wasn't interested in mundane things like food? He loved it.

He smiled down at her. "Not sure I've had those, but they sound good."

"Oh, they are." Reine took his hand, craning her neck slightly to get a good glimpse of the contents of the two trays closest to them. "Ooh. This way."

They left the dance floor and she proceeded to lead him through the crowd. At one point, Clay thought he caught sight of Rob looking after them, but he ignored him. They wanted him to network, right? Well, here he was, networking.

It was the most fun Clay'd had at one of these events in a long time.

Chapter Eight

The second hors d'oeuvres tray did have shrimp puffs. Reine let go of Clay's hand and took two as the waiter navigated the crowded edges of the dance floor. Turning back to the American, she handed him one of the small breaded balls.

"I don't know how they make them, but they are amazing." She watched as he popped the entire thing into his mouth and ate it.

His eyes widened. "Wow. Those *are* good."

Reine beamed at him. "I thought you would like them." She ate her own shrimp puff in two bites—even all these years later she hadn't forgotten her mother's etiquette training—and eyed the next passing tray. It held several types of cheeses, held together by fancy toothpicks, as well as a tiny sandwich she recognized as vegetarian, but couldn't recall the name of.

For the next few minutes, they grazed the various hors d'oeuvres, casually meandering around the ballroom. Every once in a while, Reine made eye contact with someone she knew and nodded politely. In a few cases, conversation was unavoidable.

She wasn't high enough up in the hierarchy that anyone cared much if she spent the evening dancing with an American, but now and again she noticed they were garnering a few judgmental looks. She ignored these.

The conversations...were a little trickier, but she was pleased by how well Clay handled them. He was polite and complimented Denquayan hospitality where appropriate.

"You are better at navigating all this than you give yourself credit," she said eventually, when they were back on the dance floor again.

Clay ducked his head. "Not really, but thanks."

"Modest, too."

"That part's not hard." He chuckled, and the husky rumble sent butterflies spinning around in Reine's insides again. "I'm out of my element here."

"You're doing well." She smiled at him, wondering suddenly what it would feel like to run her fingers through the curling hair at the nape of his neck. The thought drew her up short internally. When was the last time she'd thought that about a man?

"Only because I'm with you." Clay smiled at her, but beneath the flirtation, his hazel eyes held a serious note. "I don't believe I've ever met anyone quite like you, Reine Delgado."

Oh, he didn't even know the half of it. Reine bit down on the inside of her lip. What would he say if he knew what the *other* half of her job entailed?

She had a sudden, mad urge to tell him—to let a few hints drop. The sensible part of her brain immediately squashed those thoughts. In the four years she'd worked for the Intelligence Division, she'd never told a single person what she really did.

She couldn't abandon her training and blow her mission now, just because she'd met a man who interested her in ways she'd never thought she could be interested.

Her mission...

Reine's breath caught in her throat. She'd been so absorbed in getting to know Clay, she'd almost lost track of the real reason she was even here tonight. What time was it?

Her internal clock told her it was close to 10pm, but she needed to check. To that end, she opened her clutch and tapped her cell phone. The screen flashed white numbers.

9:52pm.

It was almost time.

"Everything okay?"

Reine glanced up to find Clay looking at her, his expression keen and interested. His words were light, but she sensed something behind them. In that moment, she had the strangest sensation. Somehow, she knew without being told in words that if she was in trouble, this man would do his best to help her.

She offered him a sunny smile. "It is nothing." She snapped her clutch closed. "Merely checking to make sure my boss hasn't decided to make me work tonight and sent me instructions on someone specific to talk to." Her smile turned wry. "That happens, sometimes."

"I can imagine." Clay glanced over his shoulder. Reine suspected he was probably checking for his partners in Blackthorn Security.

A little thrill shot through her. It was nice, for a change, to have a man's full attention instead of knowing he was only interested in talking to her until someone more important came along. She didn't have much experience with that.

Unfortunately, she could feel time slipping past. She had work to do.

Reine looked up into Clay's face, regret blossoming in her chest. For the first time in a long time, she hated to leave one of these parties. It was strange—Clay's company had turned a nearly two-hour slog into a chunk of her evening that had vanished in an eyeblink.

She was so glad to have met him—

—but now she had to figure out how to leave him without letting him know she was leaving him.

Her heart wrenched. Whether she wanted to or not.

Her country came first.

Letting her smile turn a little shy around the edges, Reine lightly touched his arm and then nodded toward the exit. "If you'll excuse me, I need to powder my nose."

Chapter Nine

As he watched Reine's beautiful, purple-clad form disappear behind a knot of guests, Clay's smile slowly faded. A thoughtful heaviness formed in his chest. Something told him she wasn't coming back.

He didn't understand how he knew that, he just...did. Something between them had changed after Reine checked her phone. He'd never claimed to be especially attuned to the way a woman's mind worked, but he'd grown attuned to *her* over the past two hours, and she was...different...after that.

It felt like an invisible shield had gone up between them, like she was trying to figure out how to politely extricate herself from his company.

Clay took a deep breath. Maybe he was reading more into the situation than was warranted. Nothing more than that.

But...he couldn't shake the feeling that something wasn't right.

He'd always been had a good sense about people. He was naturally observant and was used to keeping track of what was going on around him. In the military, you didn't make it outside the wire if you wandered around oblivious to everything.

That instinct had saved his life on more than one occasion.

Now, Clay wished he was a little more clueless. If he wasn't quite so observant, he could spend the next hour telling himself that Reine would come back, that she'd only gotten pulled into a conversation with someone else and would reappear at any moment. He'd tell himself that they'd laugh about it when she came back, and then she'd spend the rest of the night in his arms.

His instincts knew better.

He'd gotten a glimpse of her phone display when she'd checked it, and there hadn't been any text, emails, or other notifications. But something *had* changed.

Was it the time? Did she have an appointment with somebody?

Clay suppressed a snort. If he was anywhere else, the thought of somebody having a political appointment at ten o'clock at night would have been laughable, but they *were* in Washington D.C. *and* Reine was in politics.

Once again, he resisted the urge to scrub a hand through his hair. It figured. He finally met a woman he wanted to spend more time with, and she pulled a Cinderella on him.

His lips twitched in a rueful smile. Minus the glass slipper.

The second that thought crossed his mind, he wanted to groan. He was crazy. Worse, *she* was going to think he was crazy.

The room suddenly seemed to shrink around him, the air growing close and stale. The combined sound of the music and dozens of conversations grated on his nerve, making him wish he could clap his hands over his ears and shut it all out. He wanted to leave the Embassy, wanted to escape out into D.C.'s night air. It might be muggy as hell, but it had to be better than staying in here.

Clay took another breath, willing himself to stay frosty. Mentally, he shook his head. Oh, if Rob got wind of this, he'd never let Clay hear the end of it.

Head over heels for a woman he'd only just met—a woman he'd

probably never see again after tonight? Rob would get mileage out of that for *months*.

A hand clapped him roughly on the shoulder. Clay started, his hands automatically forming fists as he turned, but then he realized it was Rob. He forced himself to relax before they drew attention.

"Rob." He shot his friend a warning look. *Speak of the devil.*

"Where's your friend?" Rob looked around with interest, his dark eyes scanning the people closest to them. He was tall and wiry, with a thin face and dark hair that was going prematurely gray at the temples. The lankiness of his form threw people off; Rob was much faster and much stronger than he looked. He was also a crack shot and had an aptitude for strategy.

"More importantly," Rob rested an arm on Clay's shoulder, "*who is she?*"

None of your business, Clay wanted to retort, but instead he shrugged carelessly. "One of the Ambassador's secretaries. Good dancer."

There was so much more he wanted to say, but he held it back. Rob wouldn't care about Reine for any of the reasons Clay found her fascinating. Neither would Naomi.

If Reine didn't have the connections to get them a good paying job, neither of them would consider her of any further use. Or worth any more of Clay's time.

"Huh." Rob looked around again, before he straightened and let his arm fall to the side. He pinned Clay with a considering look. "Well, I'm glad you've had a good evening so far, but it's probably just as well you're taking a break." His eyes narrowed slightly as he lowered his voice to add, "Don't forget why we're here, Dawson."

"Perish the thought," Clay said lightly, though the last thing he wanted to do right now was stand here and have this conversation. When Rob's considering expression didn't change, he rolled his eyes. "Rob. Don't worry. I'm focused."

That was probably stretching the truth a little, but... Clay was *always* focused. He didn't relax much, he didn't take much time off from the job. He'd never had a reason to.

Until now.

Not that Rob would appreciate the timing of that realization.

Still... Clay held his friend's gaze until Rob slowly nodded. "Okay, then," he said, before melting back into the crowd of evening gowns and tuxedos.

Clay watched him go out of the corner of his eye and saw a glimpse of a woman in burnt orange moving Rob's direction. Great. He let out an irritated breath. Now Naomi and Rob were conferring. No doubt he'd get an earful later.

Okay, maybe he'd stretched the truth a little, but, whatever. Clay brushed that thought aside. So what if they didn't think he was focused? They both knew how much he hated soirees like these. They weren't his style. Never had been, no matter how many times Naomi told him he'd eventually get used to them.

That wasn't the point right now. The real point was that if he had to choose between work and talking to Reine some more...Clay would choose Reine. Hands down.

He wasn't exactly sure what that said about his future with Blackthorn Security, but at the moment he didn't care. He'd think about that tomorrow.

Right now, he needed to find Reine.

Chapter Ten

The ladies' restroom in the hall outside the ballroom was a fancy affair, all black marble and hardwood and gleaming silver fixtures. A discreetly hidden air-freshener sent a periodic cloud of something that smelled tropical into the air. As Reine slipped inside, she immediately noted that one of the stalls was occupied.

Her eyes narrowed. That would delay her just a bit. Ducking in a stall at the end, she pulled off one of her gloves and waited for the other woman to leave. She had a very narrow window of opportunity.

As soon as she heard the faint swish of the door swinging open, Reine bolted out of the stall. She hurried to the left side of the ornate black marble sink. Her eyes flicked to her reflection in the large oval mirror that stretched sideways along the length of the black counter. She looked calm, a little pale around the edges, but calm.

For a split second, she wondered what Clay saw when he looked at her. Then she promptly banished that thought. She didn't have time to worry about anything like that.

Instead, she plunged her ungloved hand into the round hole that had been carved into the marble sink top for trash and felt around on the underside of the counter. Her questing fingers encountered soft fabric and electrical tape and relief surged through her. Yes—there it was.

Exactly where she'd hidden it the day before.

Reine ripped the little package off the underside of the sink where she'd fastened it and pulled it out. She held a small black bag with strips of black electrical tape on it. She'd fastened the bag in a corner of the sink's underside, where the cleaning staff would be unlikely to see it in the shadows when they emptied the trash.

Opening her clutch, Reine dumped the bag's contents inside. She now possessed a small burner cell, a small Y-shaped USB connector with a micro-SD card reader on one side and a USB-C connector on the other, and a couple of other small items she might need for tonight's mission. She then dropped the empty bag into the trash. She couldn't risk coming back for it.

That done, it was the work of seconds to tug her elbow-length glove back on. She checked her reflection once more in the mirror. Good. Not a hair out of place. Coolly, she glided out of ladies' restroom and back into the hall.

Reine started toward the doors to the ballroom, but stopped partway, shaking her head as though she'd just remembered something. She abruptly turned around and hurried over to the staircase that led up to the next floor. It was roped off with red velvet cords, to warn the birthday party guests they were not allowed to go that way.

One of Ambassador Ambrose's security men should have been posted here, but he was nowhere to be seen. Reine suppressed a frown, glancing up and down the hall. She'd had a story prepared to feed him, but it looked like she wouldn't need it.

The hair on the back of her neck prickled uneasily. Strangely fortuitous, that. Why was Gregorio not at his post?

For a nanosecond, she wondered if she should write tonight's mission off. This was an unforeseen wrinkle and she didn't know what it meant. Maybe it would be better to try again another time instead of risking it.

In the next nanosecond, Reine dismissed that idea. Too much rode on tonight's mission, and there was nothing that overtly indicated she might be walking into a trap.

No, she needed to stay the course. She was more or less invisible. That was why the Intelligence Division had recruited her in the first place.

She was the only person at the Embassy tonight who could do this job.

With one last glance over her shoulder, Reine ducked under the velvet rope, hurried up the thick carpeted stairs and turned the corner at the landing. She took the remaining stairs at the same brisk pace—no need to draw any unnecessary attention to herself on the building's internal security cameras by doing anything out of the ordinary—and emerged into the darkness of the wide hall that connected the offices on the top floor.

Frames containing some of the Ambassador's favorite pieces of Denquayan art lined either side of the hall. In the faint light from the stairwell, the frames cast strange shadows along the cream walls. Reine walked the hall from memory, heading for the second door on the left, the office she shared with several other members of Ambassador Ambrose's staff for the duration of her stay at the D.C. Embassy.

Ultimately, she needed to get into Ariane Montoya's office at the other end of the hall, but to keep her cover intact, she'd have to start here. She could claim she was checking on a reply to an important email she'd sent earlier to one of the diplomats back in Denquay. That wasn't a lie—she did need to make sure that response came through.

Reine had cultivated a reputation for being quiet, careful, and thorough. She did her best to handle all aspects of her job seamlessly. If anyone—from the Ambassador and the First Secretary all the way down to the Embassy's security—checked security footage later, they'd just roll their eyes at her compulsive need to be thorough. No one would think anything of her leaving the birthday party for a few minutes.

Even so, Reine's heart beat a little faster in her chest as she booted up her computer, and then opened up her secure email client to check on the status of that email. Once she did this, she would need to get into the Embassy's security cameras.

Nothing happened. Frowning, Reine hit the login button again.

Still, nothing.

She blinked once, twice, and then checked whether or not the internet was working. A faint wave of shock coursed through her when she realized it was out.

That had never happened before. Not at this Embassy. Actually, she couldn't recall the internet ever being out at any of the Denquayan embassies or consulates she'd ever served at.

In this modern world of global communications, Denquay prided itself on ensuring all its citizens had access to fast, cheap, reliable internet access. That included their embassies and consulates world-wide.

This was new.

A wave of frustration rolled through her, so intense that she actually ground her teeth together. She wanted to stamp her foot on the carpet like her best friend back in Denquay's three year-old daughter had done the last time she visited. All this planning, all this anticipation, and now the stupid internet went out right before she needed it?

Insufferable, she thought. *Absolutely insufferable.*

And then her mind flashed back to the missing security guard at the bottom of the stairs. Reine breathed in through her nose, pressing her lips into a thin line. *It's probably a coincidence.*

The fact that the internet was out and Gregorio wasn't where he was supposed to be were *probably* unrelated.

Probably.

Reine bit down on the inside of her lip, staring at the pale glow of her unresponsive email client on her computer screen. She didn't believe that, however. Something twisted uneasily in the pit of her stomach.

This wasn't right. She didn't know what it was, exactly, but something was definitely off.

She resisted the urge to glance at the security camera she knew was hidden in a corner of the office. The camera was all but invisible during the day and didn't give off any light at night.

The Ambassador had pushed for—and received—a digital upgrade to the Embassy's CCTV system a couple of years earlier. Reine couldn't claim to know the intimate details of how the system worked, but she did know that even if the cameras couldn't sync with their server until the internet came back on, they still recorded everything locally.

Which meant that her mission might be officially kibitzed now.

Disappointment tangled with anxiety in her stomach. On her own, she didn't rank anywhere near high enough to be able to access the Embassy's cameras, but...*she* didn't have to. The burner cell phone in her clutch Erica had provided her, courtesy of the Intelligence Division, contained a copy of the app that interfaced with the security system and they had provided her with login credentials.

Unfortunately, though, without the internet, she couldn't even access the app to do anything with the cameras—and she was almost out of time.

Her window of opportunity had nearly closed. On the security cameras, her presence up here for much longer would be too suspicious.

Unable to restrain a disappointed sigh, Reine closed her email client and shut her computer down. She then picked up her clutch, straightened up and moved to one side so she could roll her chair back to its place in front of her desk.

At that moment, a shadowy figure suddenly filled the doorway, blocking out light from the hall.

Heart in her throat, Reine looked up just as the office light snapped on, temporarily blinding her.

A familiar male voice asked, "Everything okay?"

Reine's voice hit a high note in her surprise. "*Clay?*"

Chapter Eleven

Clay watched Reine stop in the hall and turn around, as though she'd forgotten something, but he still couldn't shake the feeling that something about her was off. What was she doing? Frowning, he edged out of the men's restroom as he watched her vanish up the staircase that led to the Embassy's top floor.

He glanced from side to side along the hall, but it was still empty and quiet, save for the noise from the ballroom. Everyone else in the Embassy seemed to be enjoying the party. He crossed the hall to the stairs, his footfalls making barely a sound against the lush pile of the carpet. Ducking under the red velvet rope just as Reine had done, he slowly followed her upstairs.

Clay swallowed uneasily. He'd done plenty of surveillance before, in his career as a Marine, but this was…different. Following Reine like this made him question his own motives.

I feel like a stalker, he realized belatedly.

Granted, it was out of a desire to help, but… He smiled ruefully to himself. Reine might not see it that way.

Still… He'd made it this far—and he *still* couldn't shake a gut sense that something was wrong. Maybe it was better to ask forgiveness than permission, in this particular situation.

And if Reine didn't want to ever see him again after this… Clay clenched his jaw, then forced himself to relax. Well, it was a small price to pay for his peace of mind. At least he'd have the satisfaction of knowing she was okay.

When he reached the top of the stairs, part of him expected to hear warning shouts from below. He wasn't supposed to be up here —and a place like this most definitely had security cameras. Any minute, someone would sound an alarm and a guard would be dispatched to quietly escort him back to the party.

Clay's lips twitched again. Or he'd be kicked out of the Embassy entirely. Wouldn't Rob and Naomi *love* that? He could just imagine the lecture Rob would give him on the business he might have cost them.

He pushed thoughts of his fellow members of Blackthorn Security aside to focus on the situation at hand. The hall was quiet and empty—and dark.

Clay narrowed his eyes. Reine hadn't turned on any lights. That was…strange.

He edged down the wide hall, moving quietly along the dark carpet. The tropical scent of the Embassy's air-freshener seemed a little stronger up here. The pale walls were covered in framed pictures, though in the semi-darkness he couldn't make out if they were art or photographs.

Doors led off of the hall at staggered intervals—probably offices. Most of them were closed, but there were two open. One was toward the far end of the hall, and the other was a yard away on his left. Clay listened for movement to indicate which direction Reine had gone.

He didn't hear anything.

His confusion deepened. What was she *doing* up here? His eyes tracked from the open door to his left to the one at the end of the hall and resolve hardened in his chest. He'd have to check both of them.

He considered the closed doors, but dismissed them off-hand. He hadn't heard a door shut—and unless these doors were *insanely* quiet, he'd have heard that.

Clay took a breath, his training kicking in and helping him regulate his heartbeat and his breathing. *You're just checking rooms to see where an attractive woman went,* he told himself. *It's not like you're facing possibly getting shot at when you poke your head around the doorway.*

At least, he *hoped* not.

Given that he really didn't know what was going on here, there was a probably a tiny chance that he *was* about to be shot at.

In the back of his mind, Clay thought wryly that if the guys manning the security cams weren't on their way to him yet, they would be. He knew how suspicious he looked.

But, he wasn't dumb enough to just blindly walk into a dark room, either.

Flattening himself up against the wall, Clay edged close to the doorway. He peeked around the doorframe—just far enough to see inside—and felt a knot inside him unwind.

Reine leaned over a desk, her face lit with the pale, unearthly white glow of a computer screen. Her entire body radiated irritation, but she was otherwise alone and seemed perfectly fine.

She's fine.

Clay wasn't sure if it was relief or courage or insanity—or some combination of the three—that precipitated his next movement.

He stepped into the doorway, right hand reaching instinctively for the light switch that was probably right there. Reine looked up just as his fingers touched a light switch panel. Warm golden light flooded the room.

"Are you okay?" he asked, remaining in the doorway so as not to startle her further.

It took a second for his eyes to adjust, but he saw the moment

Reine's eyes adjusted and she recognized him. Her mouth fell open in astonishment. "Clay?"

She looked and sounded so surprised and taken aback, standing there in that shimmering purple gown that made her look like a goddess, that guilt flickered in the pit of Clay's stomach. He opened his mouth to say something—what, he wasn't sure—but Reine beat him to it.

Drawing herself up to her full height, she propped her hands on her hips and regarded him sternly. "What are you doing up here? Unauthorized personnel are *not* allowed up that staircase." She nodded firmly in the direction of the stairs.

Clay swallowed, even as his stomach sank. Yep, this had definitely been a bad idea. The nascent, half-formed ideas he'd entertained this evening of seeing Reine after tonight popped like so many fragile soap bubbles.

"I just wanted to make sure you were all right." He lifted a hand to the back of his neck, feeling sheepish. If he been afraid earlier that he'd reverted to his awkward teenage self, he felt like he'd gone all the way back to silly little boy now. "Reine, I—"

He broke off as a burst of distant gunfire shattered the stillness that permeated this floor of the Embassy.

Chapter Twelve

Reine froze in place standing behind her mahogany desk, her eyes wide with shock. She felt as though someone had just thrown a bucket of icy water over her head. Gunfire? In the *Embassy?*

The familiar environs of the rather luxurious office she shared with several other of the Ambassador's staff members took on an alien cast. The gold curtains draping the windows, the bright artwork on the cream walls, the shiny computers, flatscreen monitors, and other assorted paraphernalia cluttering all three desks—it all suddenly looked otherworldly. The edges were too sharp, the colors too bright. The scent of the sandalwood incense that Clara, Ariane's secretary, kept on her desk threatened to make Reine's stomach revolt.

Another burst of gunfire sounded, followed by distant shouts and screams, and her knees almost buckled. She grabbed for the edge of her desk, gripping it so tightly her knuckles turned white. Her eyes sought Clay's.

For one crazy second, she wondered if he knew what was going on. He was a former soldier. Gunfire was his thing, after all.

But Clay's hazel eyes were just as wide and surprised as her own. Realization slapped Reine with the force of a real blow. She was being ridiculous. Of *course* he didn't know what was going on either. He was a guest at the Embassy tonight, for Pete's sake.

She took a breath, trying to get a grip on herself, and opened her mouth. Words died in her throat as another series of shouts pummeled the air, these sounding a little closer.

That was when Clay exploded into motion.

In one breathtakingly smooth motion, he slapped the light switch panel to kill the overhead light and bounded across the office to the desk where she stood. Wrapping an arm around her shoulders, he pulled her down behind the desk beside him.

"Kill your computer," he said, his voice barely audible.

His body was a warm, solid presence beside her. Reine felt the heat from him soaking into her side. When had she gotten so cold?

With shaking fingers, she reached up over the edge of the desk and pressed the button to turn her monitor off. Then she grabbed her clutch from where she'd laid it on the desk's surface and sank back down behind her desk, crouched on the thick carpeted floor next to Clay in her high heeled shoes. Darkness flooded the room, save for a swathe of faint illumination that fell through the doorway from the distant lights in the hall at the bottom of the stairs.

Reine was amazingly hyperaware of Clay. She could feel every inch where the hard planes of his body pressed up against her side. She could feel the strength in the muscled arm wrapped protectively around her shoulders. Sparks seemed to radiate out from wherever he touched her.

A shuddery breath escaped her lips. She should probably feel annoyed that he'd followed her up here, but in this moment, all she felt was relief and a profound sense of gratitude that she wasn't alone.

For a nanosecond, Reine let herself imagine what it would be like to be up here by herself, facing whatever was happening tonight completely cut off from everyone else in the Embassy. A fine shiver worked its way down her spine.

It wasn't a pretty picture.

"Any idea what's going on?" Clay asked quietly, breath warm against her ear.

Reine shook her head, before belatedly remembering that he couldn't see the movement in the dark room. "No."

She thought Ambassador Ambrose and his wife, of all the people she'd come to know during her stints traveling back and forth between Denquay's various embassies and consulates. Dread roiled inside her. Fear pressed clammy hands against her chest, making her heart hammer.

Was anyone dead? Were they hurt? What was—

"Breathe." Clay's arm tightened around her shoulders. "Just breathe. Nice and slow. It's going to be okay."

His words were little more than a whisper, but they sank into Reine like raindrops on parched ground. She drew in a shaky breath, trying to calm herself.

Clay's clean, comforting scent surrounded her, making her feel safe. That was a little surprising, given that they'd only known each other for a couple of hours, but Reine wasn't about to question it. For a couple of heartbeats, she let herself lean against him.

Clay briefly rested his cheek on the top of her head, lending her strength, before he straightened. Alert. Ready for whatever would happen next.

Reine's heartbeat was so loud in her own ears she wondered if Clay could hear it. She inhaled again, slowly expanding her lungs in an effort to stave off hyperventilation. She needed to *think*.

Terrorists were trying to take over the Embassy. Reine pressed a hand to her heart. Maybe even had *succeeded* in taking over the Embassy.

But why? And why tonight? Because it was Karina Ambrose's birthday, a high-profile event?

Beside her, Clay shifted position slightly. "Do you have any idea who's down there?"

"No."

"Does the Ambassador have any enemies capable of pulling off something like this?"

"I don't know." Reine tried to think back, closing her eyes as she cycled back through hundreds of memories from the past couple of years. "Maybe?"

"What about politics back home?"

Reine stilled, drawing in another deep breath. Now *that* was a distinct possibility.

She couldn't tell Clay about the investigation that had been launched into Ambrose's staff. Or her part in it. But now she couldn't help wondering if they were related.

Of course, there were other issues too. She swallowed. "The President has...implemented a few rather unpopular policies concerning renewable resources and some of Denquay's rainforests."

And he'd declared a crackdown on the production of illegal drugs. That hadn't gone over well either. In some quarters of the world, drugs made certain individuals even more money than controlling renewable resources.

Reine couldn't tell Clay that either, even though she suspected he was probably already familiar with that particular fact.

"Environmental crazies with guns?" Clay sounded doubtful. She couldn't blame him. "Always thought chaining themselves to trees or gluing themselves to paintings was more their style."

"It's complicated." That was probably the understatement of the year. "There is a lot of money involved on either side."

Another series of faint screams carried up the staircase and down the hall to them. Reine trembled. If it weren't for her mission, she'd be down there right now. She glanced sideways through the darkness at Clay. They'd probably still have been dancing.

Her mission. She tightened her grip on her purple clutch, which was nestled in her lap. Embassy takeover or no, she still had a mission to accomplish.

Erica and the rest of the Intelligence Division would expect no less. She could almost hear her handler's voice in her ear. *It's a dangerous situation, but it's an excellent distraction. Take advantage of it.*

Reine breathed in and then breathed out, imagining her fear flowing out of her like early morning mist burning away as the sun grew brighter.

Her eyes widened as another disturbing thought struck her. "Do you think anybody outside the Embassy knows what's happened yet?"

"No idea," Clay said grimly, his voice still a barely audible. "Depends on whether or not anybody's managed to call 911 or get a text out." He shifted a little closer to her. "What's Embassy protocol for a terrorist attack?"

A hot flush of embarrassment suddenly flared in her cheeks. That...was an excellent question. What *was* the protocol? She couldn't remember.

"I'm not sure," she said sheepishly. "One of the security chiefs gave a presentation a few months ago, but I don't remember much of it. He didn't say much other than for us to get to a secure room and barricade ourselves in. Seemed to think that in the event something *did* happen, Embassy security would be able to handle it."

They'd gotten complacent—and now they were paying for it.

"This one of those offices?"

Reine shook her head out of habit. "No. The Ambassador's office and the First Secretary."

She fumbled in her clutch for her cell phone. Hers, not the burner she'd been given. If she was going to call for help, it had to come through the correct channels.

Just as she unlocked her phone, a low rumble of male voices carried down the hall. She and Clay both froze.

Reine instinctively flipped her phone upside down on her lap, hiding the glow of the screen in her skirt while she hit the power button to shut the screen off again.

Her heart hammered in her chest. The thick carpet throughout this floor made it almost impossible to hear footsteps.

Was someone coming? Were they searching the offices?

She almost couldn't breathe. If the terrorists *were* searching the offices, was it because they knew she, specifically, was missing, or was it just a general sweep?

Clay removed his arm from around her shoulders and straightened. Reine immediately missed his warmth. He pressed a hand to her shoulder, warning her with a touch to stay down.

Then, with a faint rustle of his tuxedo, he rose to his feet and crept around her desk.

From her position on the floor, Reine watched his shadowy form through the thick legs of the desk. Clay picked his way around the office, staying in the black shadows to one side of faint wedge of light coming through the doorway. When he reached the wall beside the door, he flattened himself against it.

Reine pressed a hand to her mouth. Was he doing what she *thought* he was doing?

Her heart leaped into her throat as, for the second time that night, a shadow loomed in the doorway.

Chapter Thirteen

Clay pressed his shoulders to the wall just far enough away from the light switch that a questing hand wouldn't accidentally brush up against him. He turned his head sideways so he could watch the door and waited.

The terrorists were coming for them. Didn't matter if they knew anybody was up here or not. Anyone with the guts and smarts to execute a takeover of an embassy like this would have their people sweep the place for strays.

The only question was how much time he and Reine had.

Turned out it wasn't long.

Less than a minute later, a shadowy figure loomed in the doorway. A hand reached around the doorframe, searching for the light switch.

Clay grabbed that wrist before the person found the light and hauled the shadowy figure inside the office. The man—it was a man—hadn't been expecting that.

Clay used that second's worth of surprise to his advantage. Jabbing the man in the throat with his free hand, he stripped the man's rifle out of his hands before he could squeeze off a shot and tossed it aside into the black shadows at their feet.

Gasping and gagging, the man tried to put up a fight.

Clay kicked him in the knee and then grabbed him in a headlock, but not before the man slammed his head into the doorframe.

They grappled for a handful of seconds that felt like hours. The man clawed at Clay, trying to reach his face and gouge his eyes out. Grimacing, Clay squeezed harder, putting inexorable pressure on the man's carotid artery.

His opponent kicked and thrashed, but he'd been caught off-guard and Clay was *strong*

In a moment, it was over. The man went limp in Clay's grip. Clay remained frozen in place, however, straining his ears for any sign that the sound of their struggle had drawn attention from someone else out in the hall.

Nothing but the pounding of his own heartbeat met his ears.

Quickly, he dragged the man to one side of the dark office and lowered him to the carpet. Out of the corner of his eye, he glimpsed movement through the darkness, but it was only Reine. Ignoring her for a second, Clay knelt and rifled through the man's pockets.

He emerged with a wicked-looking fold-out knife, a cell phone, and a handful of zip ties. No wallet.

Clay narrowed his eyes. That meant no ID, which meant there was no way he'd gotten into the Embassy the normal way. He set the knife and the cell phone aside and quickly used the zip ties to bind his unconscious opponent's hands and feet together.

"Does he have ID?" Reine asked in a whisper.

"Not that I can find." Clay pressed a button on the cell phone, but of course the screen was locked. He turned the light on the unconscious man's face. "Do you recognize him?"

The cell phone screen's bright light illuminated a man of Hispanic origins, with a thin nose, a black goatee, and neatly trimmed black hair. He was dressed in evening wear, just like everyone else at the birthday party.

He heard Reine swallow. "I've never seen him before in my life."

"Not surprised. He's an underling. Can't believe they only sent one guy up here. Sloppy, that." Clay slipped the man's cell phone into his left pocket so he wouldn't get it confused with his own phone and then recovered the rifle. "AK-47." He shook his head, slinging it over his shoulder. "I swear, the bad guys *always* have these."

In the darkness, Reine's eyes looked huge in her face. "I don't understand."

"It's okay. Just know that I'd be more concerned if this guy was toting something American-made."

Swiftly, Clay stripped off one of the man's shoes—expensive dress shoes, by the feel of them—and one of his socks. He stuffed the sock into the man's mouth as a makeshift gag and then reached down and grabbed his zip-tied ankles. He dragged the man over to one of the other desks and stowed him behind it.

"We can't stay here," he said softly, when he returned to Reine's side. "You said your security protocols call for you to hole up some-place else?"

She stared at him for a few seconds, long enough that he wondered if this beautiful, amazing woman had finally gone into shock on him.

"Reine?"

Reine blinked. "Yes. The office toward the end of the hall. We can go there."

Clay reached out his left hand and clasped her right hand in his. Even through the gloves she still wore, her fingers felt cold. "Follow me."

Chapter Fourteen

The hall outside Reine's office was mercifully empty. Clay shepherded her out of the office and quietly closed the door to her office. Then he escorted her to the other end of the hall, keeping his body as a protective shield between her and any potential attackers who might appear from the stairs.

Reine couldn't help notice that he moved with a smooth grace that told her he had long practice with operations like this. Clearly, whatever Clay had once been in the United States Marines, he'd been good at it.

She'd secured her clutch to her wrist again, but she gripped it tightly anyway. If only Clay knew what was inside that tiny little bag…He'd probably have questions. Lots of questions.

Anxiety and fear swirled together inside her, making her stomach churn. Ariane's office was exactly where she needed to be right now…but Reine had *not* anticipated having an audience along for the ride. She felt Clay's quiet, solid presence behind her and guilt mixed with the fear and anxiety.

She wasn't stupid. The odds of her breaking into Ariane's

computer and cloning her hard drive without Clay realizing something was up were extremely low.

They reached the dark doorway of the office. In one smooth motion, Clay whisked her inside and pushed her down to the carpeted floor. He shut the door with a quiet 'click' and then hit the lights.

They both winced as their eyes adjusted. Reine crouched low, her eyes wide, her mouth dry, and her heart hammering in her chest. The lingering cloying scent of Ariane's perfume filled her nostrils.

Clay swept the barrel of his acquired rifle in an arc through the room, searching for potential targets, but the ornate office was empty.

Just like Reine had hoped.

She sagged in relief, but Clay's alert posture didn't change. Lowering the rifle, he sought her with his gaze. "Can you lock the door?"

It was only then that she realized he was bleeding. A stream of blood covered one side of his face from a gash at his temple. Probably where the terrorist had slammed him into the doorframe.

Reine's fingers itched to touch him. "You're bleeding."

Clay blinked, one hand rising to his temple. His fingers came away wet with blood. He inspected them, then shook his head. "We'll worry about that in a minute. Can you lock the door?"

"Yes." Reine rose to her feet, nearly stepping on the hem of her purple evening gown in the process, and stumbled over to the discreet, fancy security panel mounted into the dark wood paneling beside the heavy wooden door. Her knees felt like they were made of water again. She keyed in her emergency code—she did remember *that*—and listened as the door locked with a rather ominous-sounding 'snickt'.

She started to lean against the door, but Clay shook his head.

"No, no. Come away from the door. In case somebody tries to shoot through it," he explained, but she was already moving.

They both looked around at the luxurious office they now found themselves in. A brown leather couch stood along one wall below the windows that faced the street below. The emerald green curtains were currently drawn, covering the windows. An ornate low-slung mahogany filing cabinet stretched along the wall to their right, beside a door that Reine knew led into a private bathroom.

An assortment of picture frames and a crystal tray with a crystal decanter of rum and matching shot glasses stood atop the smooth, glossy surface of the filing cabinet. On the other side of the office stood a small bookcase. Colorful paintings of Denquay's mountains and rainforests were scattered on the walls.

Clay lifted his eyebrows. "Wow." He nodded to the large mahogany desk in the center of the office, with its shiny Mac computer and equally shiny desk paraphernalia. "This the Ambassador's office?"

"No, it belongs to the First Secretary, Ariane Montoya."

Clay turned in a slow circle in the middle of the floor, inspecting the office's corners. Reine knew what he was looking for even before he asked, "Any cameras in here?"

She shook her head. "There are a few places in the Embassy that are more private than others. This is one of them."

She'd been banking on that fact. She'd just needed to tinker with the cameras that covered her office and the hall so that she could get into Ariane Montoya's office undetected. Now, it didn't matter.

Reine flattened a hand against her churning stomach, looking around. Ariane was an excellent First Secretary. She was intelligent, efficient at running the Embassy for the Ambassador, and cool under pressure. She wasn't a cuddly person, or especially inviting, but Reine had come to like her quite a bit.

Maybe that was part of the reason she was having such a hard time with this mission. It was hard to imagine this woman selling out her country for financial gain.

"We need to shut the lights off."

Reine snapped her attention to Clay. He was looking at her, his expression almost apologetic. The weapon in his hand looked incongruous against his now-slight-wrinkled tuxedo, and yet...it fit him somehow. "What?"

"The lights." He gestured to the ornate light fixture in the ceiling, before jerking his chin toward the curtained windows. "We don't want to draw unnecessary attention right now. They might have eyes outside."

"And they might see the light under the door." Reine nodded in understanding, her eyes turning to the door. "I agree." She paused, tilting her head to one side. "I think there's a small nightlight in the restroom. Can we—can we leave the door open?"

She looked at Clay, hoping he understood. She didn't want to sit in the dark for the next however many hours until they were rescued...or someone came after them again.

Something in his hazel eyes softened. "I think that would be all right."

"Okay. I'm going to call 911."

Clay killed the lights, while Reine fumbled with her cell phone. She dialed 911, her fingers shaking a little more than she would have liked.

On the other end, the phone rang once, twice, and then a cool, crisp female voice said, "911, what's your emergency?"

"I am at the Denquay Embassy. Armed shooters have invaded the building and are holding everyone in the ballroom hostage, including Ambassador Ambrose and his wife." Reine took a breath and then gave the operator their address.

"What's your name?"

Reine shook her head. "I cannot give you that."

"Can you stay on the line?"

Reine's gaze darted to Clay. He shook his head, tapping one ear. She bit down on her lip, hard. He was right. They didn't know if whoever was behind this could listen in.

"No." She let her voice break a little. "I'm sorry."

The 911 operator asked a few more questions, but Reine only said, "I am sorry. I cannot tell you anything more. Please send help."

She ended the call and dropped her cell phone into her lap.

"You did good." Clay rested his hand on her shoulder for a second. The gesture gave her more comfort than she would have thought possible. "You can't be the only person to manage to call for help. Maybe somebody else can tell them more."

Reine nodded, and then belatedly remembered that he was bleeding. Stuffing her phone back into her clutch, she reached for his free hand. "You're still bleeding. There should be a first-aid kit in the restroom."

Chapter Fifteen

Without a doubt, the Denquayan First Secretary's bathroom had to be one of the fanciest Clay had ever seen. It was all silver and turquoise and gleaming white, with glistening sinks and counters and a glossy dark wood storage cabinet with decorative silver fixtures. A stand-up shower next to a door that opened up on a toilet and a bidet. The air smelled of the same perfume that permeated the rest of the office.

Clay leaned against the shiny turquoise counter in the dim glow of the nightlight plugged into the wall and let Reine patch him up. The gash in his head wasn't bad, but it had bled a lot, making him look like he'd been hurt worse than he had. Before they'd come in here, he'd shucked his black tuxedo jacket and laid it over one arm of the brown leather couch.

He watched Reine as she cleaned up the worst of the still-wet blood on his face with tissues, and then gently wiped away the rest with alcohol wipes. Her expression was serious. As she moved, he noticed that the purple fabric of her gown shimmered under even this dim light too.

Clearing his throat, he remarked lightly, "You're good under pressure, Miss Delgado. A lot of women—and some men too—would have turned into sobbing messes after going through everything you just did."

Reine's fingers stilled their ministrations as her gaze flicked up to his. "I'm in the diplomatic corps," she said, as though that explained everything.

Clay nodded, but inwardly he thought it was more than that. Some people just naturally handled crises better than others. She was one of those people.

"Tip your head back, please. This may sting a bit," Reine said presently.

Clay complied, and she cleaned the gash out with hydrogen peroxide. He winced as the liquor bubbled over his open wound, but it soon passed. Reine patted his skin dry, applied some antibiotic ointment, and then used a couple of butterfly Band-Aids to close the gash.

"I hope those stay," she said, eying the butterflies as though she wasn't convinced they'd behave.

"I'm sure they will." Clay glanced over his shoulder at his reflection in the mirror. "Looks like you did a good job."

"Thank you." Reine nodded gravely and set about cleaning up all of the trash she'd created. She dumped it all into the trashcan under the sink and then put all the supplies she'd used out of the way.

She washed her hands, and then turned to look at him halfway through drying her hands. "I can't believe I haven't asked this before now, but do you have a gun?"

"You mean besides this one?" Clay indicated the rifle he'd confiscated from the terrorist.

"Yes."

"No."

Even in the semi-darkness, Reine's surprise was so palpable that it made Clay chuckle. "What, you expected me to be packing just because I work for a security firm?"

Was that a *blush* rising in her cheeks? She waved a hand. "Well, you must admit you Americans have a certain…stereotype. Everyone knows that Americans love their guns."

"Some of us do." Clay was still smiling. "Some people hate them, and others abuse them. But here?" He spread his hands. "Your embassy has its rules and I respected them."

Reine pursed her lips in a wry frown. "It goes without saying that whoever has attacked the embassy did not."

"That's why the bad guys are the bad guys." Clay shrugged. "They don't respect the law."

Reine inclined her head in a nod. "I can't argue with that."

Chapter Sixteen

As soon as she and Clay exited the restroom to return to the office, Reine hurried over to the brown leather couch. She knelt on the middle cushion, taking care to keep her head low, and carefully—very carefully—peeked through the slit where the two halves of the emerald green curtains met in the middle of the window frame. She gasped.

She couldn't see much, but she *could* see flashing red and blue lights coming from the street far below. Relief and hope battled her fear and anxiety.

She turned back to Clay. "Capitol police are here."

"That's great." He came up beside her and leaned on the back of the couch to see for himself. Then he looked down at her. "We better get away from the windows. Just in case."

They both slid off the couch to the thick carpeted floor and Clay reached over to take her gloved hand. "Don't let your guard down." He cast a grim nod in the direction of the locked door. "There's no telling how long it'll take them to either negotiate their way out of this situation, or else put an end to it."

Reine felt cold again. "And we're trapped up here."

"Yes, we are. For now, at least." Clay fished in his trousers pocket for his cell phone and glanced at the display. Then he hissed through his teeth and shoved it back where it had come from.

Reine bit down on the inside of her lip. "Have you heard anything from your friends?"

Clay shook his head, before scrubbing a hand through his hair. It left him looking even more handsome than before, which was hilarious, because Reine knew if she'd tried the same maneuver, she'd have come out looking like she got hit by a rogue blow-dryer.

"They were in the ballroom, last I saw, and if these terrorists have any sense, they went through and confiscated everyone's phones." He smiled painfully. "It'd be too dangerous to try to contact them."

Reine nodded. She understood that only too well.

Tipping her head back against the couch, she stared up through the semi-darkness at the ceiling. Her thoughts were too loud. The silence in this office was almost oppressive, but the noise in her head made her feel like she was on the verge of over-stimulation.

One thought struggled out of the chaos. She froze, feeling a wave of horror trickle over her. She turned to Clay. "You don't think they have a list of everyone who is here tonight, do you?"

"And they're matching guests to the list to see if everyone is accounted for?"

"Yes."

Clay sucked in a breath through his teeth, running a hand through his hair again. "I should have thought of that." He shook his head. "I have no idea. They've already proved that they could bypass the Embassy's security, so it's possible they have access to a guest list too." He hesitated, then added, "If that's the case, then it's only a matter of time before they come looking for you."

Reine swallowed. "And you."

"I was a last-minute addition." Clay shrugged. "I think Rob had to pull a couple of strings to get me in. So they might not know about me."

Reine nodded, focusing on keeping her breathing steady. Focusing on not letting him know how much the idea of an additional time constraint stressed her out. "There's also the man we left zip-tied and gagged in my office," she pointed out. "They'll miss him eventually."

"There's that." Clay reached over to wrap his fingers around her gloved hand. The warmth of his skin seeped through the sheer fabric. "Let's hope the Capitol police can get the job done quickly."

Reine nodded, and they subsided into silence again.

She could *feel* time slipping through her fingers. It thrummed inside her, the knowledge that she was going to fail. Through no fault of her own, granted, but still.

The Intelligence Division had trusted her, and now she was going to blow it.

What were the odds that someone would attempt to take over the embassy the same night as her mission? It was mind-boggling. Reine drew her knees up to her chest, the folds of her shimmery purple gown draping over her legs. She had no idea how beautiful she looked sitting there in the soft glow spilling out from the night-light in the restroom; she certainly didn't feel it.

She wanted to drum her fingers on her knees, tap her feet on the floor, but she restrained herself. No need to make Clay think even less of her.

He sat beside her on the floor, back against the leather couch, long legs stretched out in front of him. The confiscated rifle lay on the floor beside him within easy reach. They'd both pulled out their phones and were searching for news reports, but even in the semi-darkness she could see the faraway look in his eyes. His thoughts were elsewhere.

Reine swallowed, a nascent plan coalescing in her mind. Her fingers tightened on her clutch in her lap. Even if the Capitol police were here already, it could be hours before they resolved the situation.

What she was contemplating was dangerous. For both of them. But...

The alternative was that she failed her mission. And far more lives were at stake than just hers. Or even Clay's.

She glanced at him out of the corner of her eye. Her grip on her clutch tightened to the point of the clasp hurting her fingers. She needed him to be unconscious while she did her job.

Could she really do that? Could she knock him out?

He'd hate her afterward. But...again... Did she really have another option?

Clay needed plausible deniability. He couldn't know what had happened here tonight. For his own sake, and for hers.

No. She swallowed, looking down at the *Breaking News* headlines scrolling across her own news app. This was the best option.

"I wish we knew what was going on down there," Clay said suddenly, breaking the stillness that had fallen over them. "Not knowing is killing me."

"Agreed," Reine said. She took a deep breath, let it out slowly. Her heart started hammering in her chest again. "I can't find anything other than a report that the Embassy is under attack."

"Me neither." Clay dropped his phone to the carpet beside his leg and changed the subject. "Do you have family back in Denquay?"

Reine blinked, surprised by the sudden change in subject, but she said, "Some extended family." She shrugged. "I was an only child, and my parents weren't from large families. So I grew up mostly alone."

"I'm sorry," Clay said softly. He reached over and wrapped his arms around her shoulders, squeezing gently.

Reine let herself close her eyes, soaking in the comfort he

provided. *Better take it now,* a stray corner of her mind said grimly. *He may not want anything else to do with you when this is all over.*

"What about you?" she found herself asking.

Clay was silent for a moment, and then he let out a soft chuckle. "I'm the middle of six children," he said. "Four boys and two girls. My family lives in Northern Kentucky."

Reine smiled. "You would fit in well in Denquay. We love large families." Her smile turned wistful as, not for the first time, she imagined what it would be like to have that many siblings. "I imagine your house was noisy growing up."

"Oh, definitely." Clay smiled reminiscently. "We had our share of scuffles, but at the end of the day I always knew they had my back." He shrugged, a little self-consciously. "Kind of like my team back when I was a Marine."

Reine shifted a little on the floor to angle herself toward him so she could see his face better. Beside her, Clay did the same. Around them, Ariane's office seemed to take on an intimate air, like the problems and the dangers beyond the locked door had faded away and all that remained was a little bubble around the two of them.

Reine found herself yearning to know more about this man, to get to know him better before she ruined everything. Maybe it was masochistic on her part, maybe she'd have been better off trying to distance herself, but she couldn't help it. Clay drew her with a powerful attraction like they were two magnets. They could circle each other for a while, but inevitably, that force would pull them together.

"Why did you join your friend's security firm instead of going back home to Kentucky?"

Clay shrugged, shaking his head. He looked away, and in the faint glow of the nightlight spilling out of the open restroom door, Reine watched a muscle in his jaw twitch. She realized in this moment that she had touched a deeply painful subject.

Instinctively, she put a hand on his arm. "You don't have to answer if you would prefer not to."

He looked at her then, his eyes dark, and sighed. Slowly at first, he said, "I've seen too much, been through too much, to be able to go home and get on with a 'normal'—" he made air quotes with his fingers, "—life. The town I grew up in seems so…small." He shook his head, his right hand opening and closing into a fist where it rested on his lap. "I know there's more to the world, and I know I'm a different person than I was when I left for the Marines. I just—I can't go back. I've got to do something else with my life."

Reine digest that for a few heartbeats, turning his words over in his mind. That was an eminently sensible way of looking at things. "I can't see anything wrong with that."

"You'd be the first."

"I'm sorry," she said simply.

The understanding in Reine's voice soothed a rough spot in Clay's heart. He hadn't realized how badly he'd needed to talk to someone about this. He rubbed a thumb over the back of her hand, wishing her gloves weren't in the way. It would have been nice to feel her skin.

"Anyway," he forced a smile, "my parents don't understand. They weren't real keen on me joining the Marines in the first place, although they came around eventually. But now?" He lifted a shoulder in a deliberately careless shrug and left it at that.

"What about your siblings?" Reine leaned a little closer to him, her bare arm pressing into his, with only the sleeve of his white dress shirt between them.

"Mixed bag. It's hard."

"Sounds like it."

Clay glanced at her and found Reine looking at him, understanding and empathy written all over the beautiful lines of her face. The dim light enhanced her features, making her dark eyes positively luminous. His mouth went dry.

His gaze darted to her lips. She was close enough that he could kiss her. All he had to do was lean in just a hair and…

No. He swallowed, unconsciously leaning a little away from her. Downstairs a bunch of people—including his friends—were being held hostage. He couldn't be up here making out with Reine, no matter how amazing and beautiful she was.

Even if there was absolutely nothing he could do to help resolve the current situation, he still had standards.

Clay swallowed again and glanced down at his feet. Kissing her would have to wait until this was all over.

If they got out of this. And if Reine wanted to kiss him.

He hoped she did. Clay rested his neck against the back of the couch and stared up at the ceiling. He *really* hoped she did.

Chapter Eighteen

Clay wanted to kiss her.

Reine didn't consider herself an expert on such things, but she wasn't completely oblivious. The look on his face, the way his eyes had dropped to her mouth… He wanted to kiss her.

That knowledge filled her with a heady giddiness. In that moment, the anxiety and the fear and the stress of their current situation temporarily fell away, leaving just Reine—a woman who was delighted that this man she found so attractive was just as attracted to her.

A slender needle of reality popped her giddy balloon. He hadn't kissed her. Why hadn't he kissed her?

Don't be an idiot, a wry voice whispered inside her. *You are currently holed up in here hiding from armed terrorists.*

And then another thought occurred to her, and Reine's spirits sank all the way to the Embassy's basement. She could use the fact that Clay wanted to kiss her. This was the perfect opportunity.

All of a sudden, she wanted to cry. Because she still had her mission, and now the perfect opportunity to complete it had presented itself. And when it was done, when it was over, Clay would hate her.

The back of her throat felt tight, but Reine forced the emotion away. *You're saving lives*, she told herself, as she opened her little clutch and pulled out a black tube of lip gloss. Popping the lid off, she applied a quick, careful coat to her lips. She then flipped the tube around, unscrewed the hidden lid, and applied an even quicker coat of the substance at the other end.

"Really?" Clay asked dryly from beside her.

Reine's heart jumped into her throat. There was no way he knew what this was. No way.

She widened her eyes in what she hoped was innocent curiosity. "What?"

Clay looked amused. "Sorry, it's just..." He gestured to her tube of lip gloss. "Always thought that was a stereotype." He waved to their surroundings. "We've got a dire situation on our hands and you're worried about lipstick?"

He was observant, too. Reine liked him even more...even if the fact that he was so observant was a bit of a problem at the moment.

She flashed him a weak smile, stowing the lip gloss back in her clutch. "Nervous habit. My lips feel dry."

He just smiled, shaking his head again, but she didn't miss the way his pulse jumped at the mention of her lips.

Reine inhaled slowly, despite the way her own heartbeat had quickened. For the next moment or two, she'd have to be very, very careful not to lick her lips. Otherwise, it'd be lights out for her instead of Clay.

That...would be a problem. She'd never used knock-out lip gloss before, but Erica had given her a thorough explanation of the dangers.

She touched Clay's arm. Words rose inside her—everything she wanted to say before it was too late. "I know everything is crazy, but —" emotion swelled in her breast; she let it color her voice, "—I'm really glad we met tonight. I enjoyed our evening earlier, and—" she laughed a little, gesturing helplessly to their surroundings, "—if I was going to be hiding from armed terrorists in the Embassy, I'm glad you're here with me."

Clay smiled at her, and in the dim light from the open restroom door, he looked even more handsome than he had standing in the middle of the ballroom downstairs.

He took a breath, pressing his lips together, a strange vulnerability in his eyes. "I'm glad we met too." He nodded to the door. "Maybe, when this is all over, we can go out for dinner or something? I'd really like to see you again."

Reine smiled at him, bittersweet emotion coursing through her. She put her hand on the side of his face, holding his gaze. "I would love that."

And then she kissed him.

Chapter Nineteen

Clay felt like the luckiest man on the planet. His eyes slid shut automatically as Reine kissed him, hope burgeoning inside his chest. He had his standards, but it was good to know she wanted him too.

The kiss was sweet and chaste and over far too quickly, but it was glorious. Her lips were as soft as they looked.

Clay smiled at her as she pulled away. She looked a little nervous, but her gloved hand still cupped the side of his face. He couldn't resist the urge to nuzzle her palm. Her lip gloss tasted like cherries.

Slowly, Reine let her hand fall. Clay reached out and caught her glove fingers, tangling them with his. His smile widened into a teasing grin. "How very modern of you, Miss Delgado, initiating the first kiss."

He watched her breath hitch in her throat, and then she shrugged, tossing her head. She was smiling though, shyly. "Someone had to do it."

"On a serious note," Clay said, rubbing his thumb over the back of her gloved hand. "It's a good thing we live in more modern times. A while back something like this could have ruined your reputation, spending a couple of hours locked in an office with a man like me." He wiggled his eyebrows at her.

Reine laughed, thankfully, but then her shoulders slumped. "Honestly, it still might," she admitted. "Not to that extent, thank God, but..." She sighed and then laughed once. "I will probably never be able to convince anyone this was perfectly innocent." She waved her hand between the two of them.

Well, Clay thought, *maybe not* perfectly *innocent.* But he knew what she meant.

Reine's shy smile suddenly turned wicked. She leaned in a little closer to him, raising an eyebrow, and he caught the scent of her perfume again. "What about you? Will your friends believe that you were in here with me for hours and never laid a finger on me?"

Clay opened his mouth to answer, and then shut it. Ruefully, he shook his head. "No. Unfortunately, I'll probably never hear the end of it."

He started to say something else, but at that moment the world grew fuzzy around the edges. He felt like he was floating away, darkness encroaching on his peripheral vision. Clay tried to raise his hand, tried to speak, but his mouth was full of cotton and his limbs weighed five hundred pounds.

The last thing he saw before blackness took him was Reine, her dark eyes wide and mournful in the semi-darkness.

Chapter Twenty

The knock-out lip gloss took longer to work than Reine expected. She almost wondered if she'd done something wrong, but at the same time, she cherished every second she had with Clay. Their time together was limited, precious.

Even if he didn't know that yet.

When he finally lost consciousness, his head slumping back against the seat of the brown leather couch, something inside her relaxed. She could complete her mission now.

At the same time, guilt churned her stomach. He really was an amazing man.

Reine shook Clay's shoulder lightly and said his name a couple of times, just to be sure, but he did not stir. He was out. She swallowed, and then rose to her feet. Erica had said this stuff caused a loss of consciousness for anywhere from forty-five minutes to three hours, depending on body mass and dosage.

The clock was ticking.

First step was to get this stuff off her lips before she accidentally knocked *herself* out. Reine hurried into the restroom and quickly wiped her mouth with several thick squares of toilet paper she pulled from a fresh roll in the little dark wooden cabinet next to the toilet. She discarded the toilet paper and hid it underneath the bloody alcohol wipes and other trash from cleaning Clay's head injury.

That done, Reine hurried back out into the office. She did not move Ariane's chair—she wouldn't put it past the woman to have positioned it precisely so she could tell if anybody interfered in her office—but instead leaned over the desk and turned on the First Secretary's Mac with her gloved finger.

While it booted up, Reine dumped the contents of her clutch on the desk. Her own cell phone, the lip gloss, her small wallet, and a couple of other things went back into the clutch. The rest remained.

Step one of Phase one: check for bugs. Reine doubted anybody else could have bugged Ariane's office without the First Secretary's knowledge, but the Intelligence Division believed it was possible that the woman might bug her own office to keep tabs on things when she wasn't around.

Picking up a small black rectangular that reminded her of a TV remote, Reine spent a couple of minutes walking around Ariane's office waving it over everything. To her everlasting relief, she found nothing. The office was clean

Its job finished, that device went back into her clutch, and Reine then picked up her Y-shaped USB cord. She plugged the standard USB end into Ariane's computer and then plugged the USB-C plug into the burner cell phone she'd been given. Her elbow-length gloves made this process a little more unwieldy than normal, but she'd spent time practicing this.

She couldn't leave fingerprints.

That done, she unlocked the phone and opened the app that was supposed to crack Ariane's password. She tapped the 'start' button, praying that it worked. A little status bar popped up, flashing through letters, numbers, and symbols too quickly for the eye to see.

While she waited for the app to finish, Reine detached a tiny plastic square containing two micro-SD cards that had been stuck to the card reader. She carefully extracted one micro-SD card and partly inserted it into the small card reader on the other side of the Y-shaped USB cord in preparation for phase two. The other micro-SD card was a backup, in case something went haywire with this one.

Her hands were steady, even if her heart thundered in her chest, part of her anticipating either Clay to wake up unexpectedly or else someone to bang on the office door. She knew computers. This part, she could do with her eyes closed.

On her burner cell's screen, the little status bar filled up and flashed green, indicating that the app had indeed cracked Ariane's password.

Reine pulled the keyboard tray just far enough out from the desk that she could touch the mouse. She hit 'enter', and watched as she was logged into the computer.

Phase one complete, she thought grimly. *Two more to go.*

Unplugging the burner cell from the USB connector, Reine pushed the micro-SD card in the rest of the way into the card reader. Once it was mounted, she poked around the insides of Ariane's computer.

That was when she discovered that the First Secretary had a secondary hard drive as well—not standard issue for the Embassy's computers.

You've got to be kidding me. Reine shut her eyes in consternation. Then she gritted her teeth and shook her head. *Focus. First things first.*

She needed to clone the main hard drive. Then she could deal with the other one. Erica *had* said the Intelligence Division wanted everything they could get their hands on.

Reine cast a grim eye at the other micro-SD card sitting on the desk's glossy surface. *You better work.*

Cloning the main hard drive took an agonizing twenty minutes.

Reine spent part of that time alternating between glancing from the computer screen to Clay to the door and back, and part of that time reading live updates from D.C.'s main news stations on their situation. Nobody really knew what was going on yet; the terrorists had yet to release any statements themselves.

The second the clone of the main hard drive finished, Reine scrambled up from her spot on the carpeted floor behind the desk and turned her attention to the secondary hard drive. She swapped out the micro-SD cards and set about cloning the second drive.

A warning dialogue box immediately popped up: the secondary drive was encrypted.

She'd need to input a password before she could access it.

Still leaning awkwardly over the desk, Reine dropped her head to her chest in frustration. She suppressed a growl. Of *course* it was encrypted. Had she forgotten who she was supposed to be dealing with?

She bit down on the inside of her cheek. She was running out of time. If Clay leaned more toward the forty-five minute end of the spectrum, it wouldn't be long before he regained consciousness.

Fighting a sudden burst of panic, Reine plugged her burner phone back into the USB connector and pulled up the password-cracking app. This time, the process seemed to take forever. Not surprisingly, this password was apparently a lot more complicated.

"Come on, come on," Reine muttered under her breath in her native French, watching the progress bar slowly fill. "You can do it."

Anxious tension corded the muscles in her shoulders and neck. Reine straightened and rolled her shoulders before leaning over the desk again. She'd need a good massage after this.

If we make it, whispered a dour voice in her mind.

We'll make it, she thought fiercely. There wasn't room for any other outcome.

She almost wilted in relief when the progress bar finally turned green.

"Yes," she hissed, clicking the 'enter' button.

Seconds later, Reine straightened with a shuddery breath. The cloning process was successfully underway. This hard drive was smaller than the main one, so in theory the process should be quicker.

Phase two was almost complete.

All she had to do was make it another fifteen or twenty minutes.

Carefully gathering her skirts, Reine sank back down on the carpet beside the desk. She was shielded from view from the door here, and she could easily reach the computer. That was important —if Clay regained consciousness before the cloning process was finished, she should be able to kill everything and shut the computer off in time to keep him from suspecting anything.

Her mouth twisted into a grimace. Emphasis on the *should*. In the event that happened, the Intelligence Division would have to be content with what they could get.

She closed her eyes, scrunching her fingers into the thick pile of the carpet. This had to work. She'd come this far, risked this much.

It *had* to work.

Chapter Twenty-One

It took seventeen minutes and forty-two seconds to clone the secondary hard drive. This time, the torture of waiting was almost unbearable. Reine kept imagining she heard Clay stir, or that she heard footsteps and shouts from beyond the secure, locked office door.

Halfway through the process, someone banged on the door.

Even though Reine had been anticipating something like this, the sound still caught her off-guard. It was so loud and brutal. Angry, muffled shouts in French followed.

She froze, fear and horror rushing through her. Had they found the missing terrorist and concluded the people who bested him were in here?

Or did they know she, specifically, was in here?

The pounding on the door continued unabated. Reine pressed her lips together so hard that it hurt. *Not now. Oh, God, please not now. Don't let them get in here now.*

Not when Clay was lying on the floor a few feet away, unconscious. Not when she was so close to finishing her mission.

They can't break down the door, she assured herself. *And even if they do drag the Ambassador up here to unlock the door, it'll take time.*

She'd finish her mission first, whatever else happened after that.

Whoever was beating on the door and shouting suddenly stopped.

Reine strained her ears, listening as hard as she could. They'd given up.

For now, anyway.

She released a breath she hadn't realized she'd been holding and turned her attention back to the progress bar. Only a few minutes left. She briefly shut her eyes.

It was a selfish hope, but she really hoped that Clay was conscious again before the terrorists returned.

She opened her eyes. Three minutes and counting.

Reine spent those last three minutes watching the progress meter, unable to look away. She was so close. So close.

When the cloning process finally finished, she lunged for the mouse and immediately unmounted the micro-SD card from Ariane's computer. She then pulled the tiny card from the card reader, slipped it back into the tiny plastic square case with its sister, and slipped *that* behind the little pocket flattened against her sternum created by the underwires in her bra.

Her fingers only shook a little.

Next, she unplugged the USB connector and shut Ariane's computer down. Those were the two most important components of Phase three: safely hide the micro-SD cards on her person, and make sure the computer was in the same state as it had been when Ariane left the office.

Just as Reine swept the burner cell and the USB connector back into her clutch, she heard a groan behind her.

Clay was coming to.

A million butterflies erupted in her stomach, but she didn't lose her focus. *Finish the mission.*

The final touch was to push the keyboard tray back into place. That done, Reine scrambled back over to Clay as quietly as she could.

She'd just sunk down on the carpet beside him when he groaned again and opened his eyes. They were unfocused at first, and he blinked a lot, but he seemed to regain control of his faculties rather quickly. He sat up a little, taking in his surroundings, before he turned to look at her.

Reine watched recognition flood those gorgeous hazel eyes and felt guilt and grief mix inside her.

"Hi." She braved a concerned smile. "You're awake."

"Wha—what happened?" Wincing, Clay put a hand to his head.

"You passed out." Reine infused as much innocent concern into those words as she could. She put a hand on his arm, even though it felt dishonest. "I'm glad you're okay."

And she was. That part was probably one of the truest things she'd said to him tonight.

It was just too bad that from here on out she'd have to lie to him.

Chapter Twenty-Two

He'd passed out? Clay blinked in the semi-darkness permeating the First Secretary's office, trying to clear the cobwebs fogging up his mind. Why? What had happened?

"I must have hit my head on that doorframe harder than I thought." He winced; his head was pounding. "I see we haven't been rescued yet."

"No." Reine shook her head.

Clay regarded her a little woozily. The way she was looking at him, her eyes dark and worried, as though it was somehow her fault, prompted a smile. Of course it wasn't her fault. How could it be?

His smile turned teasing. "The last thing I remember is you kissing me."

Those words echoed in his mind. The last thing he remembered…

Clay went very still. Slowly, he rested his head against the seat of the couch, regarding Reine through hooded eyes. Nah. It was a crazy thought. There was no way it could be true.

And yet...

His mind, though still a little fuzzy around the edges, flashed through the evening's events. Reine had left the ballroom just before the attack went down, conveniently removing herself from immediate danger. She'd been up on this floor in her office, ostensibly trying to work, but...was *she* responsible for the security cameras going down?

Was it *possible*?

Something wrenched in Clay's chest. He didn't want to believe it. Didn't want to fathom that this beautiful, witty, intelligent woman could be involved with the madness happening downstairs.

But she'd lost her parents to political unrest in Denquay. He knew too well how a loss like that could drive someone to seek vengeance. A hurt that deep and a vendetta could create a vicious, never-ending cycle of destruction.

Confusion poked through the scenario playing out inside his head. If that was true, why had she knocked him out? What could she have possibly hoped to gain?

If in fact she *was* responsible for his sudden loss of consciousness.

It niggled at him though, a sense of wrongness. He hadn't thought his head injury was severe enough to have caused him to lose consciousness. He'd taken hits like that in the field before and kept fighting without any issues.

"What?" Reine sounded a little unnerved. "Why are you looking at me like that?"

"You're not involved with those terrorists, are you?"

The words slipped out before Clay realized that was what he was going to say. He didn't take them back, just kept looking at her.

"What?" She reared back, her eyes widening in shock.

Genuine shock, Clay thought. He'd caught her off-guard. He lifted an eyebrow. "You sure?"

"No!" Reine was suddenly on her feet, her gloved hands

clenched into fists at her sides and her chest heaving with anger. "I mean, yes! I'm sure. I would never—" She shook her head, as though the mere suggestion was too much to bear. "How could you think that of me?"

Clay continued to regard her steadily. He thought he glimpsed tears sparkling in her eyes. Part of him felt guilty for making her cry, but the other part, the part that had kept him alive outside the wire, had to be sure.

Bonds formed quickly in extreme situations like this, but it didn't change the fact that trust was a fragile, precious thing. Easily broken, and difficult to regain.

He wanted so badly to trust her.

Reine swallowed, visibly composing herself, and then she sank back down on the carpet in front of the couch by his side. She spent a moment arranging the folds of her gown around her knees before she met his gaze again. Her brown eyes still sparkled with unshed tears, but that sudden anger had dissipated.

Her shoulders shuddered as she drew in a deep breath, and then she lifted her chin. "What makes you think I could possibly be working with those—those monsters?"

"I didn't say you were. I just asked." Clay wanted to reach out and take her hand, but he restrained himself. Now was not the time. His head was still pounding, though it had started to subside.

Reine just looked at him. Waiting. Like she was on trial and he was about to hand down the verdict. It was a weird vibe.

Clay mustered a wry smile. "You have to admit, your timing is a little coincidental." He shook his head. "You leave the ballroom just before a terrorist takeover? Anybody with half a brain is going to ask that question."

Dead silence greeted these words, and then he watched recognition dawn in her eyes, immediately followed by horror.

Reine buried her face in her hands. "Oh, my God. That's terrible."

Clay waited for a moment, but when she said nothing further, he reached over to poke her in the knee. Gently. "So... Are you a political terrorist, Miss Delgado? Did you stick me with a needle when you were bandaging me up earlier to knock me out?"

He kept his voice somber, but one corner of his mouth twitched in a semblance of a smile. Her reactions were genuine. He still couldn't shake the certainty that *something* was going on with her, but...he didn't think she'd had a hand in this evening's terrible events.

Still...that old adage floated across his mind: Trust but verify.

Chapter Twenty-Three

Disbelief, horror, and a strange kind of morbid amusement swirled around inside Reine's head. She pressed her gloved hands to her face, squeezing her eyes shut. Her cheeks felt hot, even through the sheer purple fabric. How had all of this gotten so complicated?

Clay was an intelligent man. He'd taken circumstantial evidence and the evening's sequence of events and put them together to form a narrative. He'd put them together *wrong*, of course, but that was beside the point.

No one could have foreseen the terrorist attack on the Embassy tonight. Not unless they were in on it.

A helpless laugh escaped Reine. *Oh, this is such a mess.*

If someone like Clay could paint a picture that made her out to be a terrorist, then her colleagues here at the Embassy—with all of their combined years of experience with politics and intrigue and backstabbing—most certainly could paint the same picture. They might even find a few details Clay missed.

Would anybody believe she was innocent? Would the Intelligence Division and Denquay's Department of Defense admit that she'd been operating on their instructions, or would they let her be swept up along with the terrorists in order to keep the investigation from being blown?

Reine honestly didn't know the answer to that—and not knowing terrified her.

She struggled to keep her breathing even, trying to keep Clay from sensing the fear rising inside her like lava from a volcano. *What do I do?*

From out of the distant past, a memory of her father came to her. She heard his voice saying, *Lies are poison that tastes sweet, little one. The truth is always best, no matter how painful.*

Her breath hitched. She had been seven or eight at the time, and she had broken an expensive sculpture while playing with some of the other children at the Embassy. Frightened, she'd lied about it. Her father had gone down on one knee, drawn her to him, and talked with her gently.

She still remembered the earnest look on his face. *Lies are poison that tastes sweet, little one.* She'd forgotten about that.

She knew from her study of his Ambassadorship that her father had never wavered on that front, though stretching the truth here and there would have benefited him greatly at times.

It's a wonder he survived in politics as long as he did, she thought wryly. The old pang of grief came, but she let it glide through her like water through a lazy river. *Thank you, Papa.*

Resolve flooded her, calming her fear. The Intelligence Division had chosen her not only because they believed she was brave enough and strong enough to accomplish the missions they gave her, but also because they believed she could adapt to unforeseen situations.

Well, she thought, dropping her hands from her face and opening her eyes, *this is me adapting.*

She looked Clay full in the face. "What I'm about to tell you cannot leave this room." She waited for him to nod once in understanding before continuing, "I'm not a terrorist. I had nothing to do with tonight's attack. But I did have a mission to accomplish tonight, and you weren't supposed to be here." She flashed him a grateful smile. "I am very glad you were here tonight, or that man in my office would have gotten me. But..." Her heart started pounding in her chest again. "You need plausible deniability. Trust me, you don't want to be a foreigner tangled up in Denquayan politics."

"What exactly is *that* supposed to mean?" Clay narrowed his eyes at her.

She squared her shoulders. *Be brave, Reine.* Her mother's voice, this time.

"It means that I had to drug you." Reine didn't wait to see the shock register on his face, but kept going. Best to get it all over with at once. "I know that doing that put your life in danger, given our current situation." Her voice wavered. "I'm really sorry. But if I had to do it again, I would."

If her heart beat any faster, it would probably beat itself right out of her chest. Clay was staring at her like she had suddenly morphed into an alien creature from an old science fiction horror movie. If she had ever had a conversation harder than this one, she couldn't remember what it was.

Reine swallowed a painful knot in her throat and spread her hands. "There is something rotten in this embassy, and I was tasked to help investigate. I can't tell you anything more than that." She shook her head. "You have no idea how many of my peoples' lives are at stake. My life, even your life, is a raindrop in a lake in comparison."

Pressing her lips into a thin line, she looked away. She couldn't bring herself to meet his eyes for this next part; it was too intimate. "I...understand if you would rather not go out for dinner after this is all over."

A pregnant pause ensued. Clay said nothing; he merely sat

frozen. She'd expected anger, perhaps an outburst, but this calm silence was far worse.

Hot tears pricked the back of her eyes; she held them back. She'd done the best she could with the hand she'd been dealt. That was all anybody could do.

The truth *was* painful. A corner of her heart felt like it had shattered into a thousand tiny shards, and all of them were currently stabbing her. But…she'd still be able to sleep at night, if they made it out of this.

Pulling her diplomatic training around herself like a shield, she forced herself to look Clay in the eye. "I know you don't have any reason to trust me, but, please…no one can know about this. For both our sakes."

Still, Clay remained silent. He studied her, his expression inscrutable. They were close enough to touch, and yet Reine felt a chasm had opened up between them. Awkward, uncomfortable tension filled the office, sticking to her skin like an almost tangible film.

At last, Clay blew out a breath and raised both hands to rub his temples. "Let me get this straight." His voice was terse. "You're not a terrorist, but you left the ballroom because you're investigating your colleagues here at the Embassy?" He shook his head, his expression confused and suspicious. "What are you, some kind of spy?"

Under different circumstances, Reine would have laughed. It sounded so ridiculous on the surface. She knew for a fact that nobody except her recruiters at the Intelligence Division thought she was spy material. There was nothing glamorous or exciting about her life or her work.

As it was, she only lifted one shoulder in a shrug. "Something like that."

Chapter Twenty-Four

Until tonight, Clay had never found himself in a position where one of his grandmother's favorite expressions—'you could have knocked me over with a feather'—was so apropos. He was reeling, and he felt like the tiniest nudge would send him flying. Information zipped through his mind, realization after realization.

His instinct that something was up with Reine had been correct. His instinct—crazy though he'd thought it had been—that she'd had something to do with him passing out had *also* been correct.

The worst of it was that he'd never seen that part coming. How had she done it?

Clay drilled Reine with a hard look. "How'd you drug me?" He tipped his head toward her clutch. "If I dump out everything you've got in there, will I find evidence to corroborate what you've told me?"

"You'll lose your plausible deniability." Reine's voice was calm, but her beautiful face was so pale Clay began to wonder if *she* was about to pass out. "I didn't use a needle, but I can't tell you anything more than that."

Maybe it *was* her lip gloss. Clay eyed her clutch again, a wild laugh bubbling up in his chest. That was crazy spy stuff, right?

He swallowed the laugh. If he let that loose, he'd probably scare her, and even after everything he'd just heard, he didn't want to do that.

Instead, he frowned. "You're damn lucky that nobody broke through that door while I was out." He shook his head, his stomach twisting in horror. "If that had happened…"

Reine ducked her head, looking guilty. "Somebody did bang on the door about fifteen minutes ago," she said in small voice. "But they couldn't get in. They went away after a few minutes and they haven't come back yet."

"What?" Clay sat bolt upright, adrenaline spiking through his veins. "And you're just now telling me this?"

Reine just gave him a look that said they hadn't gotten to it until now. "They won't be able to get in without using the Ambassador to manually override our emergency protocols."

Clay looked at the door, and then back at Reine. His mouth worked, but no words emerged. Just about everything about this night had gone sideways.

What could he even say at this point?

He understood duty to one's country and the greater good. He also understood impossible choices.

He scanned Reine's face in the faint glow provided by the nightlight in the bathroom. Anxiety and stress were written all over her face, but the expression in her brown eyes was sorrowful.

Those moments right before she'd kissed him floated through his mind's eye. The words she'd said…the way she'd looked at him…

"We're a pair." Clay laughed a little, shaking his head. This woman. This wonderful, brave, *amazing* woman.

"What?" Reine tilted her head to one side, wary confusion flooding her face.

"Come here." He reached for her hands, and then wrinkled his nose. "Will you take those off? You don't need them anymore, do you?"

"My gloves?" Reine's confusion deepened as she held her hands out in front of her.

"Yeah. Take 'em off."

Silently, Reine removed the gloves and stuffed them into her clutch purse.

"Thank you." Clay reached for her hands again. Her fingers were cold, but he felt that spark of electricity ignite between them the second he touched her. He wrapped his hands around hers. "Look at me. Please," he added, a little belatedly.

When Reine reluctantly met his gaze, he offered her a lopsided smile. "We're going to have a hell of a story to tell the grandkids."

"What?" She was so surprised her hands went slack in his, her eyes widening to the size of saucers.

"Oh, yeah." Clay rubbed his thumb over the back of her hand, immensely satisfied to be touching skin instead of fabric. "They'll think we're kidding, what with a terrorist attack, and all." His tone turned serious. "No more drugging me, though, okay? Have to draw the line somewhere."

Chapter Twenty-Five

Clay must be having a bad reaction to the knock-out lip gloss. Reine stared at him, torn between panic and hope. Either that or he'd lost his mind. Because he couldn't possibly be talking about *their* grandchildren after everything that had just transpired between them, could he?

His hands holding hers were an immense distraction. So was his closeness. The chasm between them seemed to have filled itself in, though Reine wasn't entirely sure what had changed.

"We've only known each other for a few hours," she said weakly. "Are you—are you saying you *do* still want to have dinner with me when this is over?"

Clay looked at her, and the expression in his eyes made butterflies explode in her stomach. "I do."

Reine had to be sure. "Even though I knocked you out in the middle of all…this?" She gestured to the embassy as a whole.

"Yep."

"Even though I can't tell you everything?"

"Yep."

"Even though I'm Denquayan and you're an American?"

"Aren't you in diplomatic relations?" he countered. "People from different countries have relationships all the time."

"What about your friends and your company?"

Clay brushed that aside with a wave of his hand. "It'll be fine. They'll find somebody better suited to mesh with the two of them."

Reine blinked. The calm assurance in his voice was comforting, but… she shook her head in bewilderment. "But what about you?"

"What about me? I'm a man of many skills. I've got options. There's a whole world of possibilities out there."

Emotion swelled in Reine's chest; the sweetness of his words made her want to cry. "Why?"

Clay just shrugged. "Because I knew when I met you tonight that you were something unique. This—" it was his turn to gesture to their surroundings, "—just proves it." He lifted an eyebrow at her. "I'm serious about the not knocking me out again part, though."

"I won't," Reine said faintly. Then she lifted her chin. "Not unless I have to."

He looked askance at her, and she thought he'd take everything back. But then his bearded face split in an endearing grin. "I think I can live with that."

Reine had thought most of this night in general was the most surreal experience of her life, but this moment? This moment topped everything else. The world—the entire universe—fell away until it was just her and Clay sitting on the floor of Ariane's office.

Hazel met brown as Clay searched her eyes, and then he closed the gap between them and kissed her. The touch of his lips against hers—gentle, but confident—sent sparks racing through her, spreading from her mouth to her chest and out through all of her limbs.

Reine kissed him back, her heart swelling with hope and warmth and something it was probably too early to call love. This time—this time there was no guilt, no ulterior motive, just the slide of his lips against hers.

Clay pulled back long enough to search her face again. He must have found what he was looking for, because he leaned back in, letting go of her hands in the process. She didn't have time to mourn the loss before he wrapped his arms around her, pulling her to him in a hug that felt like coming home.

Reine hugged him back, sliding her hands over the solid muscles beneath his white dress shirt, and for a glorious moment there were no words.

All too soon, they broke apart.

"I would love to kiss you forever," Clay said softly, resting his forehead against hers, "but we do have a situation on our hands."

"Yes, we do," Reine replied, rather breathlessly. She skimmed her fingers over his rough cheek and then used his shoulder to steady herself as she pushed herself back into a proper sitting position.

Her eyes fell on something lying on the carpet on Clay's other side, and a snort of laughter escaped her. It probably wasn't appropriate, given that everyone else in the embassy was still being held hostage right now, but she couldn't help it.

"What?" Clay lifted an eyebrow at her, his hazel eyes dark and his hair rumpled.

Reine nodded to the AK-47 rifle lying beside him. "I can honestly say that before tonight I've never been kissed in close proximity to one of those before."

The kiss earlier didn't count. *She'd* kissed *him*, and it had been a means to an end.

Clay looked down at the rifle. "Oh." He shrugged. "It's a tool." His mouth firmed into a line. "One I'm really hoping I don't have to use tonight." He glanced sideways at her. "Contrary to popular stereotypes, we're not all trigger-happy morons."

Guilt rose inside her. "I never—"

He brushed that aside with a flick of his fingers. "It's fine. Honestly." He took her hand. "But know that if they'd managed to break in here, I will do my best to defend you."

She knew he would. Reine could feel it in her bones. There was no bravado, no macho swaggering. Just a simple declaration of fact.

He would protect her.

A little staggered by how that made her feel, Reine drew in a deep breath and tried to clear her head. Her gaze fell on her clutch, and she reached for it.

Extracting her cell phone, she turned to Clay, only to find him holding his own phone. They'd had the same idea. That warmed something inside her.

"Our little corner of the grid square is secure for now," Clay said. "Let's see if we can find out how everybody else is doing."

Side by side, they leaned against the brown leather couch and pulled up news updates. All they could do now was wait and hope and pray.

Chapter Twenty-Six

Two hours later, Reine's phone vibrated with a flurry of incoming messages. Her screen lit up, the bright light banishing some of the late-night darkness permeating Alison Montoya's office. She bolted upright from where she'd been leaning against Clay, hope blossoming in her chest.

She hadn't had a single text all night—surely, *surely* this meant it was over.

No one had returned to bang on the door again. Nor had the terrorists brought either the Ambassador or the chief of security to unlock it. She and Clay hadn't been quite sure what to make of it.

They'd concluded that either the terrorists no longer cared that they were in here, or else the question of whether or not this office was occupied no longer mattered.

Reine picked her phone up from her lap and input her pin with shaking fingers. She and Clay were still sitting together on the carpeted floor, their backs against the brown leather couch. The air in the office had grown cooler over the past several hours, but they both become accustomed to the lingering smell of Ariane Montoya's perfume.

They'd spent their time alternating between talking and sitting in silence, both their thoughts turned in the direction of the ballroom and the events unfolding there. They'd debated crazy schemes for sneaking out of here and trying to see what they could do to help, but eventually abandoned all of them. After all, there were only two of them, with one weapon between them, and even if Reine wanted to disclose her one advantage to Clay—being able to turn security cameras on and off—she couldn't use it with the internet still out.

Now, she eagerly scrolled through a series of texts demanding to know where she was and whether or not she was all right, and pressed a hand to her chest. It looked like everyone was okay.

Eyes shining, she looked over at Clay. "It's over. I don't have any details, yet, but—it's over."

She paused on a text from Ariane Montoya, requesting a status check. That one, she'd better answer in person. She hit the 'call' button.

Beside her, Clay glanced up from his own phone in alert curiosity. He was busily tapping out messages to Rob and Naomi.

The First Secretary answered on the first ring. Words tumbled out of her in a staccato rush. "Reine. Where *are* you? Are you all right? Everyone is accounted for except you."

Reine blinked. The First Secretary's usually calm, cool voice was rather frayed around the edges. *Getting held hostage for hours will do that to a person.*

She infused as much calm as she could into her voice. "I'm fine, Ms. Montoya." Nervousness fluttered wings in the pit of her stomach, but she ignored it. "I'm actually locked in your office." She glanced sideways at Clay. "With one of our American guests. He saved my life tonight."

Surprised silence met these statements. Reine did not wait for Ariane to find words, but immediately asked, "Are the Ambassador and his wife all right? Is everyone else all right? What happened?"

On the other end of the phone, the First Secretary seemed to gather herself together. "Everyone is fine. And I do mean everyone."

"What happened?" Reine asked quickly. She didn't think she could wait any longer to find out—and it would be a shame if she learned what had happened in her own country's embassy from an American news station.

"It's quite a long story, but suffice to say, Ambassador Ambrose was able to reach a compromise with the…terrorist ringleader. It has to do with the rainforest deal back home." Ariana paused, and Reine could picture her pursing her thin lips together. "John Renaudin is under arrest for assisting with tonight's debacle. He confessed to using diplomatic pouches to smuggle illegal weapons into the Embassy."

"Renaudin?" Reine gasped. John was an attaché to the Trade Secretary. Only a few years older than Reine herself, he was charming and well-spoken. She hadn't considered him a political hothead.

"I am sure there will be more to the story," Ariane said dryly. She paused, then said in an even drier tone, "Just as I am sure there is more to your story."

If Reine didn't know better, she would have been alarmed by this. As it was, she narrowed her eyes, but kept her tone open and eager to please. "Yes, ma'am."

"You might," Clay said quietly from beside her, "tell her that there is a man locked in your office and that I have his weapon."

Reine had almost forgotten about that man. She quickly relayed the message to Ariane, who absorbed it in stride.

"Very well," the First Secretary said. "We will send an escort up to collect you and bring you down to the ballroom." She paused. "I'm glad you're all right, Reine. We were…worried."

This time, Reine's response was genuine. "Thank you." The call ended and she dropped her phone to her lap.

"So they're sending somebody to collect us?" Clay raised an eyebrow at her. "Is that normal?"

Reine laughed. "Considering the circumstances? Yes."

"Okay, then." Rising to his feet, he picked up the rifle off of the carpet. "I'll be sure to put this where they can see it as soon as they walk in." He set the rifle on the First Secretary's desk, and then approached Reine, holding out both hands toward her.

She let him pull her to her feet, but Clay didn't stop there. Instead, he looped his arms around her, and studied her upturned face. "How long do we have?"

"Not long." She shook her head. "They'll secure my office first and then come here."

"Understood. Then I guess I better do this now, while I still have the chance." Bending his head, he swiftly kissed her again.

Reine closed her eyes, leaning into him and returning the kiss. She flattened her hands against the warm, hard planes of his chest, marveling at how this man could make her feel safe and yet fill her veins with fire at the same time. It must be one of those unexplained mysteries of the universe.

They broke apart only when a series of hard knocks resounded from the direction of the door. Clay let go of her and started to turn in that direction, but Reine stopped him with a hand on his arm. "Are you sure about this?"

He searched her face. "Sure about you?"

She nodded wordlessly.

Clay grinned, and it was like the sun breaking over the horizon. "I've never been more sure about anything." His grin widened a little. "Except maybe joining the Marines."

Reine nodded slowly. She could accept that. She took his hand and marched across the office to unlock the door.

The standoff at the Embassy was finally over—and she'd accomplished her mission.

The only things she had to do now were make it through whatever debriefing Ariane had in mind for her and smuggle the micro-SD cards hidden in her bra to her handler.

A warm, giddy feeling rose in her chest, like the bubbles from the champagne she'd pretended to drink earlier—a lifetime ago. No, that wasn't all. She looked up at Clay and smiled. His fingers were warm against hers, his lean body a solid presence at her side.

They'd made it through everything tonight together, and now they had a future to explore.

Together.

Acknowledgments

I've loved writing down the stories in my head since I was tiny. It's a mostly solitary endeavor, but art doesn't happen in a vacuum. I am so blessed to have family and friends to cheer me on

For my husband, Tim: thanks so much for always encouraging me to keep pursuing the dreams and talents the Lord has given me. Thanks for putting up with a wife who regularly writes down what the voices in her head say. ::grin:: (I promise I'll stay away from psychiatric facilities.)

For my children: thanks for keeping things to a (mostly) dull roar.

For my mom and siblings: thank you for your encouragement and support.

A big thanks to Connie Trapp, for being a fantastic beta reader. Your insight over the years is much appreciated.

Thanks also to Kristine Kathryn Rusch, who read *Danger at the Embassy* and gave me the feedback that ultimately resulted in my decision to write *The Spy at the Embassy*.

Thank you also to Kim Burns and Heather Stearns for being excited readers, great friends, and great listening ears when I need to talk about writing.

A very special thank you to all of the people who supported the Kickstarter I ran for *The Spy at the Embassy Special Edition*. Thank you, Johanna Rothman, Pauline Baird Jones, Virginia Skye, Kimberly Burns, Susan Jones, Patty McGregor, John Idlor, Amanda Balter, Amanda Eschmeyer, Kathryn Kaleigh, Dean Wesley Smith, Author

Lia Huni, Audrea Martin, Peggy Kurilla, Lu, Anonymous Reader, Jenna Hendricks, L. Simpson, Anthea Sharp, and Eron Wyngarde.

Y'all are amazing and I am so grateful for your support and involvement!

Thanks also to Lori Christie, Sarah Reschar, Chelsea Stevens, Hannah Hatton, Sarah Gharib, Emily Bare, Kristie Sullivan, Felicia Bridge, Meta Clark, and many, many others for your encouragement and support.

Newsletter Sign-up

I value honest feedback and would love to hear your opinion in a review, if you're so inclined, on your favorite retailer's site. Thank you!

Be the first to know!

Just sign up for the E. R. Paskey newsletter and keep up with the latest news, releases, and so much more, including the occasional giveaway.

Go to www.erpaskey.com or scan this QR code:

About the Author

E. R. Paskey fell in love with mysteries and science fiction and all their possibilities at a young age. She is the author of over a dozen novels, including the *Finder* series and a Christian science fiction series, *The Guardians*. She currently lives in Southern Indiana with her husband and their six children.

You can find her website at: ERPaskey.com or scan this QR code: